THE
BARONS

PARRIS

AFTON BONDS
NEW YORK TIMES
BESTSELLING AUTHOR

THE BARONS

THE TEXICANS ★ VOLUME TWO

NEW YORK TIMES BESTSELLING AUTHOR

PARRIS
AFTON BONDS

MOTINA BOOKS PUBLISHING

Text copyright © 2024 by Parris Afton Bonds
2nd Edition
All Rights Reserved. Printed in the United States of America
Published by Motina Books, LLC, Van Alstyne, Texas
www.MotinaBooks.com

Library of Congress Cataloguing-in-Publication Data:

Names: Afton Bonds, Parris
Title: The Barons: Volume Two of The Texicans
Description: Second Edition. | Van Alstyne: Motina Books, 2024

Identifiers:

LCCN: 2024940101
ISBN-13: 979-8-88784-043-7 (paperback)
ISBN-13: 979-8-88784-045-1 (e-book)
ISBN-13: 979-8-88784-044-4 (hardcover)

Subjects: BISAC:
FICTION/Romance/Historical/American
FICTION/Romance/Western

Cover and Interior Design: Diane Windsor

Dedicated to Joy Ross Davis
Your Irish Spirit Dances on Sunshine.

THE TEXICANS
GENEALOGY

THE BARONS

Alejandro de la Torre y Stuart

Sixth Baron of Paladín

m.
Fiona Flanagan

Kerry	Tara	Wade

Niall Gorman

m.
Rafaela Carrera

Jamie	Catarina

Amarillo
Red River
Brazos
Fort Worth
Dallas
Nacogdoches
El Paso
Brazos
Trinity
Austin
Rio Grande
Houston
San Antonio
Galveston
Nueces
The Barony
Corpus Christi
Gulf of Mexico
N
Rio Grande
Rio Grande City
Brownsville

TEXAS

PART

I

SMUGGLERS DEN
REPUBLIC OF TEXAS
DECEMBER 1844

It was cold. Or, in southwest Texas lingo, "cold as the Baron's heart."

Texas had more than a few barons—justly entitled or self-proclaimed—but none matched the Baron of Paladín. Fiona Paladín could swear to that.

In this love match with Alex Paladín, the Fiona Flanigan of old wondered if the disputed land grant would ever cease to be a source of semi-pleasurable contention between her and her rakehell of a husband.

A cutting wind—the same kind that had scuttled gray clouds above the Gulf of Mexico's miserable Port of Matamoros exactly nine years earlier on her debarking in the Tejas colony—now whiplashed the flag of the Lone Star Republic hoisted at the Bay of Corpus Christi.

Its choppy water hurled against the flimsy pilings of the smugglers' den, with its stockade and clusters of brothels, saloons, and gambling places. Better known as Kinney's

Trading Post, it hosted the closest port to her land grant.

Well, to *their* land grant—a compromise which she had reached upon her wedding Alex de la Torre y Stuart, Sixth Baron of Paladín, seven months after her arrival. That ceremony had united her tempestuous temper and his tempestuous lovemaking, and their marriage continued to do so.

Their lighter neared the rickety wharf. She anchored one hand on the wide brim of her brown silk traveling bonnet against the salt-laden wind. The expensive bonnet was most decidedly different than the scruffy cottage bonnet she had worn when first she had sighted what was then Tejas.

However, there was a lot different about that Irish lass who, at twenty, had emigrated from impoverished County Kerry to notorious Five Points, New York, and from there to the war-torn Mexican state of Tejas y Coahuila.

Three years of shuttling between London and Paris with Alex, the Republic of Texas's *chargé de affairs,* had wrought changes of Pygmalion proportions in Fiona Flanigan. Sharing that magical time with her raven-haired husband had literally breathed transformational life into her sprite of a body.

Few would suspect that the lovely, cultured twenty-nine-year-old woman, freckles and all, had once been both a cleaning lady and tutor in Madame Margie's house of ill repute.

From behind, Alex's powerful arms wrapped around her waist. So much taller, he had to bend his head to slant his lips against her nape. The light kiss nevertheless sent a delicious tingling through her, even after all this time—and three babies.

"Eager to be home again?" His voice held that distinctive rasp, like a farrier's file on a horseshoe.

He related to her all too well. Not, "Eager to see Liam?" or "Eager to see our old friends again?" He understood her Irish's soul-deep need to drop to her knees and run her fingers through The Barony's alluvial soil.

It was not her quasi-adopted son Liam, nor her and Alex's close friends, Rafaela and Niall, who awaited her and Alex's disembarkation, but the President of the Republic of Texas himself. Almost as tall as her handsome husband, Sam Houston greeted Alex with one of those arm-over-and-under bear hugs.

"You old reprobate. What in God's name are you doing this far southwest of Austin?"

Her licentious husband did not believe in God, but she wisely said nothing, rather politely focusing her attention on his distinguished mentor.

Houston's grizzled mutton-chop whiskers tweaked with the grin made by the deep bracket at either side of his mouth. Over his street clothing, the flamboyant general wore his usual Indian blanket. "You don't think I'd allow just any feller to welcome you back to God's country, do you?"

An erudite and eloquent statesman, Sam only resorted to such homespun homilies when with a purpose in mind. Her eyes narrowed.

Sam turned to execute a courtly bow over her extended

kid-gloved hand. "Madam, your rare beauty blights Texas wildflowers."

"Ever the adroit charmer." She smiled, dipping a curtsey. But behind her easy smile, concern crouched.

The Republic of Texas's President had not traveled all this way merely to welcome his protege back home. With Sam's presidential term ending in two weeks, Alex's services as chargé were likewise ending—as was the country itself. When annexed at the end of the month by the United States, Texas would become its twenty-eighth state.

So what nefarious scheme was the old hero of San Jacinto concocting for this next phase of his life?

And what did he want of Alex?

Once the three—along with Kerry, almost eight, five-year-old Wade, and the toddler Tara—were ensconced in Houston's big yellow coach, its four horses were off in a cloud of rolling dust. Behind the great carry-all, Houston's driver, Joshua, handled the reins of a wagon, loaded with the Paladín's traveling trunks, baggage, and three year's accumulation from living abroad.

"You know, Alex," Sam began, approaching his objective in his crablike fashion. "The white bean survivors have just been released from prison in Perote Castle."

While in London the year before, Alex had been working with Great Britain's foreign minister to Mexico. Fiona had heard a terse account of the horrific Black Bean episode from Alex.

According to dispatches, one hundred and seventy-six Texicans taken prisoner in the Mier Expedition against

Mexico had been ordered executed for their attempted escape from the Perote prison. Diplomatic efforts by Great Britain's foreign minister had led Santa Anna to compromise that only one in ten would die. Blindfolded, the Texicans were ordered to draw from a pot in which 159 white beans and seventeen black beans had been placed. Those who drew the black beans were executed before a firing squad.

A friend of hers and Alex's, Captain Ewen Cameron, had drawn a black bean. He had refused to confess to a priest and declined the offer of a blindfold. Instead, word went that he had declared, "For the liberty of Texas, Ewen Cameron can look death in the face." He then had opened his hunting shirt and yelled at his executioners, *"¡Fuego!"*— Fire!

Alex settled a squirming Tara onto one knee. "Great news, Sam. I heard Big Foot Wallace figured out for himself that the black beans were larger and fingered the bean crock until he drew a white one. But then, he always has been too wily, even for the devil."

"These Mexican depredations must end, Alex. Next month, when we become a state in the Union, we need to shore up our border with Mexico. I have been mulling over the—"

"No!" Fiona shifted a sleeping Wade into the crook of her arm. She knew too well the old general's methodology.

The heads of both men and red-haired Kerry, who thought he was being reprimanded for one of his pranks, swiveled toward her.

Her lilting brogue was pleasant enough, but there was no mistaking the narrow-eyed volley she fired off at the two men. "We've been away from The Barony for too long. We have a ranch to run and a family to raise." She turned a more pleading gaze on Houston. "Sam, surely Alex has paid his dues for Texas.

The old general reached across and tousled Wade's dark curls. "More than enough, madam. I am just trying to forestall this little one's life-rendering service on behalf of the United States. With Texas coming into the Union as a slave state, I am most apprehensive about a rift splitting our mother country." A fine patriotic sentiment, but Sam Houston, great orator that he was, knew how to play to an audience—and her wicked Alex knew how to play her like a finely-tuned fiddle.

Tonight, he would doubtlessly pleasure her in their bed until, like always, she could not say no to his finely tuned fingers—or to his political inveigling. Well, not this time!

STARING OUT THE COACH window, Alex could finally make out the big live oak on the bluff overlooking the Nueces River—and below it, the adobe house erected nearly a decade ago from stones remaining after his late brother's house was burned to the ground by raiding Comanche.

Starting with two rooms, Alex and his intrepid *Paladineños* gradually added five more and an upper story around a central patio. They then built a mesquite corral, an adobe barn, and a lookout tower with two small cannon pointing south and west—toward the raiding Mexican bandidos and the savage Comancheros. Inside, some parts of the house resembled an arsenal. In one over-sized room, he had stored more than eighty Enfield rifles.

Even from a distance, he realized how shabby their place looked—much like his own finances. Mexican and Anglo cattle rustlers, Indian raids, and drought had all taken a toll.

His fiery-haired Fiona had drubbed into him her deeply-felt belief—that family and land meant everything—and he meant to keep intact the original royal Spanish land grant of 1767, come hell or high water. Though the former was more likely to come than the latter, given the drought.

Their vast grassland in the nation that was becoming the state of Texas was proving expensive to keep up, even for a man of his resourceful means—means that he had, in earlier times, derived from shrewd investments, gambling winnings, or occasionally through marginally legal actions.

Because of the Texas Republic's depleted coffers, he had been forced to finance out of his own pocket too many of his official *chargé* expenditures, as Sam had been forced to do his presidential outlays in Austin.

Tiring as the coach trip home was, Alex was pleasantly surprised by the sea of faces waiting at the main house to greet his family. Old Winnie and Frederick, who had been with the Paladín family in London when Alex was but a boy in pantaloons, were standing outside beaming.

Frederick, shortened even more by the passing years,

doffed his cap. His rheumy eyes glistened as the Paladíns stepped down from Sam Houston's coach.

Winnie, with her comfortable-looking features, delivered Alex one of her typical scowls, belying the moisture present in her age-hooded eyes. "Been away long enough you have, Master Alex."

Solely for Fiona's benefit did the countenance of the stout old housekeeper soften. "Missed you mightily we did, Mistress."

Present too was Niall Gorman, the Irish Traveler himself. Once the baron's hired hand, Niall had fought alongside Alex at San Jacinto and had been rewarded for that service with a parcel of land outside San Antonio.

Alex hugged the younger, much shorter man. "Your beloved writes us that you've parlayed your horse-trading business into a successful company."

"*Somewhat* successful. Rafaela and I are still scratching it out like chickens."

"Providing carriage horses to local society, are you?"

"Aye, but I'm also cross-breeding what I call quarter horses—much more agile and cattle savvy than those dray horses that pull our wagons and plows. And you, Alex? Still planning to expand The Barony into that vast empire we used to talk about?"

"By hook or crook." Alex stooped to sweep up Niall's brash and perky four-year-old, Catarina, tugging fiercely at her father's coattails. "What a little sprite, you are Catarina. You were but an infant in swaddling when last I saw you."

She dimpled and giggled.

He turned to Niall, setting the girl on her feet and scanning the candle-lit *sala*. "Where's your other offspring?"

Niall nodded over his shoulder. "Over there, with your Kerry. The boys are hero-worshiping Houston."

Alex's sooty black eyes moved past his own son to eight-year-old Jamie Gorman, the image of his mother Rafaela and just as sweet-tempered.

At that moment, his mother was smiling at something Fiona was describing with a lively gesturing of her small hands. For all Rafaela's regal beauty and elegance, he would be forever relieved that he had never consummated his engagement to her.

In order to sustain himself in Tejas, and to defray the cost of substantiating his late brother's land grant, Alex had bartered his baron's title for her bridal dowry. A deed he readily acknowledged as one of his serious weaknesses—the expediency that let nothing interfere with his own self-determined course, whatever cost he might incur.

The highborn Spanish woman lacked Fiona's vibrancy, but she had suited well Niall's convivial and more temperamental nature.

"Where the bloody hell is Liam?" Paladín knew he shouldn't be surprised at Liam's absence. Even as a lad, he'd turn up missing for a day or so. At first, Fiona would be frantic, but eventually, she abandoned her effort to train him differently and reluctantly came to accept the little shit's lackadaisical temperament. For his part, Alex had never trusted Liam and never would.

"The kid's come into his juices," Niall said.

Alex raised a cynical brow. At eighteen, Fiona's 'adopted' son was no kid. "Too busy in The District to be home to greet us?" The District was nearby San Antonio's vice zone.

Three years ago, when Alex brought Fiona and their children with him to London and Paris, it had seemed a good decision to leave Liam in Texas. Winnie and Frederick could look after him at The Barony or, on occasion, he could learn the horse training and breeding trade with Niall and Rafaela in San Antonio—and, just maybe, learn responsibility.

"You and Niall got a few minutes?"

Alex turned toward Houston. "Sure, Sam." At last, Houston was getting around to his true reason for beating a path to The Barony. "My office?"

The old commandant's desk, hauled from the Matamoros *presidio* that he had won in a game of Faro a decade ago, dominated the small office. It was one of the *hacienda's* original two rooms from where his floundering cattle operations were overseen.

Slouched in a hide-bottom chair, Alex stretched his lengthy legs. He propped his elbows on the chair arms and, staring over interlocked fingers at Houston, waited. What further dangerous machinations might be coursing through the old man's devious mind?

Houston wasted no time launching into his purpose. "President Polk covets this continent clear out to the Pacific Ocean. As soon as Texas is annexed, he means to protect our disputed Rio Grande border."

The General paused to light his pipe from the candle on the desk. "As luck would have it, my esteemed friend Polk, anticipating a potential war with Mexico, is planning to send troops right here to Fort Lipantitlan."

Luck? Or due to Fiona's four-leaf-clover necklace, as she would doubtlessly claim? Regardless, Alex's racing mind hurtled the possible benefits and risks from such an act.

The abandoned army post squatted at the intersection of the north Nueces River, claimed by Mexico as its border, and the overgrown San Patricio Trail, beaten out by Irish in 1830 to connect nearby San Patricio with San Antonio.

Soldiers bivouacked anywhere in the area would need beef to eat, as well as horses to ride and to draw supply wagons. Both would provide almost instant salvation for the struggling Barony.

"If you could wrangle from Polk a contract for The Barony's beef, as well as a contract for Niall to provision wagons to transport goods from the Army supply depot in San Antonio—what in turn would you require of us?"

Houston removed his pipe and tamped down its tobacco. "It is enough merely for me to know that southwest Texas has two such devoted citizens."

Niall, arms folded, braced one spurred boot against the stucco wall. "Spies, you mean, Sam? Or is me English less fluent than me Gaelic?"

Houston's smile was disingenuous. "Mere semantics, my dear fellow."

Privately, Alex was certain Fiona would never accept Houston's trifling designation. What Houston had in mind

would demand Alex's time, much of it away from home—
and for him, Fiona was his home.

She knew his weaknesses and his neediness. That
neediness had led him straight into her arms. After all, it
was she who fired the weapon that saved his life—and his
property. That pivotal moment had proved her worth, as
well as her value to him.

Eventually the guests retired, and later that night in their
bed, made by a San Antonio German cabinetmaker
expressly for Alex's long frame, he concentrated on taking
Fiona and himself on that sweet journey to that heart-
stopping moment between life and death.

They conjoined in that age-old rite of the mating of the
bodies—and the souls, if one was so lucky. Perhaps that
was why a soul as black as his could never get enough of
her light.

"*Abre tus ojos.*" He lapsed into the native language of his
childhood. When he could look into her eyes, see deep
inside her, only then did he know she was his. Otherwise,
she belonged to the world at large.

Her hands gripped the muscles that ridged his upper
arms, her nails digging into his sweat-sheened flesh. Her lids
fluttered open, her hazel-green eyes fixed on his. "If ye stop
now, I will kill ye, I swear!"

Kill him she most assuredly would if she found out he
was back in Houston's spying game as he and Niall had
been during the Texican revolt against Mexico.

THE SMUGGLERS DEN
NOVEMBER 1845

To avoid the cutting norther that was shredding the few leaves left on the trees that evening, Liam O'Brien ducked into the doorway next to the saloon. Keeping watch for the army captain who was the third and final player to arrive for the poker game Liam had arranged, he stared out at the Gulf of Mexico, fanning out from the mouth of the Nueces River.

He knew all about storm-wrecked treasure and galleons at the bottom of Corpus Christi Bay, as well as the fabled riches of the area's long-lost El Dorado mine, hewn out long ago by the earliest *Conquistadores.*

What he knew equally well, and which was safer and more assured, was smuggling—goods he purchased in New Orleans and sold illegally in Mexico and vice versa. In the past year, he had forsaken the fleshpots and dens of inequity of San Antonio for the more lucrative ones of Corpus Christi Bay.

The most lucrative was gambling, which he deemed

robbing the robber. That Devil's spawn, Don Alejandro de la Torre y Stuart, had taken him aside when he was still a skinny nine-year-old refugee from Five Points and taught him the fine art of winning at poker—and the not so fine art of coming in second place in family concerns.

That one shaming image, reinforcing what was to be fifteen-year-old Liam's role in the new family, still haunted him—when Paladín had found him in the adobe barn trying to fook a *Paladineños* fourteen year old daughter.

Surprising Liam, Paladín had hauled him off the girl by the scruff of his collar. "I do believe you're supposed to be helping move stones for the new well, not satisfying your own stones. I suggest you cease shirking your responsibilities."

Liam had squirmed loose. Ignoring the cowering girl, he glared back at Paladín. "As if ye're of any better character."

The towering man's disgusted expression had changed to one of mocking amusement. "Character? You will learn, whether I teach you or life does, that one is not born with character. It is learnt. Now is as good a time as any to tell you that Fiona and I and the boys are leaving for England shortly—and I am leaving you here to learn just that. Character."

With that, Paladín and Fiona and their 'rightful' children had left the Republic of Texas. And left Liam.

At nineteen, he was still pissed that he had missed out on the land promised to all the patriots after the Texican Revolution. Even now, almost ten years later, he ached inside to admit with gut-sickening certainty that the Baron's natural son Kerry, not he, would eventually inherit The Barony.

Not too different from his mentor Paladín, Liam had considerable resources—except Liam's skills were not financial or military but finagle and flimflam.

And General Zachary Taylor's troops had sweetened immensely the area's gambling prospects.

Earlier that fall, Liam had spotted white canvas sails poking above the endless Gulf horizon. Soldiers and horses soon waded ashore and cannon were unloaded. Within hours, more white canvas appeared on land—a sea of tents, rippling in the onshore breeze where grass as high as a man's head once grew.

Almost 3,600 American soldiers were camped along the Nueces River, which Mexico continued to insist was its border with Texas. The presence of the U.S. Army was a bold declaration that the United States was preparing to back its rights to the Rio Grande River, farther south, as its border with Mexico.

To round out that evening of cards, Liam's table in the back room of the grog shop awaited only the last mark— and then Liam spotted him, arcing forward against the punishing wind. Approaching Liam along the boardwalk, the blue-uniformed captain strode briskly on his horseman's bowed legs. At five foot eight inches, Liam was the same height as the captain.

Inside, seated within his table's wreath of cigar and pipe smoke, Liam deftly dealt the cards while studying his marks. Military men, Liam believed, were confined and constricted by their servitude to superior ranking officers, who likely had never had a superior thought.

The Yager Colonel, Jefferson Davis, was clearly a gentleman and a scholar. His fingertips showed no calluses.

Next to him, Sergeant Rusk, who had the annoying habit of constantly sniffling through his broken nose, was more than likely a boxer. Liam expected him to be an aggressive player.

Finally, Liam examined the last arrival, Captain Ulysses Grant. A natural horseman, Grant displayed deep concentration, ignoring the raucous drinkers in the outer room. To this one, Liam decided, he would give a wide berth.

Combining his winnings with his losses, Liam let his wins grow gradually compared with those of the other three players, as the pots grew larger and the drinking more frequent. Jefferson Davis, to his credit, maintained his cordiality, the brutish knuckles of the sergeant's left hand rapped continually, and Grant chewed pensively on the butt end of his unlit cigar.

Davis and Grant sat out the following round. It was Liam's turn to deal. The two officers watched from beneath the brass oil lamp suspended overhead as Liam dealt himself and Rusk two cards each. Nearly inaudible inhalations circled the table.

Rusk showed the high ace, the spade.

The Irish in Liam took pleasure at the old superstition that it was the card of death. "Aces in the pockets. Paladín always told me aces win the small pots and lose the big ones."

"Paladín?" Rusk sniffed. "You know him?"

"Me stepfather—sort of." Although that would hardly qualify him to legally inherit any property of the Paladíns, let alone The Barony.

Then he began to deal afresh . . . three kings face down to Rusk. Liam knew, because he had nicked the card edges. The chips Rusk anted up indicated he had to be feeling very confident—with good cause. Slowly, Liam turned over his cards. A straight.

Smiling broadly, he raked in his winnings. As Rusk glowered at Liam, two other pairs of eyes observed him gravely.

"Thank ye all for yuir contributions to the Irish famine fund." Liam grinned as, leaving the table, he bowed at the trio with a dramatic sweep of his tweed cap.

That he had duped two West Point graduates gave him great pleasure, because he was one of those lowly and detested Irish scrappers. His Irish immigrant parents had died of typhus within days of their ships docking in New York. His own confinement on the overcrowded 'coffin' ship had been a nightmare he recalled too clearly, but upon the death of his parents, his life had been a living hell. He was left alone to scrabble for sustenance and forced to shelter in alleys teeming with fierce rats and, worse, people bent on having their way with a scrawny eight-year-old.

True enough, Fiona had rescued him from that life. Hauling him from Five Points to Matamoros, Mexico, she had passed him off as her son. Only he was never that. Not really. Paladín's older son by her would inherit it all.

For this, he could forgive none of the three. Not Paladín. Not Kerry. And not Fiona. He and she were both from the old world, from Eire. She was supposed to have rescued him from having to fight for food and a place in this world, wasn't she? Yet, because of Paladín, here he was, reduced to the same state he was when he was eight and had lost his parents. He had been abandoned all over again.

He swaggered through the grog shop's crowded outer room. Over on Chaparral Street, a Mexican girl with flashing dark eyes was waiting just for him. They spent ten minutes groping one another in a nearby darkened alley before he arranged to meet her at her *jacal* after retrieving his mount from the livery.

As he strolled past the ammunition magazine—behind the sand embankment the soldiers had built as a windbreak to protect from Texas northers—he felt only for a blinding instance the crushing blow that drove him unconscious onto the sand.

SAN ANTONIO

Niall Gorman watched his elegant wife, the former Lady Rafaela Carrera, mingling among the few guests invited for dinner that evening. Few, because the San Antonio house Niall had purchased was small, even after he added a room to the adobe block-walled and pine-floored homestead.

Discounting the outdoor kitchen, the house consisted only of a sala and three bedrooms, one of which served as the office for his cattle and horse-trading business, as well as his newest enterprise as a military contractor—thanks be to the looming war with Mexico and Paladín for that negotiation with Houston.

Niall's expansion into provisioning the American troops posted near San Patricio was the reason for tonight's dinner. Or rather, the Baron Karl von Hesse-Lippe was.

Taller even than Houston and at eye-level with Paladín, the polished German nobleman had studied law at the renowned Philipps University near Bonn. After peasants in his native Germany burned and pillaged estates of the wealthy, Karl had departed his fatherland for the growing German colony that Prince Braunfels was establishing in central Texas.

Finally settling in San Antonio, Karl was serving as liaison for the Adelsverein, the Nobility Society set up to assist German immigrants fleeing persecution in their homeland by helping them to become established in Texas.

Although San Antonio could not point to any splendid castles, the city did have a few noble families. More than a hundred years earlier, in 1731, seventeen families had been brought from the Canary Islands to settle the Spanish colonial outpost of San Antonio de Bexar. Spain's King Philip conferred upon them, as first settlers as well as upon their descendants, the title of *Hijos de Algos* or "Hidalgos."

Since then, the more Spanish heritage a resident could claim, the higher one's rank in local Hispanic society. The Hispanic caste system also included the higher level of "grandees" and included in the hierarchy all white people of Spanish lineage.

Counted among San Antonio's present nobility was the tall, graceful, and patrician Rafaela. She was considered by local society as the *chatelaine* of San Antonio. Now twenty-eight, she had grown into her loveliness.

At eighteen, when Niall had first set eyes on his friend Alex Paladín's fiancée, she had been a tall, standoffish debutante with a nose too large for her face and too-rarely glimpsed dimples.

Perhaps it was those dimples—or more likely her innocence, that of an untried filly—that had driven him to pursue her to war-torn San Antonio after she had fled her forthcoming marriage to Paladín.

In bringing her back to Alex's headquarters at *La Espada presidio,* Niall had lost his own freedom. In a real sense, he became Rafaela's willing captive.

As an Irish Traveler of Gypsy heritage, Niall would have been at the very bottom of the Spaniard nobility totem pole. Nevertheless, the San Antonio colonials, proselytized by more egalitarian American virtues, instead looked upon Niall as foremost a hero of the Texican war for independence. Almost reluctantly, with Rafaela as his personal lodestar, he had become one of San Antonio's most eminent social icons.

The candelabra suspended from the bead board ceiling cast a heat-withering glow. Fiona snapped open her fan, swishing it rapidly. "Have ye seen anything of Liam lately, Niall?"

He shook his head. "Sent him out more than a week ago with a wagonload of rifles for Fort Lipantitlan's dragoons. Should have been back by now." He shrugged, withholding what else was on his mind.

He did not have to say anything. She sighed. "Which explains his tardiness. What with Kinney Trading Post in easy reach, the laddie is either bedding its wenches or five-fingering some poor soldier's pay."

Fiona's "laddie" was old enough to cover his own carcass. He had the heart of a fighting cock. Niall remembered catching Liam, as a boy, cooking a rabbit he had killed over a fire.

Why Fiona was overly concerned puzzled Niall—unless she was displaying her legendary Irish gift for premonition.

Legendary or not, Niall was feeling some uneasiness himself, and it had nothing at all to do with Liam, he felt sure.

Still puzzled, he could not yet put his finger on the worry, could not yet give name to what was bothering him. His uneasiness continued to linger in his wee office, where he was closeted with Sam Houston, the lantern-jawed Baron Karl von Hesse-Lippe, and Paladín.

His friend hunkered one hip on the rickety table that served as Niall's desk. Karl had chosen the ladder-back chair, its woven rush bottom in danger of unraveling. Newly elected U.S. senator for the recently annexed Texas, Houston sat opposite the table. Saying nothing, he listened attentively while carving a letter opener from a pecan branch with his pocketknife.

Alex explained his proposition. "Obviously, Karl, you are the best legal talent available in south Texas."

Karl glanced at Houston, who smiled wryly. "I vouched for you, son."

"I would like to hire you as our legal counsel," Paladín continued. "Represent me on my land acquisitions—and represent Niall's and my partnership as military contractors. With the recent influx of soldiers, our contracting business has boomed beyond anything we had imagined."

To his credit, Karl made no attempts at false modesty. From all accounts, he eschewed gun-toting, opining that it only led to more violence rather than the protection from violence.

"Thank you." For all his mild countenance, his blue-eyed gaze was direct and assessing. It settled first on Houston, then on to Niall. "The Gorman name has come to mean 'expert horseman' in southwest Texas."

Karl's measuring gaze moved on to Alex. "I hear your vaqueros call themselves Paladíneños—Paladíns' men. They are law-abiding, industrious workers. That says a great deal about the kind of man you are. Why don't both you and Niall draw up a joint contract? I will look it over and we can proceed from that point."

No, nothing at all to make Niall feel uneasy there.

He was, indeed, an expert at divining the nature of animals. His understanding of humans came a close second. His preference for the company of either was in the same order. Karl was congenial, highly intelligent, and capable. Moreover, he represented the essence of his nobleman's baronial title—a noble man.

Still, after they adjourned to take a fashionably late

dinner with the ladies, Niall's unease followed him like a relentless ghost.

PRESIDING OVER THE SMALL dinner party that evening, Rafaela was happy. Rarely was she able to experience the conviviality of such warm and easy friendships there in San Antonio. Its Old Guard looked to her and Niall to set the local hallmark for social propriety.

Catarina, Rafaela's lovely daughter—and the bane of her life—and Jamie, her son, were tucked in bed, so at last she could enjoy herself. Fondly, her gaze flitted over her dinner guests to alight on her former fiancé.

At thirty-five, Alex was now more handsome, if that was possible. Fiona . . . their three children . . . The Barony . . . perhaps these additions to his life were responsible for muting the harsh lines on his face and easing his reactions to the rest of his life as well.

Whatever he was becoming, she knew Alex's eyes were those of a man who had seen too much, done too much, felt too much. He had willingly bartered his baron's title for Rafaela's dowry.

When she first met him, she realized that the roue he admitted to being was too cold and calculating for her own more tender inclinations. She felt fortunate that his fabled passions had found a better match with her dear friend Fiona.

Resilient and fearless, the year-older woman was blessed with a liveliness Rafaela envied. A decade earlier, pending the settlement of a land grant dispute with Alex, the Irish lass had needed work and a place to stay for her and nine-year-old Liam.

For whatever might then have been his true and possibly nefarious reason, Alex had offered her a temporary position as Rafaela's companion until his marriage with Rafaela would be solemnized a month later.

Maybe Alex felt Fiona's presence as his betrothed's companion would forestall Matamoros's wagging tongues. Or, he might even have contrived that arrangement to facilitate his seduction of the lass. More likely than any other possibility was his need to hinder Fiona's attempts to validate for herself a land claim they both disputed.

Rafaela would not have put anything past the blackguard. Regardless of his self-serving assertions that he lacked both heart and honor, she knew Alex to be a man whose word one could rely on, but further, a man wholly committed to keeping safe what was his—his family and his land.

She thought Niall, with his seductive hound-dog eyes and Irish temperament, would have been better suited for Ireland-born Fiona. But no, the gypsy enchanter's mellifluous voice and his gentle way with animals had cast its spell over herself instead. He had won over her damaged girl's heart.

Over the years of their marriage, Niall had finally healed her mistrust of all men that was wrought by both a distant father and a surrogate father—one who had forcibly taken her innocence and raided her savings.

Her eyes moved past the table's candelabrum, pausing

briefly on that beloved friend and patriarch Houston, then encountering her third guest, the Baron Karl von Hesse-Lippe. His reddish-blond head inclined in a reassuring nod with a faint but polite smile that suggested to her his introspective nature.

Flustered a bit by that conclusion, she sipped from her champagne flute. The German baron reminded her of the glittering London society she had forfeited to come to the Texas frontier as Paladín's fiancée.

Arriving in San Antonio only the year before, the red-haired nobleman was fresh from the courts of the Grand Duke of Baden. The mere presence of the urbane and rather handsome German stimulated Rafaela's innate imagination, as well as her intelligence.

When she looked up, she noticed the steady gaze of her rough-edged husband regarding her somewhat quizzically and she felt a pang of guilt, although she knew not why.

DEAD HORSE DESERT
APRIL 1846

A long line of the Army of Occupation cavalry trotted slowly across El Desierto de los Muertos—the Desert of the Dead. Behind their draft horses, U.S. artillery caissons bumped along. Behind them tramped the infantry—and Liam O'Brien.

Dust and sand abraded his cheeks, fine grit clogged his eyelashes and teeth, and his sweat created muddy tracks through his own filth.

He looked over his shoulder at the miles after miles of wagons bringing up the rear, each wagon drawn by six large mules. Mules and wagons alike provided by The Barony Ranch Transport Partnership.

If before this adventure Liam had ever thought he disliked Paladín, in his present circumstances, he flat out hated him.

Legally, at least, Sergeant Rusk had good reason to be pissed about the card game last October—which had landed Liam in the stockade for three months. He vowed to be more circumspect at cards the next time he played. Or, at least, to keep his gob shuttered at the table.

Truth be told? Rusk had taken an intense dislike to Liam the instant he mentioned Paladín's name. In post-independence south Texas, that name meant power. Ruthless power or beneficial power. Depending, of course, which side of the fence someone occupied.

Alongside the marching army, The Barony Ranch unscrolled seemingly into infinity. Could well be, in his present condition, why he wanted the property so deeply. Once he owned the place, he believed The Barony's vast open spaces would banish forever his own confinement nightmares.

Those months in the stockade had been for Liam the second darkest pitch of his soul. It reminded him every second of his boyhood years in Ireland's Ballingarry coal mines.

Small back then for his age, he had been put to work at six each and every morning as what the foremen called "a trapper." He opened and closed wooden doors so air could ventilate the mine. Twelve hours a day, he sat in the dark, with only a wee candle for light and not one soul to natter with.

In the army stockade, he had not had even a candle for company. When Rusk had hauled Liam out to join this bloody march, Liam had raised his shackled wrists to block the blinding sun.

Today, the sun was blistering everyone, the air itself wrung out of any moisture. The army was already halfway to the Rio Grande River, but ahead, Liam knew were sixty-odd more harsh miles of sand dunes, cat claw cactus, and scrub brush—with the ever-present specter of the Grim Reaper himself hanging over every man jack in the stumbling line.

Mick Mallory, another stockade dweller who was shackled to Liam, whispered that General Arista's sizable army was ready to defend the Rio Grande border. Those Mexicans, Mick said, kept their fury focused and were on alert waiting to greet General Taylor's advancing troops with rifle and cannon.

The ruddy-faced Mallory, a huge Irishman who could effortlessly lift any misguided man off his feet with one hand and shake him till his teeth rattled, had been found guilty of stabbing another soldier in a dispute over who would go first to get some whore's favors.

Liam, who was not even in the army during the card game, was charged with felony theft by the army provost marshal. What felony that might apply to him no one in authority ever told Liam, nor when or whether he would be tried for his offense.

He sensed that Captain Grant or the soldier-scholar Colonel Davis were aware of his incarceration and were ignoring his plight.

Bloody hell! He was a civilian, not some soldier boy. A newly conscripted one at most.

"'Tis telling ye, I am," Mick muttered as they trudged along, "the army considers us Irishmen inferior to themselves. We get all the filthy jobs. Ye can forget about any chance of promotion. Worse, we get no Catholic services—only the protestant."

Liam was no believer in Catholicism, or even in God. What kind of fookin' God would allow the child he once was to fester deep inside a pitch dark mine day-in and day-out, or put him in this hopeless situation?

"Defect then, Mick."

"What? And when I'm nabbed, at best, I get a 'D' branded on me cheek—or, at the worst, I swing from the gallows?"

Lowering his booming voice, Mick leaned closer. "I'll tell ye something better—those Mexicans are offering land and money to anyone who deserts the Americans and joins them. Why, ye might even be a hero across the river."

Taking in Mick's news, Liam almost convinced himself that was a plan to consider.

Whatever happened when they got to the big river, Liam was going to make a run for it once Taylor's army arrived there. His first year in Texas, or "Tejas" as it was called a decade earlier, Liam spent many a night in Matamoros, right across the river. He knew the lay of that particular land better than any of these bloody Yankees ever would.

His escape plans were postponed by General Taylor's orders to set about at once to building a gigantic earthen fortress on what was once a cattle rancho next to the Rio Grande. Its perimeter was to be 800 yards all told, with walls more than nine feet high, a firing parapet fifteen feet wide, the whole surrounded by a moat fifteen feet deep and twenty feet wide.

Tents were erected, and guards posted. After that, the grunts shoveled.

With each shovel of earth Liam dug for what they were already calling "Fort Texas," he told himself that was one more shovel of dirt he would throw on Paladín's grave one day.

What really galled Liam was realizing that just across the river in Matamoros, 4,000 Mexican troops were doing the same thing—shoring up a fort, lining up cannon—each side warily watching the other while swatting at buzzing green bottle horseflies and starving mosquitoes.

ON MAY FIRST, GENERAL Zachary Taylor deemed himself ready. He had prepared Fort Texas to withstand a siege by the Mexican army while he moved most of his force, about 1,800 soldiers, to protect his supply base—Fort Polk, some twenty-odd miles north at Point Isabel on the Gulf coast. He left Fort Texas garrisoned by only 500 men of the 7th Infantry, including Liam and Mick.

The following night, blood-blistered hands clasped beneath his shaggy, blond ringlets, Liam lay awake on his cot. Right before dawn he decided would be his best time to escape.

Next to him, Mick yawned. "You're going over, ain't ye now?"

"Go to sleep."

But once again, Liam's escape plan was scuttled. That morning, at five a.m., Mexican artillery opened fire against the newly established six-sided fort. American troops of the 7th Infantry quickly responded with their own artillery fire.

When more cannon fire erupted from Mexican positions up and down the riverbank on the opposite side, Fort Texas commander Major Jacob Brown pointed his guns into the city of Matamoros and fired a volley.

Shellfire continued on both sides until well into the following night. Like a fireball streaking out of the night sky, a shell landed next to Liam. His immediate thought was a raging, "No—Paladín first!" But the shell never exploded. At the realization that he was safe, the breath whooshed from him and his bollocks unknotted. Well, he was safe—at least for the moment.

In time, however, the artillery exchanges gave way to a prolonged standoff. Despite the continuing Mexican siege of Fort Texas, the earthen walls Liam had helped erect withstood the salvos. Mexican leaders apparently acknowledged their lack of success, because during the next few days, firing on the fort continued only sporadically.

Liam found himself marking time, too. True, he was now armed with a rifle and a Bowie knife, with which he would cheerfully gut Sergeant Rusk from sternum to pelvis should he ever cross paths with the man. But alas, that opportunity had not presented itself because Rusk was most likely with Taylor's other troops, somewhere along the dusty road leading to Point Isabel.

Realizing his bombardment of Matamoros was having little effect, Major Brown called for a ceasefire. The Fort Texas soldiers would have to wait for General Taylor to march back to their rescue.

For the next few days, the 7th conserved their ammunition, offering only brief flurries of return fire, while they concentrated on bolstering the fort—that meant Liam and his mates were back wielding their picks and shovels.

Six days after the siege began, most of the Mexican infantry and cavalry stopped firing on Fort Texas and marched across the Rio Grande toward Point Isabel to confront General Taylor's force.

By crossing the Rio Grande, the Mexicans gave the U.S. the legal excuse needed to declare war officially, thus laying claim to the coveted continent all the way to its Pacific Ocean shores.

The distant rumble of cannon fire down the dusty road at Palo Alto told Liam about the ensuing battle between Taylor's force and the Mexican army. Louder evidence of warfare on May ninth informed the Fort Texas defenders that fighting had reached closer to them at Resaca de la Palma.

That afternoon, as the Fort Texas troopers manned the parapets, they saw hundreds of Mexican soldiers rushing back to the reedy crossing points along the Rio Grande. Taylor's troops were victorious.

Possibly worried that friendly fire might strike their own forces retreating from Resaca de la Palma, Mexican gunners halted their salvos against the fort. Sporadically, the attacking forces of Americans fired on the fleeing Mexicans, but Liam watched more and more of them thrash across the river unscathed. Eventually, Taylor's soldiers ceased firing altogether. Most likely because they feared they might harm the Fort Texas defenders.

"Hell, it's a damned stalemate," a soldier down the line grumbled.

The ceasefire by both sides inspired Liam. If he wanted to leave, now was the time to bust out of the fort. After all, this wasn't his war to fight. These eejits were fighting a war not worth the winning—nor the dying. Grabbing his rifle and Bowie, he headed for the fort's lowest redoubt.

"I'm comin' with ye, O'Brien."

Liam shrugged and yelled in Gaelic over his shoulder, "Is fear rith maith ná drosch sheasamh!" Rapidly, he began to climb an unguarded ladder onto the parapet. Aye, a good run was better than a bad stand.

Unless one considered, as Liam waded across the Rio Grande to stagger up the cat-tailed bank inside Mexico, the bayoneted flintlock musket the Mexican soldiers aimed at his heart.

MONTERREY, MEXICO
SEPTEMBER 1846

THE ST. Patrick Battalion!

Who would have thought, once accepted into the unit, Liam O'Brien—or "Guillermo Obregon," the Spanish equivalent of his first and family names—would be made a sergeant of the *San Patricios,* as Mexico's Legion of Foreigners was identified?

Sergeant Obregon's artillery battery was made up mainly of Irish Catholics, many of whom, after complaining of the

U.S. Army's treatment of Mexican civilians and captured soldiers, had crossed over to join the Mexican side. The recruits included a number of German Catholics and a handful of other nationalities, along with a few foreigners who were living in Mexico before the war.

Liam realized that this war, this battle would be his first engagement against his former countrymen. Not that it mattered much to him. He knew Rusk would have adobe-walled him without a qualm.

The thought of Rusk reminded Liam of that bad luck poker game—and the other player, Ulysses Grant. That captain had remarked that this war was the most unjust ever waged by a strong nation against a weaker one.

Right now, to Liam, it appeared Grant was right. Neither the battle Liam was engaged in nor this war in general was going well for Mexico.

That evening, the American army, now 7,000 strong, was fighting from house to house, and had reached Monterrey's Plaza de la Capella. The Mexicans fired upon the American soldiers' volleys of musketry from the windows of the storehouses, the tannery, and the Black Fort. Regardless, the bluecoats kept coming. The conflict in the streets was hand-to-hand, the carnage staggering, beyond anything Liam had ever imagined.

He commanded a mortar unit atop the Citadel. His men, five in all, had to work fast. They loaded a powder charge behind a wet wad, then shoved into the tube a lead ball on top. The mortar had to be fired quickly before the shot itself burned through the wad and ignited the powder.

"Quick! Get the lead out."

"Lead balls are all gone, sir," a pint-sized man named O'Bannon shouted.

Bloody hell, what was artillery without shells?

"O'Brien," Mick said quietly at his shoulder.

"Obregon." Liam snapped, out of patience. An uneasy feeling, one of every Irishman's ominous hunches, was beading sweat on Liam's forehead. He rounded on Mallory. The man always followed him closer than Liam's own shadow. "Obregon, sir."

Mallory's ruddy face was smeared with black powder. "What say we find logs—of the toughest wood, mind ye—and bore them out for six-pound shells? Bind them with some strong bands and we've got ourselves a bit of firepower."

Liam threw up his hands in frustration. "Where the hell are we going to find logs?"

"Down by the river. The woods would cover someone looking to find logs."

Liam was quiet for a moment. Nightfall had quieted most of the fighting except for sporadic rifle and pistol shots. His scramble-for-survival youth in Ireland had taught him one thing, if nothing else. Take care of himself first, foremost, and always. Let the other buggers make their own way because they weren't going to give a shit about him. Wasn't the proof in the pudding that Fiona and Alex put Kerry first and foremost?

"Good thinking that, Mallory. I'll go now and find some."

He grabbed his almost useless Brown Bess musket. Most of them had been condemned as unserviceable by the British government and sold to Mexico back in the 1830s and '40s. "Ye are in charge until I return with the wood." As if he ever planned on returning to that hellhole.

At last! He knew absolutely that the timely luck of the wretched Irish was with him. Feeling his way down a cool, darkened stone stairwell, he emerged onto a parapet. A weak quarter moon revealed a fifteen-foot drop at the most, he figured, from where he stood, onto a carpet of grass spooling down toward the Santa Catarina riverbank.

He unclipped his bayonet from the musket and tossed the blade over. A soft ker-plunk was all he heard. Sucking in a deep breath, he leaped, tucking in his knees and rolling as soon as he landed.

A shot zinged past. When Liam stood, sharp pain bombarded his ankle. Had he twisted or broken it? No matter!

After grabbing his bayonet, he ran for it. Zigzagging, musket in hand, he hobbled toward the shelter afforded by scattered stands of live oak, pines, and some kind of scraggly trees. Quickly, he clipped the bayonet onto his musket barrel.

Which way to go? Should he keep to the river, hoping it would lead him back toward the Rio Grande and Matamoros? Out in the open, he was a sitting duck.

Limping painfully, he wove in and out of the trees, always keeping the shallow, moon-glinted river in sight. When he heard dried pine needles crunching behind him, he whirled around, musket at waist level.

Fifteen yards away, Mick held up both palms. From under his bulbous nose, his grin gleamed in the moonlight. "What with that limp of yuirs, I figured ye'd need a bit of help, Obregon. Uhhh . . . Obregon, *sir* "

THE SANTA CATARINA RIVER provided the two deserters with water, its banks delivering a few handfuls of berries. What it did not provide, at least not for long, was any protection. Their red and navy-blue jackets and pale blue trousers were the military uniform of the San Patricio Battalion, making them stand out among the ever-more-sparse trees lining the banks.

Away from the river, even greater danger loomed. Their white shirts would label Liam and Mallory as deserters to the Mexican civilians and as enemies to the American soldiers. Either way, they were easy targets for almost anyone's bullet.

He was twice-over a deserter, and the only good news was that his ankle was improving.

By mid-morning the following day, the sun was blazing. At the first pueblo Liam spotted from the banks, he looked for line laundry.

Sure enough, outside the splotchy-plastered adobe pueblo, several *jacales* or huts clustered within a hundred yards of the river. Hanging from clotheslines and draped over bushes he could see fresh laundry. *Camisas* and *calzones*— shirts and pants—theirs for the snatching.

At a nod from Liam, Mick hunkered low and scurried

toward the *jacales*. Liam followed. No sooner had they yanked still-damp clothing that looked to be their sizes from the first clothesline, then a mongrel bolted from a doorway, snapping, growling, and barking.

Mick aimed a hard kick at its prominent ribs. Yelping, the dog cowered into a snarling, back-pedaling retreat.

Close to Liam, an old woman, her head covered by a black, woolen shawl, was shoveling a wooden paddle with a loaf of under-cooked bread back into an outdoor *horno*. She looked up at them, eyes wide.

At the smell of the bread, hunger welled saliva into Liam's mouth. The outcry the old woman would put up if he stole her loaf was not worth the risk.

He sprinted past an already-fleeing Mallory. They ran for a good mile along the riverbank before thrashing through reeds and bulrushes to collapse against a cottonwood trunk, gasping for breath.

Mick slouched next to him, laughing hoarsely. "You should have brained that old woman with her own paddle and stolen that loaf."

Liam tucked away Mick's good advice. Mallory having no moral code that would ever hamper him might be of good use somewhere down the line.

Stolen burros shortened their trek north to Matamoros to an uneventful four days of sweltering heat, blasting sand, and blinding sun. That quiet period allowed Liam some time to plan his next move.

Eventually, he knew arrest warrants would be issued on both sides of the Rio Grande for his desertion from both the American and Mexican armies. His name change should help disguise his former identity in the United States. He doubted there were any records of his service for Mexico.

With what he had learned about cattle and horses from Niall Gorman and The Barony's *Paladíneños* he could make a living as a cattle rustler or horse thief. It would be easy enough to steal and drive stolen animals across the Rio Grande to sell in Mexico or to outlets like Cuba—or to kill and skin them on the spot, then sell their hides.

To effect that plan, he would need a horse and a safe place to work. That meant falling back on his earlier profession. With that thought in mind, he and Mick turned their footsteps in the direction of Bagdad, the Matamoros port inhabited by cutthroats and pirates. Liam meant to find a gambling hall that offered him the fullest pockets.

Before he could track one down, however, he found something even better right in Matamoros—a cockfight. But not just any ordinary cockfight. This blood sport took place in a concert hall's *palenque*. The arena's dancers and musicians alternated performances in the cockpit with the cockfights.

The wealthy and fashionable bellied up to the arena, their pockets full of riches the port of Bagdad could only wish for. The aristocrats wagered their bets vociferously and drank heartily while roosters fought to the death.

Drawn by the strum of a guitar, much as he had once been to Niall's, Liam paused outside the concert hall.

Mick shot him an incredulous look. "Has the sun boiled yuir brain? Ye'll not be thinking of going inside, would ye now?" His beefy fingers gestured vaguely at their matted hair, filthy and sunburnt faces, and their unkempt clothing, the kind only the poorest Mexicans ever wore.

"As a matter of fact, I am." Liam passed the burro reins to Mallory.

However, so as not to draw more unwanted attention, Liam kept to the rear of the spectators around the circular pit. Nevertheless, a haughty *hidalgo* in a black *sombrero* ornamented with silver braiding, looked over his shoulder. The nostrils of his high-bladed nose flared as his sharp gaze focused on Liam, the source of that unpleasant stink.

At that instant, the singular reaction of the hidalgo altered Liam's life and inspired him forever. Shame and anger burnt through him like a lit fuse.

He was standing there—without a peso to his name, smelling like shit, his belly growling for food—while somewhere that night, Paladín was seated at some lavishly spread banquet table.

A rapacious greed fueled by furious adrenaline replaced the blood in Liam's arteries and veins.

The two owners proudly placed their gamecocks in the cockpit—shorn of combs and wattles and armed with two-inch spurs—and the wagering began.

Beak to beak, the roosters flapped their wings in a frenzy, kicked their talons, and pecked ferociously at the enemy. Dust swirled. Blood splattered. Feathers flew. The destructive power of aroused testosterone and the fury of the birds fused together into a bloody drama of cruelty, violence, and ultimately death.

From his long experience as a crafty thief, Liam scanned all the spectators by habit until he stopped short. His calculating stare went back to a young woman it had passed over.

Eyes as dark as a coal mine, yet paradoxically bright with excitement, her ripe lips parted in what might later become a gasp of ecstasy. Her hands clamped the wooden railing in eager anticipation of the bloodbath about to begin again. An expensive gold-threaded lace rebozo was artfully arranged around her face, as if to disguise her identity.

Her male companion leaned over and whispered in her ear, bejeweled with diamond and emerald earrings. She flashed the man a sultry smile.

Something about her was familiar to Liam, although he could not quite place her. Certainly, he had never mingled in her social circle.

Then he heard the man address her by name—Senorita Dolores Cavett—and Liam was both surprised and delighted. Her father, a wealthy Land Commissioner, had died a decade earlier in the battle at San Jacinto.

While no great beauty, Dolores was pretty enough and obviously single, as no wedding ring graced her finger. But with some certainty, he doubted she was a virgin.

Not that it mattered—it was her money, not her maidenhead, that he aimed to acquire.

PALADÍN PLANNED TO crossbreed longhorns with the Brahmans he would be importing from India, where his early service as a raj had established him with India's most prominent and influential citizens.

Occasionally, he might make some trips to The Barony's far-flung rustic cattle camps, or he might journey back east to prospect for white-faced cattle.

Then, too, he traveled sometimes into the deserts of northern Mexico, prime cattle country, to purchase longhorns which better tolerated heat and drought.

His trips into northern Mexico accomplished more than cattle buying. Because of his part-Hispanic ancestry and his fluency in Spanish, Alex easily acquired the confidence of Mexico's *hacendados, rancheros,* and *vaqueros.*

Over glasses of *criollo* wine*., pulque,* or *aguardiente,* he learned the locations and troop size of Mexican units massing along the Rio Grande, their exact locations, and the strength of their weapons and artillery. Within days, he would relay that information to General Taylor in south Texas or to Sam Houston in Washington, who was now serving as a Texas senator closely allied with President Polk.

There was another reason for his trips into northern Mexico—Liam O'Brien.

There was still no sign of Liam, who it seemed had vanished. At Fiona's worried behest, Paladín had searched waterfronts from Corpus south to Bagdad—surely the wickedest town in the world, home to the scum of the Seven Seas—and surely the likeliest place to find the young weasel.

Paladín was completely open in acknowledging he himself was a man without honor, but Liam was a sneak. A taker. As unscrupulous as they came. Nevertheless, for all that, he was still family.

Alex accepted that if Fiona valued anything in her life more than land, it was family.

4

BROWNSVILLE
JULY 1847

Margarita Magnum, who had aged considerably since her husband Cavett's death at San Jacinto, closed the heavy-timbered bedroom door behind her and gave Liam a weary smile.

"It is twins you have, Guillermo—a granddaughter and grandson for me, *¡gracias a Dios!*" Her palsied hand made the sign of the cross.

"Good! Then a celebration drink is now in order."

"You don't want first to see your wife and her babies—Sarita and Rodrigo?"

"Roderick."

Let the ninny call his son by the Spanish version of Roderick. Liam knew its Irish translation—"famed power"—and he knew well the legend of Roderick O'Flaherty, Baron of Moy Cullen, the last recognized chieftain of the great O'Flaherty clan. That was good enough for Liam.

Something else he knew—not only had Cavett Magnum's widow failed to recognize him as the boy Liam

O'Brien, but she also had little regard for him as the man Guillermo Obregon. Not that he cared.

"No, I will see the babies soon enough." He would also be bedding Dolores again soon enough. If that spoiled harpy was not up to it yet, there was always one of the not-so-demanding brothel wenches to be bedded across the Rio Grande in Brownsville.

Also there, across the Rio Grande from Matamoros, hunkered Fort Texas—now Fort Brown, named for the foolishly heroic commander, Jacob Brown, who had died during the siege of the fort in the Mexican-American War a year ago.

With its end—and the establishment of the Rio Grande as the boundary between the two countries—the bustling town of Brownsville had sprung up around the old fort. The city's atmosphere was a brawling free-for-all, with men on the hunt for a quick profit, legal or not. Dogs and drunkards skulked everywhere. In the grog shops, taverns, and barrooms, men dueled over honor, or over nothing at all.

It was toward one of the taverns, on the U.S. side of the Rio Grande, that he would be headed that afternoon. He was a co-investor in The Horse Trough. Mallory was half owner with him, as well as bartender, bouncer, and bed maker. The Horse Trough's patrons ranged from an endless supply of border riffraff to an occasional party of carousing hidalgos.

Within months after spotting the lovely and lusty Dolores Magnum, Liam—along with Mallory—had earned a tidy profit rustling on both sides of the border. Enough to invest in the ramshackle tavern. Within a few more months, he was courting Dolores—apparently bedding her vigorously and imaginatively enough to satisfy her almost insatiable need.

In that, if no other, they were well-matched counterparts.

Marriage to her had been a sweetheart deal, in more ways than he had anticipated. Neither his wife nor his mother-in-law had a head for finances and with but little inveigling, he had been able to part Cavett Mangum's widow from a portion of her late husband's dwindling estate.

With that sum had come another sweetheart deal. The U.S. Army Quartermaster was auctioning off boats purchased by the army during the war with Mexico. Prices were incredible. Liam bought an old decaying steamboat, the *Stars and Stripes,* for $680—far less than the $13,500 the army had paid for it. Once he owned the boat, it was easy enough to win a bid to transport artillery and soldiers from Point Isabel downriver to Fort Brown, Texas.

Dolores might not be happy with his penchant for speculation—a silver mine here, a citrus farm there, a thousand dollars lost, or a pile made—but as long as his enterprises satisfied her needs, she did not whine over much. How could she, when she and her mother were gradually plowing through the fortune Cavett had made swindling would-be Texican landowners?

Leaving the Cavett House off Hidalgo Plaza later, Liam

took the Matamoros ferry across to Brownsville. The reek of stale ale, piss, and vomit assaulted his nostrils whenever he entered The Horse Trough. Even at that time of day, a dozen or so rowdy imbibers were plunking their coins on the filthy bar. Mallory, wiping down the counter with a gray towel, looked up and nodded toward a darkened corner. "He's over there, Obregon."

Liam smiled. Lord Geoffrey Brighton had taken the bait.

SAN ANTONIO
APRIL 1848

"I say, Paladín!" Geoffrey Brighton, Earl of Grantham, whistled between his teeth in appreciation of the wagon yards, stables, corrals, and loading chutes that were a part of The Barony Ranch Partnership's San Antonio enterprise. He leaned on the top rail of one of the pens. "This is quite the spread, I believe you Texan folk might declare."

Between Brighton and Paladín, six-year-old Tara and eight-year-old Wade perched on the pen's top railing, their brown eyes alight, their ink-black hair tangled like mustang manes. Paladín, his black frockcoat hitched over his shoulder by a forefinger, watched as Niall—a piece of straw anchored between his lips—approached a Kentucky saddle mare he was breaking.

According to the Irish Traveler, he never finished breaking any horse until its third birthday. Niall's current project was crossbreeding feral mustangs off the open range with finer thoroughbred riding horses because he felt the resulting animals had innate cow-sense, an almost natural instinct for working cattle.

Knotting his fist in the mare's mane, Niall sprang bareback upon her, looking like a centaur as he landed on her back without so much as a tremor. He then began trotting the mare and then loping her. He had told Paladín that the sooner one got a new horse to lope, the less chance of being bucked off.

Rising dust partially obscured Niall's mastery. When the mare was finally winded, he dismounted, rubbed, and patted the mare, picking her hooves before rubbing her legs in what appeared to be a bonding ritual.

"Your partner does seem to have quite a special way with horses."

"And with women—as do all Irishman," Paladín tossed in just to needle the popinjay. The Irish and the English had never acquired any fondness for one another.

Leaving his kids Wade and tomboyish Tara to watch Niall finish the taming, Paladín walked Brighton back to Rafaela and Niall's house, now a two-story affair with an outdoor kitchen. Built around a stone courtyard, the top floor was framed oak with the bottom constructed of native limestone blocks cemented together.

All in all, Paladín felt he and Niall had done well by The Barony Ranch Partnership, although both of them were required to be absent from home more often than either liked.

Niall, for all his wanderlust, had settled down and proved to be a diligent worker. However, he was away more than he was at home—rounding up wild horses in West Texas or buying wagons in the east. He had missed the birth of both Jamie and Catarina.

How to help reduce Niall's lengthy absences preoccupied Paladín less at that moment than the presence of the Earl of Grantham. What was the Englishman doing in Texas? How much did Fiona really value her childhood friend—the one from whom she had told Alex she had received her first kiss?

The day before, he had brought Grantham, with Fiona and their children, to San Antonio. Any business meeting, holiday, or celebration was always greeted as an excuse for the two far-flung families to get together. Two of Alex's *Paladineños* had ridden as outriders to protect the family coach against Indians, bandits, or Mexican soldiers, a few of whom still made occasional raids across the border.

Escorting Geoffrey Brighton through the cool, tiled corridor to the Gorman's sala, Paladín glanced sidewise at the lively Englishman.

He strolled with the confidence of those blessed by inherited money, droll charm, and flashy good looks. Moderately tall with brownish curls that tumbled across his forehead, Grantham was dressed in froths of lace, a gold silk vest, a burgundy frockcoat, and his fingers were lavished with a galaxy of rings.

Brighton arrived merely to tour Texas. Out of curiosity, he had told them.

Only the devil himself knew how he had tracked down Fiona. After all, The Barony was far from most civilized

Texas outposts, stuck as it was in the middle of the south-west Texas vastness.

What if Fiona had written to Grantham? She might have been the daughter of Grantham Manor's scullery maid, yet she had partaken of Geoffrey's tutoring lessons in the manor music room. She dressed in her rags, Geoffrey all in velvet. Had the fop's droopy-lidded hazel eyes once looked adoringly upon Fiona?

Did they still?

She sat on the carved slipper chair next to Rafaela's pianoforte and was taking tea with her and Karl von Hesse-Lippe, seated across from her on the deep-seated rosewood sofa.

At Alex's request, Karl had stopped by the Gorman house. Brighton had expressed an interest in establishing a syndicate that might take financial advantage of the beef bonanza brought about by the Mexican-American War.

Alex wanted the presence of his astute German lawyer for negotiating a possible contract with Grantham. The Barony Ranch Partnership was spending a mountain of cash to expand both Barony Beef and Gorman Transport while trying to keep its overall operations firmly in the black. A substantial investment of Brighton capital could likely guarantee the stability Alex sought for the Partnership.

At the sight of Brighton, Fiona set her tea cup and saucer on the marble- topped lamp table and jumped to her feet, her skirts swirling. "Well, Geoffrey? What did ye think of the yard?" Her green eyes danced with delight.

"Capital!" Grantham declared, bowing over the back of

her hand and, Paladín noticed, giving it a slight squeeze.

At that moment, Alex experienced his first-ever twinge of jabbing jealousy.

Ridiculous.

That Fiona's affections should ever be ensnared by such a dandy. Paladín thought he knew her too well. She would never succumb to Grantham's superficial manners and posturing.

. . . Or would she?

True enough, there had been a few bumps in Alex and Fiona's fiery yet mainly tender ten-year marriage. Most of their disagreements represented mere clashes of opinions—sometimes issues so innocuous as the value of her cash crops versus his cattle.

Actually, their conflict went deeper—all the way to their fifty/fifty interest in The Barony land grant itself. Her claim went back to 1835, when she first became a Mexican citizen, a 'widow with family.' His far earlier claim, to 1767, derived from the original royal land grant to Alex's family by Spain's King Carlos III.

Alex reflected that he and Fiona had invariably resolved their quarrels either through their peppery communication or through slaking their frenzied passions.

But this . . . this preoccupation with her childhood friend . . . Paladín was not sure how to handle it.

Fiona was very much a social creature. Most likely, she found the isolation of The Barony ranch stultifying and welcomed the diversion of the animated and worldly-wise Geoffrey.

Turning to the seated Rafaela, he offered her a deep bow. "A bang-up place you have here, Mrs. Gorman!"

Rafaela's smile was as gracious and regal as everything else about her. "Thank you, your Lordship. All of us hope you will consider San Antonio your second home."

"My primary home, Mrs. Gorman," Brighton turned to Karl, "that is if you approve my offer, Baron. You have had a chance to look over the contract. What do you think?"

Karl rose to his full six-feet, four-inch height. He picked up the sheaf of papers on the lamp table and pulled spectacles from his waistcoat, adjusting the wire-rimmed glasses low on his high-bridged nose. He flicked through the pages, then gave Grantham one of his most judicious lawyerly smiles. "There are a few points that need clarifying, but . . . ," he paused and glanced at Paladín.

Alex nodded slightly. He had complete faith in the wisdom and expertise of the German nobleman, who had become not only a trusted advisor but a family friend.

Karl continued. "I entertain the certainty both my clients can come to terms agreeable to both them and you, Lord Grantham."

"Uncle Karl!" Catarina hurtled through the door with her brother Jamie and Kerry, both thirteen, trailing at a more dignified pace. Kerry drew alongside Alex as Catarina threw her dimpled arms around the lawyer's waist. He set the contract aside and pocketed his spectacles.

Her head of light brown braids craned up. "Did you bring it? Did you bring the yo-yo?" Dressed in a light blue, knee-length smock and white pantalettes, the seven-year-old displayed a captivating gap-toothed grin.

"Catarina," Rafaela reproved her daughter and rolled her eyes, "what happened to curtseys?"

Karl picked her up. "Now where did I put my spectacles?"

She giggled. "Right there! In your vest pocket."

"Are you certain?"

Catarina nodded vigorously. "Silly. They are right there where you—" Her small hand dived inside and came up with a yo-yo. "Oh! You did! You did bring it!"

"There's another one there, too, for Tara." Karl winked at Alex and reached out his free arm to clap Catarina's brother on the shoulder. "Jamie, I do believe that is some muscle bunching there."

Proudly, the kid—who with his betwixt and between features looked like neither Rafaela nor Niall—hoisted one small bicep and made a fist to pump up the burgeoning muscle upon which his suspender strap at once slipped down.

"And Kerry, you have grown at least a foot. It must be grasshopper legs your britches are hiding."

Kerry grinned and properly offered his hand. "Your Lordship."

Gravely, Karl shook it. "If you two boys will look in my buggy, you will find battledores and shuttlecocks."

"Swell!" Both boys sprinted from the *sala*, which set Brighton and Fiona to laughing.

Alex glanced over at Karl and unexpectedly caught the warm gaze exchanged between him and Rafaela. From behind, Alex heard the click-click- click of Niall's spurs on the tiles and could only hope his friend and partner entered too late to notice.

Hell and damnation! Surely, he had imagined it. Surely, what he had glimpsed was merely ordinary fondness shared between Karl and Rafaela.

Unlike himself, Alex knew without a doubt that the two were both persons of absolute integrity. It must have been that foolish moment of jealousy over Fiona and that peacock that stirred in him such a hornet's nest of suspicion.

JEU DE VOLANT, UNCLE KARL called the game. Kerry watched his younger brother lob the shuttlecock just over Tara the Terror's head into the patio's double-tiered fountain.

"No fair, Wade Samuel!" His sister's mouth turned down at both ends. She and her mother called him by his first and middle name, the latter for Sam Houston, only when they were peeved.

Jamie hustled to retrieve the shuttlecock and Wade took the opportunity to shove the older boy over the fountain stone rim, face first into the water.

Sputtering, a soaked Jamie struggled to his feet, standing in water knee-deep. He held aloft the shuttlecock, its feathers shredded and soggy. He shrugged good-naturedly. "This one's a dead bird."

Kerry couldn't keep from grinning but offered to fetch another one. Uncle Karl had left his buggy beside the hitching post out front. Kerry stopped short at the sight of Catarina, crouched atop the post railing, one foot in front of the other, as, arms out-flung for balance, she tried to stand upright. His breath caught in his throat rendering him speechless.

She tottered, lost her balance, and went over the railing head first.

He leaped forward just in time to snag the brat by her ankles before her head smashed into the adobe bricks.

Upside down, her smock flapping against her face, her pale brown braids sweeping the adobes, she wriggled like a trapped snake. "Put me down this instant, Kerry Paladín."

Carefully, he set her on her feet. "What in tarnation are you trying to do, Kiddy Kat?"

She frowned and bared her gappy teeth. "Don't you ever call me that. I am trying to yo-yo." She held up the toy and grunted. "But I am too short."

"And too stupid. If you had hit your head, it would have splattered like a dropped pumpkin."

"Oh! I hate you, you copperhead!" She hurled her yo-yo at him, then flounced off toward the house.

"If you weren't a girl, I would box your ears, Catarina Gorman!" He had been called everything from "tomato-head" to "torch," and had often scuffed his knuckles in fistfights with some of the *Paladíneños'* sons in retaliation. He'd probably lost more fights than he'd won, but "copperhead"—that one beat all.

A swift peek over her shoulder to make sure he was watching, she stuck out her tongue at him. Quick as a cat, she skipped away.

He scooped up the yo-yo and stormed after her. She had taken refuge on the pianoforte bench near where her father stood. Niall's back and one boot were braced against the stucco wall where he tuned his guitar. Catarina flashed Kerry a taunting smile that showed all her teeth. Well, all but the one she was missing.

Why hadn't he thought to goad her by calling her "Jack-o-lantern?" Though five years younger, the brat usually managed to best him.

Uncle Niall's fingers were plucking out some kind of tune. The English gent, Brighton, sat in the slipper chair, his boot pumping to the music. Kerry's mother and Rafaela sat on the sofa, and his father and Uncle Karl stood behind it. All were listening as Catarina chimed in, playing a duet on the pianoforte with her father, their voices blending mellifluously.

Kerry's jaw dropped open. He had never heard anything so . . . so threatening. Like an unseen rattler warning you it was about to strike.

Only at that moment did he remember the shuttlecock he had been going after. With something close to reluctance—reluctance, of course, to miss out on delivering the brat a swatting—he backed from the room.

FREDERICKSBURG
EASTER 1848

That evening on a hill outside Fredericksburg, the traditional Easter Fire flames leaped toward the silver dollar moon.

Though the tradition of hilltop lighting of bonfires to celebrate the eagerly anticipated coming of spring had been brought to Tejas by German immigrants, these particular bonfires also celebrated the Adelsverein treaty negotiated the Easter last year with Chiefs Buffalo Hump and Old Owl of the Penateka Comanche.

It had been a tense night of parleys in 1847 and the settlers, seeing the huge fires and smoke on the hills, had not known the meaning of the signals, which increased their uneasiness. Later they learned the Comanche had been signaling each other about the progress of the treaty negotiations by lighting fires.

The treaty's provisions allowed Adelsverein settlers to go unharmed into the Comancheria and the Penateka Comanche to visit the white settlements. It also provided for a payment of at least $1,000 to Buffalo Hump's tribe.

His long, coarse black hair hanging down, Buffalo Hump appeared the most formidable of humans. Scorning every form of European dress, his body was naked save for a buffalo robe around his loins, brass rings on his arms, and a string of beads around his neck.

Buffalo Hump called Karl von Hesse-Lippe *El Sol Colorado,* the Red Sun, because of his reddish-blond hair. As the Adelsverein's representative, Karl had traveled several times to the Fredericksburg area to meet with the Chief and Old Owl.

Fredericksburg, a settlement of some eight hundred people, consisted of seventy log houses and as many huts.

They were spaced long distances apart on both sides of the main street—with the half-timbered *fachwerk* of the Vereins-Kirche set squarely in the street's center.

Nicknamed the *kaffeemühle*—coffee mill—for its octagonal shape and high cupola, it served as town hall, fortress, school, the Marienkirche, as well as worship sanctuary for Fredericksburg's few Methodists, Lutherans, and Catholics.

It was here, attending the Vereins-Kirche Catholic mass during one of Karl's earliest visits to Fredericksburg, that he first glimpsed Maria Elena Gunter. A black lace mantilla covering her head, she was kneeling before her pew, praying. He was drawn to look at her, for what reason, he knew not.

Quietly, he walked past the rows of mostly unoccupied benches to sit across from her. Her profile, with its aquiline nose, magnolia skin, caramel-brown hair, and generous lips, reminded him so much of Rafaela, he inhaled sharply.

He sat on the backless bench, his nostrils filled with the scent of the Vereins- Kirche's freshly hewn oak and waited for Maria Elena to rise and face him.

At last, she did.

Though neither as tall nor as slender as Rafaela, she did possess a pretty face. As her shy gaze met Karl's steady one, she offered him a charming half smile. He followed her outside where he introduced himself. He learned from Maria Elena that she was a recent widow, barely sixteen, and with a newborn. Her husband had come over with the first Adelsverein group aboard the *Johann Detthard* in 1844. He was a surveyor and had met Maria Elena on a supply trip to San Antonio. He died of dysentery before the birth of their son, Maximilian.

With each visit to Fredericksburg, Karl called on the young widow at the log cabin built by her husband. Karl was one of her many suitors, none of whom Maria Elena would allow to stay beyond a few minutes. Karl's friend, the Comanche Indian agent Robert Neighbors, who had helped Karl negotiate the peace treaty with Old Owl and Buffalo Hump, was also her suitor.

Maria Elena was sweet and pleasant, but she delivered none of Rafaela's incisive commentary or her sharp insights. Her education was, at best, elementary.

Nevertheless, Karl continued to call on Maria Elena. If Rafaela, who visited in his dreams, was forbidden to him, then did it matter who would fill his arms?

When the U.S. Secretary of War sent Major Neighbors along with Rip Ford to explore a wagon route between San Antonio and El Paso, that event moved Karl to the top of Maria Elena's corps of admirers. Then, a year-and-a-half ago, Maria Elena allowed him to share her bed on his occasional visits. Perhaps hoping he would one day ask her to share his name.

He hoped not. He would not want to disappoint her by refusing.

With Max between them, Karl and Maria Elena headed for the Vereins-Kirche. The three-year-old looked apprehensively at the flames leaping from the hill top beyond. She knelt behind him to tie the sashes of his tunic.

"The fires are the bunnies boiling wildflowers to make the colors for their eggs," she reassured her son.

Inside, the Vereins-Kirche appeared to be decorated more for May Day than Easter. Pink, green, and cornflower blue banners and bunting draped the eight-sided walls as well as a dais.

There, an old fiddler in *lederhosen* and red web suspenders was wielding his bow in a fast, wild polka that competed with the revelers' convivial laughter. Couples danced, ale flowed freely, and grilled armadillo and bear meat graced the table along with baked squash and fruit pies.

Off to one side of the room, children were clustered, and Karl steered Maria Elena and Max in that direction. Her son's cherubic face lit up. In a wire cage layered with shrub brush nibbled three hares—not the furry cottontail kind, but the large, long-eared breed the locals called jack rabbits.

Max had obviously inherited his father's light blue eyes and blond hair and had inherited, as well, his Nordic height. The boy was well-mannered and bright. Maria Elena had done well in raising him on her own.

Adjusting his coat tails, Karl hunkered down beside the lad, observing the hares along with the other children. She stood just behind Karl, her brown batiste skirts that matched her bonnet rustling against his spine, her gloved hand lightly placed on his shoulder.

Max glanced back at Karl. "The bunny—can we open its cage?"

"Not a good idea, son. It can hop very high—as tall as

you—and very far and fast, too."

Her hand squeezed Karl's shoulder. He turned his head to peer up through his spectacles at her. Her liquid brown eyes regarded him with deep affection. She was a good woman. A good mother.

"Baron! Baron von Hesse-Lippe!"

He stood, pivoting in the direction of the hearty voice. Over Maria Elena's head he saw Geoffrey Brighton approaching. On the handsome Englishman's crooked elbow was the stout Frau Schmidt. Red apple cheeks and merry blue eyes made her a popular figure in Fredericksburg. Her husband was the town financial officer.

"Gorman told me you were in Fredericksburg. You know *Frau* Schmidt?"

Karl bowed over her fat fingers. "Brighton, may I introduce Frau Gunter." Karl turned to Maria Elena. "The Earl of Grantham is part of The Barony Ranch Partnership."

The two women fell to talking.

"Does business or pleasure bring you to Fredericksburg?" he asked Brighton.

"Syndicate business." One of Brighton's droopy eyes winked and he lowered his voice. "I am courting the Schmidt nest egg to scale up our profits."

He had to admit that Brighton was an asset for Partnership. However, the Englishman's social graces concealed what Karl suspected was both a vacuous core and bank account. In Texas, the man evidently lived off of the good graces of others who were impressed by his title.

"By the way, my good man," Brighton smiled, clapping him on the shoulder, "I hear you are about to play once more the role of godfather."

He cocked his head and blinked. "What?"

"Catarina whispered to me that she thinks she may be getting a brother or a sister for Christmas. It seems our Rafaela is with child again."

The merry music suddenly became irritatingly loud to Karl's ears. The room felt stiflingly hot, the smell of ale and cologne and sweat were nauseating him. "If you will excuse me, your grace, we were just leaving. Give my regards to Paladín, if you should see him first."

Maria Elena was surprised by Karl's abrupt leave-taking, Max was crestfallen, and Karl was decimated. How foolish of him to hover around, like a pet hound waiting for crumbs from Rafaela, when she viewed their friendship with only deep affection. He had let his emotions distort his usual good reasoning.

That night in Maria Elena's bed, when she was wrapped in Karl's arms, she twisted so she could look up at him. Thankfully, it was too dark for her to read his features. "Did I do something wrong, Karl?"

He was aware the reticent Hispanic woman felt gauche among Fredericksburg's vigorous and forthright German personalities. He splayed his long, tapered fingers across her ample hip. "No, you did everything right, my dear."

He was smitten by the sense that the bedroom was much too warm. The scent of Maria Elena's lavender cologne had become overpowering. His silence sounded far too loud.

"I just wanted to leave a bit early, my dear, to be alone with you . . . so I could ask you to . . . be my wife."

WILD HORSE DESERT
JANUARY 1849

In awed appreciation, Fiona stared out the coach window at the herd of wild mustangs galloping across the plains. How she loved this land—with its sea of undulating grass interspersed by sand dunes, the Spanish bayonet soaring twenty-five feet skyward, and mottes of mesquite tree islands flaunting their brilliant lacy branches. They were forever green, even during this dry, winter climate.

As far as any eye could see . . . here was the empire Alex was assembling piece by piece. With Karl's shrewd legal strategy of acquiring ranchos through technicalities and tireless maneuvering, The Barony was gradually becoming all Fiona once envisioned. She had been inspired all those years ago when she read that *New York Morning Chronicle* notice offering free land in Texas to new immigrants.

Land was wealth. It lasted, she and Alex both believed, when things, even people, did not.

As a couple, they might disagree about the rearing of their three children or about the politics of slavery or even the existence of God, but they always agreed on their passion for each other and for their land. Having lost most of his property inheritance through the fraudulent dealings of unscrupulous speculators, Alex now bought land meaning never to sell it.

She knew so well her beloved husband, who sardonically claimed to be the Devil's agent on earth. He was her dark-eyed Devil.

He was hell bent to spend his last breath amassing all the land between San Patricio and the Rio Grande—that acreage that was originally part of his family's Spanish royal grant. Only a few parcels in the Rio Grande Valley, mostly citrus farms, seemed beyond Alex's reach.

Ordinarily, when he purchased an owner's land and livestock, the owner willingly went to work for him—most often as a loyal *vaquero*, a *Paladíneño*. When land acquisition was the issue, he always fought for water.

As he had fought for her.

The jouncing coach, paced by outriders sweeping through high grass, was fairly flying, its horses' manes and tails flowing. She reached across the coach's squab seating and squeezed his hand. Wherever his attention had been fixed, it shifted at once to her, and he smiled warmly. She was glad they had left their children at home with Winnie and Frederick. She and Alex rarely had time enough to be alone together.

Because Alex often carried a payroll that could amount to as much as fifty thousand dollars, he had set up stagecoach camps every twenty miles between San Patricio and San Antonio. The camps provided fresh horses, ready to gallop to safety in case of depredation by bandits or Comanche. Alex believed the Indians rode better than the best light cavalry he had ever opposed while a British officer.

As Alex had once hired Niall, he hired outriders for The Barony to serve both as scouts and for protection—as armed men who were capable of settling disputes if their assistance was needed. The Texas Code of Practice, her beloved called it—the gun was often quicker than waiting for the law to arrive, if there were any.

These days, Niall's services were more profitably focused on his and Alex's Barony Ranch Partnership. This week, Niall was in deep East Texas at Nacogdoches, acquiring a timber mill to supply raw material for the booming Gorman Transport wagon and buggy production.

Hordes of gold seekers were clamoring for Gorman wagons to carry them to California by way of the San Antonio-El Paso road, and then over the Rockies.

However, this was one of the worst times for Niall to be away. Karl had sent them word that Rafaela was in labor. Narrow of hip, she had difficult deliveries with her first two, but this must be an especially hard one for her. She asked Fiona to come and help.

Maybe it was all that Rafaela and she had shared during the Revolution's horrific Runaway Scrape that had bonded them. After all, Fiona had assisted for the seventh time in helping a mother to deliver a baby, the last one on the banks of the Guadalupe River, while waiting to be ferried across before Santa Anna could catch up with the fleeing Texican colonists.

The coach arrived at Niall and Rafaela's house late the following night. A harried Karl met them at the door. After a handshake for Alex, he turned to Fiona.

"She's been asking for you." He nodded over his shoulder at the arched corridor that led to the bedrooms.

"Where are Jamie and Catarina?"

"Maria Elena is entertaining them and Max in our home. I think she thought it best that Jamie and Catarina did not . . . well, you know." He removed his spectacles and rubbed the bridge of his nose. "I have been reading to Rafaela from *Homer* . . . trying to distract her. The maid Carmen is doing the best she can to . . . to handle the more delicate tasks." He sighed and pocketed his spectacles. "I cannot tell you how damned glad I am to see you both."

"I wish I could stay, Karl," Alex said, "but after I freshen up, I'm on to Austin."

Karl frowned. "What is going on there?"

"It seems the legislature is about to charter the state's first railroad—the Buffalo Bayou, Brazos, and Colorado. That happens, much of our wagon service is doomed."

"Even you cannot stop progress, Alex."

Her husband arched one ebony eyebrow in response. At thirty-nine, his hair was still as black as spades. "But I can delay progress—until I can afford to finance my own railroad. From San Patricio to the Rio Grande."

Hearing her husband's confident reply to Karl, Fiona blinked. Hard. Crikey, this was the first she had heard of his latest enterprise. Alex's facile mind, like his boundless ambition, always kept her guessing.

She turned toward Rafaela's bedroom. Halfway down the corridor, she could hear Rafaela moaning. In the bedroom, a Mexican girl in a loose white blouse and blue skirt was applying cool cloths to Rafaela's forehead. When she heard Fiona come in, the girl looked up, her black braid swinging over her shoulder.

"*Hola,* Carmen." Fiona stripped off her gloves. "Ever deliver a bairn?"

The maid's eyes darkened apprehensively. She gulped and shook her head, her braid whipping back and forth.

"'Tis no matter. I will need clean linens. Boiled. And squaw root. Do ye know squaw root?" She found it worked wonders as a childbirth aid. "Oh, and a knife—or some scissors."

The young woman nodded vigorously. After she left, Fiona slid onto the chair beside Rafaela's bed. Every bone in Fiona's body was still vibrating, even her teeth.

Two days of travel by coach and she wanted nothing more than to climb into bed beside her oldest friend. But first, she untied the ribbons of her bonnet and tossed it onto the commode along with her gloves.

A sputtering candle cast its yellow light on Rafaela's much-too-thin body. When Fiona placed her palm on Rafaela's forehead, she found it warm but not feverish and damp with perspiration.

By Fiona's calculation, Rafaela was a fortnight past due. *Mary, mother of Jesus! This canna be good.*

Rafaela's hand, its veins prominent, was clutching a rosary. Beneath the thin bedsheet, her body, with its burdensome mound, contorted suddenly as Rafaela drew her legs toward her waist. Another tortured groan issued past her dry, cracked lips.

She opened her eyes. A weak smile found its way onto her face, as white as the sheet. "You came." Her voice was barely above a whisper.

Fiona choked back her fear and her tears. "Of course."

"Please, Fiona . . . a priest . . . the last rites . . . Penance."

"I did not come, dearest friend, to let ye die!"

CORPUS CHRISTI, TEXAS
MAY 1852

"Pleasure, Fiona, is always equated with guilt. Equated with hell itself."

Smiling archly, Alex slowly traced a path with his sun-browned forefinger from his beloved's four-leaf clover necklace down her bare flesh, goose bumping at his touch, to the delightful valley between her small—but now turgid—breasts.

She half gasped, half laughed. He was not certain if her enticing response was due to his provocative touch or the familiarity of those words he had used in his futile attempt to seduce her that first time in the confessional, a quarter of a century before.

Staring up at him with slumberous eyes, she softly quoted the last of his refrain. "By reason then, all candidates for heaven must forego pleasure. So, I would never deprive you of heaven . . . but would you deprive yourself of pleasure, me luv?"

Her Lilliputian hand slid between their sweat-sheened

bodies, her fingertips lingeringly marking the arrow of fur aiming down his stomach—and its cylinder of muscle and flesh convulsed, as always, at her mere touch, a reaction of his that never failed to surprise him.

Here, the degenerate he had been expected to be satiated with the sprite, as with all his lovers, once he had completed his conquest of her. But no, it was she who had conquered him.

When her small hand attempted to encircle his throbbing length, it was he who gasped. "Fuck!"

Too loud, apparently, because she shushed him, her hand halting. "The children, Alex!"

"They're not children, anymore."

Indeed, Kerry and Jamie Gorman—sharing a room with twelve-year-old Wade next door—were, at sixteen, as randy as cowpokes coming off a three-month cattle drive.

And where better than Corpus Christi, with all its saloons and brothels? Sodom would have had a difficult time competing with the Texas coastal town.

Fortunately, further along the Kinney hallway and out of earshot, Alex's ten-year-old Tara was ensconced in a room with Niall's Catarina, a year older but no wiser in the ways of the world.

Henry Kinney, Corpus Christi's foremost settler, land speculator, and born opportunist, had graciously offered Alex and his entourage—his family, along with the Gormans and Sam Houston—the hospitality of his spacious residence, built of drift lumber found on the beaches and timber cut from the Nueces River bottom.

Otherwise, there was not a room to be had in Corpus Christi, what with the Lone Star State Fair being hosted by Henry himself. Some 20,000 circulars had been promoted heavily worldwide, promising lavish entertainment and prizes in various competitive displays and exhibits, in addition to generous terms for the purchase of land.

Handicapped by the remoteness of its location, south Texas needed settlers, and it was the exhibit of American inventor Samuel Colt's revolvers at the Great Exhibition at London's Hyde Park fair the year before that prompted Kinney to host the Lone Star State Fair.

"Please, my dear, do not leave off your ministrations," Alex urged in a whiskey rasp, breathing softly in her ear.

He smoothed back stray hair from her neck and inhaled her scent. Her smells that whispered not only of her femininity but of her own arousal skyrocketed his body's tension. The sputtering candle mimicked his and Fiona's panting gasps.

He watched the blush suffuse her throat and rise to her cheeks, seeing the desire flare in her eyes. She couldn't have any idea how beautiful she looked.

"That's it," he breathed. "Come with me . . . ride the wave." Keeping her gaze firmly locked with his own, his knee wedged at the juncture of her thighs, willingly spread for him, he began grinding insistently on that nub that accelerated her gasps—and his heart palpitations.

Perspiration pearled her face. "But," she protested in a faint voice. "I wasn't finished with me . . . me ministrations."

"Neither am I." He proceeded to minister to her the best way he knew how.

He at forty-two and she barely thirty-five still found themselves, after all these years, locked in the throes of all-consuming lust at the most unexpected times. Surely it wasn't normal, this ongoing need of her, this rush of wanting that tingled even his fingertips when he touched her. Like a thirsty person needed water, he needed her.

Early in the morning before they left for Corpus Christi, he had caught sight of her in her shear shift, as she bent over the dressing table. When she straightened, her nipples nudged the thin material and the dark triangle at the apex of her thighs was clearly visible. His blood had scoured through his veins like scorching lava, and he had grown momentarily dizzy with desire.

He tried to pace himself now, to temper the satisfying of his forcible passion, when a heavy thudding at the door interrupted that mission.

Head snapping up, Alex rolled off to his side on one propped arm. "Who is it?"

"Alex, it's Henry. Uhhh . . . the deputy sheriffs in the *sala*. Wade's been hurt in a fracas. At the Public Square."

"What? Wade?" Alex squinted at the fireplace mantle's clock. Barely past midnight. He began scrambling into clothes cast off from the night's feverish fandango. "I'm on my way, Kinney."

"I'm coming with you." Fiona nearly shoved him off the bed and rapidly gathered up her hip-length, copper-red hair into a knot at her nape.

"Wait here." He struggled into his pants, shirt, and vest.

"He needs me, Alex." Her voice was brisk and purposeful, as mothers were apt to be when faced with danger to their offspring.

"He needs you alive—and Corpus Christi's Public Square after dark reduces those odds of longevity—even more so now, during the fair." The town was notorious for its public drunkenness and lawlessness. "Never fear, I'll return with our son." He buttoned his frockcoat and tugged on his wide brimmed hat. "Alive, both of us."

He, Kinney, and the deputy sheriff got no further than Fogg's Livery, next door to a quite boisterous saloon. Out of breath and jerking on his sleeve, Fiona caught up with them. "Wade's my son, too, and he needs me wherever and whenever."

When distraught, Fiona was not a female to buck up against. And neither was Sally Skull, whom it seemed was in some way involved, according to the little information supplied by the deputy sheriff.

Alex was aware of her reputation in the wild border country on the Rio Grande. An Amazon of a woman, Sally already had several marriages behind her. She could handle a bowie knife with the equal reckless skill she did a revolver—from either hand, it mattered not which. She was a woman prudent men did not provoke into a row.

Though apparently, one had. The poor cuss lay groaning out his last breaths, his blood clotting the stable straw.

Sheriff Berry, a former Texas Ranger, had the woman's

wrist cuffed to the door handle of one stall. "Just the usual fracas our Sally here triggers when in town," the skinny sheriff explained, shooting the woman a disgruntled look.

In front of the next stall, back against its slatted door, sat Wade, one knicker hitched up past his scuffed and bloodied knee. His lank black hair swagged over his forehead, clipping his nose. At his father and mother's approach, he glanced up and gulped.

"Might I ask what brings you here, without my permission?" Alex demanded of his younger son in a gruff tone that concealed his immense relief.

"Fine young man you got there." The hard-featured Sally spit a wad of tobacco juice into the straw at her feet.

"Wade Samuel Paladín," Fiona snapped, dropping down next to him, her full satin skirts billowing around them both. "Just what do you think you are doing out this time of night?"

The relief of Alex's beloved was evident not only in her own sharp tone but also in the way she converted her fear to energy, as she set to fussing over the boy's injured knee.

"'Tis nothing, Ma. One of the bullets ricocheted off the horse trough. Barely skimmed me."

The sheriffs grin augmented his buck teeth. "Take the kid on home and beat the tar fire out of him tomorrow."

Such was Alex's gratitude—with Wade none the worse off for his nocturnal escapade than a nick from the bullet— that he reserved his reprimand to a single, stern, "You can muck the pig sty when we get back, son."

It turned out the thirteen-year-old had wanted to sneak

into the fair's Colt Exhibit, already closed, to study the display case of newfangled revolvers.

"Can't blame the lad," Houston said the next evening, walking stick in hand, as they all strolled along Water Street's promenade. "I even lobbied President Polk last year to adopt the Colt .45's for the U.S. military."

Alex and his retinue were headed to the Maltby Circus. That day, two-thousand visitors swarmed a town of not more than fifty families to see the horse races, bull fights, and cock fighting, as well as the exhibits.

Dodging a carriage pulled by four horses, Alex, Houston, and Karl shepherded their troop of kids down the dirt street toward the circus tent erected on the plot next to Anderson's salt mill.

The women—Fiona, Maria Elena, and Rafaela—were lingering at a taco vendor's cart, laughing as Fiona tried daintily to consume the untidy, dripping cuisine.

At least Fiona and Maria Elena were laughing. Rafaela managed a somber smile. Her still-born baby three months earlier still cast a pallor on her spirits.

Although the Irish Traveler never addressed that loss, Alex knew his friend anguished for both it and his wife's grief. He was missing the fair, his presence required by a work stoppage by the Texas Wheelwrights Association.

Still, this neglect nettled Alex. He had not forgotten that warm exchange he had glimpsed between Rafaela and Karl. Could he have been wrong?

For Christ sake, is it my demonic need to possess and protect what I consider mine that I fault others?

Karl wanted to see the horological and surgical exhibits and Maria, Rafaela, and Catarina were interested in the musical exhibits. Seven-year-old Max, whom Karl had officially adopted, wanted to sample the dried meat biscuit for which Gail Borden, a transplanted Texican, had taken the Blue Ribbon. Alex himself was interested in the electric telegraph and barometers.

Eventually, his interest reverted to the steadily growing desire to resume his dalliance with Fiona that had been cut short the evening before. Something about being in a different locale, away from the ordinary, sent all his senses on alert and aroused his desire for her to a heightened degree.

With closing time approaching, everyone regrouped and headed back toward the Kinney residence. They got no further than the nearest streetlamp when Fiona's gloved hand on his sleeve tightened. She stopped short. "Alex!" He looked down at her blanched face. "What, my love?"

"That gentleman, across the street—in the top hat."

He glanced up to see a short male, accompanied by a colossus of a man, round the corner, out of sight. "What about him?"

"He looked so familiar. The way he walked . . . the way he held his shoulders." She shook her head slowly. "My imagination, I suppose. But I thought he might be—"

Her puzzled expression turned to a sharp, pained one, and he inclined his head over hers. "What? What is it?"

Her hands flew to lace over her stomach. "I think I am going to be sick."

"Are you . . . " he lowered his voice, "Are you with child?" Fear struck him. She was so small, had such trouble with her three previous deliveries. And had not Rafaela nearly died in delivering her still born? What if . . . . What if . . . .

Saying nothing, Fiona shook her head adamantly.

Karl raised a brow at Alex. "The tacos?"

Alex wouldn't be surprised. The Spanish word referred to the pieces of paper used to wrap gunpowder for excavating Mexico's silver mines, and hell if these tacos weren't as hot as sticks of dynamite.

He scooped Fiona up against his chest and looked to Houston and Karl. "Can you two escort the rest of the group back?"

The two nodded and Rafaela volunteered, "I'll see to it that the children get settled in."

Cradling Fiona, whose shoulders were shaking, as if in fever, Alex strode resolutely back down the boardwalk and hailed the hackney out front of the nearest saloon.

As the town was without a doctor, the Negro driver hauled up the hackney before the apothecary's residence. For all Alex's banging on its screen door, no one answered. Meanwhile, Fiona had thrown open the hackney door and was retching violently.

Returning to the carriage, he directed the driver to the Kinney homestead. He found his handkerchief and, taking her small jaw in one hand, began gingerly patting clean her sweaty face.

"Better you had eaten the *mezcal* worm than eaten the

street vendor's taco," he tried to joke.

In answer, she clapped her hand over her mouth—only to spew between her fingers, over her slippers and his boots.

He sighed, once again gently swiping her trembling lips.

"Oh, God, Alex." Her eyes squinched closed. "'Tis verra sorry I am."

"Have no worry, my love. We'll set our young, wayward Wade to cleaning our shoes."

"No, no—'tis sorry I am about the horrid feeling that came over me, at the public square."

Abruptly, his own stomach wrenched with worry. Then, she was, indeed, seriously ill.

She fingered her four leaf clover pendant as if it were an amulet. "Alex, t'was the *an da shealladh* I felt back there."

He sighed more heavily. That damned Irish second sight—and her finely-tuned sense of looming, and unalterable, doom.

PART
2

THE BARONY RANCH
SEPTEMBER 1856

According to local custom, any opportunity for people to get together was a grand treat in the near-empty expanse that was southwest Texas. For weeks, word of a shindig would go out to every *rancho,* saloon, and cow camp.

From the army depot in San Antonio to the bullrings of Brownsville to the tepees of the Penateka Comanche, news of The Barony's grand *fiesta*—always a cherished three-day event—was broadcast everywhere throughout the region.

This weekend-long celebration was staged in honor of *El Patron's* son, Kerry, who was going off to college—at Baylor University in Independence, Texas—and Niall's Jamie, off to St. Mary's Institute in San Antonio.

Not that Fiona was too thrilled by their son's departure. Alex stood at his office window, only half watching his *Paladíneños* entertaining Barony's guests that morning with feats of calf roping and bronc riding in the corrals.

In fact, both she and Rafaela were behaving overprotectively with their sons' approaching departures.

Understandably, Rafaela, with the stillborn death of one child four years before, insisted Jamie attend St. Mary's, where she could keep a sharper eye on him.

Fiona, being Catholic at heart, had encouraged Kerry to do the same—join Jamie at the college in nearby San Antonio. But Kerry was determined to attend Baylor to study their curriculum of intellectual philosophy. *Intellectual philosophy?*

What their son needed to learn was ranch management!

Outside the hacienda, tents and wagons of guests from near and far peppered the ranch. More cherished guests were sharing the *Paladlnenos* bunk houses. There had to be eight score or more merrymakers coming and going over the three-day event whose revelry continued unchecked.

Behind him, Brighton continued, "I have established reputable connections in Brownsville. They feel a public stagecoach between San Antonio and there would be an outstanding investment for The Barony and a boom for their economy. I would urge you to jump on the prospect."

Alex turned back to him—and Niall, Houston, and Karl. They had taken the opportunity provided by the celebration to attend to The Barony Ranch Partnership business. "I have some doubts about your suggestion, Brighton."

Quite the dandy in his lavender blue vest of silk and deep purple frockcoat, he had yet to marry. Alex had the impression that Brighton's amorous interests had never been set on Fiona—or any other female, for that matter— much to Alex's ease of mind. Get his dander up and he would have to send a second to deliver a challenge to the English earl.

But then, Fiona could be just as jealous tempered. Now that Alex's former lust, Thérèse del Valle, had married the hatchet-hewn pastor Daniel Engler, Fiona was acting the grand and gracious hostess to the couple, who had traveled up from Brownsville, along with Moses and Charlotte Solomon, for the weekend festivities.

Niall ceased tinkering with his guitar and looked up. His sloping eyes held a note of nostalgia. "The wagon trade in all its forms—'tis going the way of the bison and the mustang. Soon to be extinct."

Hands clasped behind his back, Karl was pacing the tiled floor thoughtfully. The lawyer turned to look at Niall. "What would you suggest?"

The Irish Traveler's blue-gray eyes flicked to Alex. "As much as it pains me arse to say this, I think 'tis time we put Alex's plan into effect—the railroad from San Antonio to Brownsville. What say ye?"

Alex walked to his desk and picked up his glass of sangria. Rafaela had made quantities of fruity wine to quench the guests' parched throats after the morning's rodeo was over. By midday, the temperature would be soaring.

"I think the Partnership could possibly defray the initial outlay—with the help of some state funding. But the clock is ticking."

He glanced to Houston. "Did you not say the state's legislative special session will soon adjourn?"

The old general nodded without looking up from the miniature tomahawk he was whittling from a pine branch.

Alex turned back to Niall. "Can Gorman Transport handle the logistics with our esteemed congressmen in Austin?"

From his curt nod, Niall's over-long butternut curls tumbled across his brow. "I can head back to San Antonio a day early and prepare a business plan—that is, if Rafaela and the kids can catch a ride back on the next wagon load through here after the fiesta? I know Rafaela would like to spend more time with Fiona."

Alex nodded. His friend might be near illiterate, but when it came to numbers, the Irish traveler was as skilled as he was with horses. A hard worker, Niall was. In reality, Alex thought he worked too hard.

Alex looked at Karl. "Can you take care of the charter legalities?"

"Of course. I will do that right after the *fiesta.*"

"Brighton—can you secure any additional financing for us?"

The Englishman rose to go, flipping his frockcoat's tails. Alex's vanity was pleased to note that while his own hair betrayed only the faintest threading of that odious gray at the temples, the popinjay's hairline was receding in inverse proportion to the man's belly growth. "As I said, Paladín, I have excellent sources in Brownsville. With Texas cotton being exported from Pointe Isabel, nearby Brownsville shippers are raking in the chips."

"Then I propose a toast to the Rio Grande Valley

Railroad."

The five raised their glasses, but Alex noticed Houston's taciturn silence. After the others took their leave, the old general set aside the whittled tomahawk and picked up his hickory cane. Still seated, gnarled fingers overlapping its knob, he leaned forward and gave Alex one of his patented eagle-eye stares. "I am thinking about running for governor of Texas."

"You would win that election like a cakewalk. But talk to me, Sam. That is not all that is on your mind."

The old man's fingers rubbed his cane's worn-smooth knob.

"Well?"

"As U.S. senator, I am still privy to secret legislation going on in Austin. Someone in Brownsville is putting forward a bill preventing private corporations from building railroads with state funds."

"Who?"

"Not sure exactly. I have heard the name 'Obregon Enterprises' bandied about in discussions. Seems that firm has pillaged some Rio Grande Valley citrus farmers out of their land grants. Many of its real estate schemes have been acquired at a pittance, I understand—paid for with funds Obregon earns running a fleet of steamboats on the Rio Grande. Naturally, railroads in the Rio Grande Valley would doom his steamboat business. I have a nasty feeling you will have a devil of a time getting your charter approved."

"Ahhh, but you should know, Sam, the devil and I are in league with one another—and besides, you still owe me one for San Jacinto.”

EVERY MORNING ON THE BACK patio near the pump, Kerry shaved what his father termed peach fuzz.

This morning, he and Jamie were leaving before sunup to get in some hunting before the banquet that evening. Celebrated down on the Nueces beneath the shade of the native pecans and giant triple-trunked *huisaches*, the banquet would bring the three days of partying to a close.

He stole into the silent kitchen, though his rowels clinked on the tile floor. Evidently, Frederick, the old leprechaun, was up early as well and had started a fire. Its flickering light had yet to reach the enormous kitchen recesses. Either Winnie or one of her three kitchen servants had already hung a huge kettle of pinto beans on the fireplace crane.

Furtively, Kerry palmed a couple of *buhuelos* from the dozens set out to cool on one of the larger tables. The fried, puffed tortillas sprinkled with sugar and cinnamon and piled on plates for holiday gifts to neighbors would get him and Jamie through breakfast.

Bunuelos in one hand and his expensive two-trigger muzzle loader in the other, he made it as far as the door.

“Kerry Paladín, put down those *bunuelos*. You are as bad a thief as your father was.”

Was? Everyone knew his father drove a hard bargain with the intention of driving out competitors. Recently, he had issued a stockman a draft for $167.52, payable only at the Bank of San Antonio, where the stockman could cash it only for notes or silver at twenty-seven cents on the dollar.

"As a lad in London, your father stole tarts set out to cool in the kitchen window and ye do no better."

He turned his most beguiling smile on her. "Awww, Winnie, please?"

Her rheumy blue eyes twinkled. "All right, be on with yourself, ye redheaded rascal."

He bent down and planted a kiss on her heavily jowled cheek. "I know I'm your favorite."

Jamie was already in the stables, their horses saddled. He was mounted astride one of The Barony's sorrels. Like his father, Jamie was a good judge of horseflesh. In Texas, owning a fine horse was an important social consideration.

Kerry's father had told him how General Sam had ridden nags during the Runaway Scrape, but the day before his Texicans were to meet up with Santa Anna's armies at San Jacinto, Houston had spent what little he had on acquiring a handsome white stallion on which he was to lead his men into the epic battle.

Dawn's early light was shafting through the thrown-wide stable doors. Kerry planted a fist on his hip and stared up at Jamie. "You do not look too good, mi amigo. Your face is as white as Winnie's pastry dough."

Jamie wiped the back of his hand across his forehead, damp with sweat despite the stable's relative coolness, and managed a sheepish grin. "I think it was that all-nighter with Gussies Girls."

Despite Rafaela's worried hovering, Jamie was determined to try his spurs.

The week before The Barony was to host the fiesta in their honor, he and Jamie had decided to do their own celebrating in the Den of Inequity that was Corpus Christi. Jamie had hitched a ride early to The Barony on one of the Gorman Transports wagons and, together, Kerry and Jamie had ridden to Corpus Christi to participate in a Bacchanal of drunken orgies.

But Jamie had been looking a little rough around the edges this past week. Yesterday, he had spent the day abed. Rafaela had brooded over him like she was Florence Nightingale. Kerry sincerely hoped his best friend did not have a case of the clap.

All that morning, he and Jamie, protected by their shotgun chaps, prodded their mounts through the thorny chaparral and thickets of devil's claw acacia in search of bedded down deer. The Barony was a vast, unforgiving terrain beset by sudden floods, long-lasting drought, blistering sun, rattlesnakes, and feral hogs, not to mention the occasional Indian party or band of Mexican marauders.

The hunt appeared to be wasted effort. Jamie trailed sluggishly behind him, and even he was ready to call it quits. But then, he sighted a buck with a big rack, poised beneath the scanty shade of a mesquite forty yards away and ready to make a dash for it. He held up his hand, signaling Jamie to freeze.

Slowly, Kerry raised his highly prized rifle and peered through its V notch. The big white tail would help supplement the banquet's lavish table that evening. Barely daring to breathe, he cocked the hammer then set the front trigger.

A light touch on the rear trigger fired the rifle, its recoil slamming Kerry's shoulder and its *ka-boom* ear-ringing. The buck dropped.

Rapidly and efficiently, he—with Jamie's lethargic help—skinned the twelve-point buck, quartered it out, saving everything for use, and loaded up to head back.

The Big House and *vaquero* quarters turned out to greet them with their cargo. Even the guests' children—those old enough to grab the colored cloth off a calf's tail—deserted the arena and their chance at a prize to gawk at Kerry's buck.

As he and Jamie dismounted, Uncle Karl and Maria Elena, with flaxen-haired Max between them, left the veranda to admire the buck's rack, strapped to Kerry's saddle.

The usually shy Maria Elena sniffed and, with a laugh, pinched her nose. *"¡Híjole!"*

Max clamored to see and his stepfather hoisted him to his shoulder.

Diego, the ranch's *mayordomo,* and Kerry's brother Wade left off tossing horseshoes. With the cowboy's rolling gait, the two ambled over to take a gander at the kill.

Tara the Terror strode out of the stable. No skirts for his sister, but pants and work boots. The fourteen-year-old took one look at the rack and sneered. "A twelve-pointer is the best you can do?"

The usually pesky Catarina hung back to watch from the veranda. He strove mightily not to strut like some damned peacock in front of the others, but he did wink at her as, shouldering his hefty saddlebags, he headed for the kitchen. Hell, the bags were heavy, but there was no way he would let her or anyone catch him dragging them.

As he passed her by, her pale brown eyes raked over his bloody hands, boots, and chaps, riding low on his hips. Her tongue tsked. "Clodhopper!"

He shot her a lopsided grin. "Kiddy Kat."

She tossed her chin and flounced back inside the house.

Jamie struggled with his own heavily packed saddlebacks. "I am headed for bed, Kerry. I have a hell of a headache. Wake me for the banquet tonight and not before."

Kerry's mother had a hip bath of hot water ready for him. "'Tis verra proud of ye yuir father is." She grinned and, standing on tiptoe, reached to yank off his filthy low-crown, large brimmed hat.

"It'd be nice to hear him say so."

"Acck, we both know he will never let a bragging word leave his lips. And if ye get any taller, son, 'tis a step stool I shall be needing. Ye've got his height and military bearing, ye do."

Once she left, Kerry began stripping. His thoughts lingered on his father. Both he and Uncle Karl were trying to persuade him to enlist in the military. Robert E. Lee, Commander of the Military Department in San Antonio and a friend of Uncle Karl's, was even a party guest that night.

Something in Kerry bucked against a society that placed a great premium on forced conformity. Still, his father, who had served with 'His Majesty's' troops, had a way—with just the lift of one brow—of intimidating.

As Kerry dressed and tamed his red curls into some semblance of order, his thoughts wandered from his father to Catarina. What an irritating child. Although he could not help but notice she was growing cabbages. What was she . . . thirteen? Fourteen? She and Tara were about the same age, but his tomboy sister defied human age estimation.

With cabbages lingering on his mind, his imagination rocketed to the daughter of the paymaster at the army depot in San Antonio. What was her name? Gladys? That was it. He had plans to claim her hand for a dance that evening, a Paso Doble or one of the cuadrillas—and more than mere dancing, if she would let him.

It would seem, at the moment, his mother had her own plans for him. He had started down the cobblestoned path to the river, where the banquet tables were set up beneath the trees hung with lanterns. Though twilight was still half an hour off, guests were already mingling.

She hailed him from a blanket spread beneath one leafy bower. "Kerry, I want ye to meet me old friends from Matamoros—the Englers and the Solomons."

Two couples sat with her. Hunkering on one knee, he shook the proffered hand of the nearest gentleman, who wore the puritan's white bibbed collar. "A pleasure, Reverend."

She made the other introductions, adding, "They have turned La Espada Presidio into a school."

Kerry was born there and he vaguely recollected his

father had leased out the presidio to the other gentleman, Moses Solomon, a smallish man, for a dollar per month. Somewhere, Kerry figured, there had to be a payoff for his father.

The other two women in their beflowered sunbonnets, Mrs. Engler and Mrs. Solomon, were all right in the looks department he reckoned, but his mother took the prize for pretty, hands down.

He spotted Jamie's mother coming down the path toward them. Her skirts swishing gently around her ankles, Rafaela moved with a grace her brat of a daughter completely lacked. "Jamie is not with you?"

He had completely forgotten. He shot to his feet. "I will get him—he's taking a nap. We rose before dawn."

Leaving Rafaela to chat with his mother and their Matamoros friends, he headed back to the Big House. When he opened Jamie's bedroom door, he halted abruptly. "Oh, God!"

Jamie sat at the edge of the bed, palms braced on its mattress. Blood streamed from his nostrils and the corners of his mouth and eyes.

ALEX FELT JAMIE'S FOREHEAD. It was dangerously hot. Thin trickles of blood traced lines of agony from his eyes, nose, and mouth. His half-masted eyes were yellowed. The lad, supine in the bed, was nearly unresponsive to his questions.

Alex rubbed his jaw. He had been cutting across the patio on his way to join the others at the banquet when his anxious son waylaid him. "You and Jamie were in Corpus?"

Kerry nodded. He had the grace to look abashed.

"Find Diego. I want him to bring back your Uncle Niall. He is on his way to San Antonio. As small as Diego is, he will ride faster than any jockey. Where is your mother?"

"Down by the river—with friends of yours from Matamoros." Kerry swallowed hard. "Jamie's mother is with them. She was looking for him."

"Say nothing to anyone, son." Once word was out, the guests would panic—and that would help nothing.

Having dispatched Kerry, he left Jamie's bedroom and with reluctant but brisk steps, strode down to the Nueces. By now the sun had set and the lanterns were lit. He took only a respectful moment to greet his old Matamoros friends, all seated on the spread blanket, then drew Fiona off to the side.

Above her confetti freckles, her eyes were questioningly wide. She knew him so well. "What is wrong, luv?"

He looked over her head. Though Rafaela was listening to something Thérèse was laughingly sharing, he could see Rafaela's curious gaze straying to him and Fiona.

He would have preferred to talk to his wife alone. However, she could offer Rafaela comfort. A gift for which he woefully lacked. "Find an excuse to draw Rafaela away. Meet me with her in the bedroom we have given over to Jamie."

Her lips flattened into that all too familiar stubborn line. "I asked ye what is wrong, Alex Paladín."

He had seen the epidemic once with the East India

Company in the tropics. A ship carrying tropical fruit had docked in a seaside village. Within hours, the citizens who boarded the vessel to buy its produce began showing signs of yellow fever. From there, the epidemic had spread, though not even the best doctors knew why or how. And even as good as Fiona was with herbs and poultices, he knew her skill could not stop this scourge.

He said in a *sotto voce,* "Jamie. He has the Yellow Jack."

Her fingertips flew to her lips. "Bloody hell! No!"

DESPITE ALL FIONA'S DESPERATE ministrations— quinine, opium, laudanum, and comanche—she failed to save Jamie.

Even though Niall had yet to return, Alex arranged for the burial early the next morning because of the heat. He ordered his carpentry shop to build a casket. Three of his *vaqueros* dug the grave—at the apex of the bluff, where the huge live oak tree spread its fifty-foot canopy.

Alex did not know how he would manage if he were to lose one of his children. Niall would take it hard, but Rafaela . . . life had been difficult for her these past few years.

Candles were lit. She, Fiona, and Alex sat up with his body all night. The guests became the mourners. Throughout that night, one by one or in pairs, they stopped by the bedroom to pay their respects.

At dawn, lanterns still lit, the mourners gathered yet again. Kerry, eyes red from surreptitious tears, culled four white horses from the herd to draw the funeral wagon.

Beneath the great live oak tree on the bluff, three tombstones already commemorated lives that had come and gone—Alex's older brother Enrique, his adoring and frivolous wife Graciela, and their three-year-old daughter Rosa. Gone, too, were the Paladín estates back in England, with only a few crumbling walls left to attest to a barony that had once been of regal regard.

Houston, Karl, and Brighton, along with Daniel Engler, Moses Solomon, and himself, served as the six pall bearers. On the right arm, each mourner wore a black crepe band that Thérèse and Charlotte volunteered to sew from an old black silk dress of Fiona's. As there was no priest, she gave the rosary, her usual Irish lilt a raw monotone.

During all this, Rafaela had not broken down once. Not a tear. Not an outcry. Not a palsied hand. She was a beautiful Madonna made of marble. Her stoicism was unnerving. Paladín knew, sooner or later, her pent-up grief would have to shatter her.

After the services, most of the guests left. That evening, he stood in the shadows of the patio's colonnaded portico, where it was cooler. He bit off the end of the after-dinner cigar he intended to smoke. He was not a social creature like Fiona and was grateful for the respite for the few solitary moments to reflect with only the fountain's splashing water to distract him.

How would he break the news to Niall when he arrived? Or perhaps Diego had already told him . . . if indeed, Diego had caught up with Niall yet. Fiona was concerned not only about Rafaela but also Catarina. The brash girl seemed only slightly fazed by her brother's death. Perhaps she had yet to absorb its reality.

Suddenly, the French doors leading from the library onto the patio were flung open. Rafaela hurtled into the arched corridor. The library's candlelight silhouetting her, she appeared a black wraith. She flung her arms around the portico's nearest column in a fierce grip. Had she possessed the biblical Samson's strength, she would have tumbled the columns. Her forehead dropped against the hand-carved wood and her shoulders began heaving. Her deep gasps affected Alex as pain made audible.

He had thought she was alone. Then Karl stepped through the doorway. He crossed to her and aligned his arms over hers, cradling her back to his chest. "Go ahead, Rafaela. Cry. Cry, my dear."

A sob broke from her. She whirled into his embrace, her palms clasping his shoulders. Her anguished face tilted up to his. In the moonlight, his countenance was just as anguished.

"Oh, God, Karl . . . what would I have done without your friendship?" Her voice amplified. "Over the *years* . . . *and* now? Now this. Another child taken from me. More than I . . . more than I can bear. Do you hear?" Her fists thumped on his chest. "Do you hear me? Do you hear me, God?"

Karl's head lowered. His lips claimed hers in a silencing kiss that even the village idiot would know was not one of solace. Arms locked around his neck, she clung to him. As if he were her life buoy. A half-sob, half-sigh escaped from her.

Alex stepped forward into the moonlit patio and cleared his throat. "I think it is time we rejoin the others in the parlor."

Startled, both broke away from each other. With another tortured gasp, Rafaela buried her face in her hands. To Karl's credit, he made no excuses. "I think you are right." He grasped Rafaela's elbow solicitously, propelling her toward the open French doors.

Alex followed the two inside. A sick anger roiled in his gut. His first reaction was to call out Karl. Alex was a crack shot, but he could not bring himself to kill his associate, who, besides, never packed a pistol.

Alex sincerely liked Karl and had depended on his counsel over the years. German speakers outnumbered both Hispanics and Anglos in San Antonio, making Karl a valuable asset in Texas' largest town.

Nonetheless, Karl's indiscretion, planned or not, with the wife of Alex's best friend, could only cause constrained relations between Alex and his associate for the rest of their lives.

Most importantly, from this day forward, Alex would have to conceal carefully his acrimony for Karl from Niall . . . because Niall was even better with his pistol, and his wild gypsy blood mixed with his hot-headed Irish temper might just well result in the killing of not only Karl but Rafaela.

SAN ANTONIO
SEPTEMBER 1858

In the woods down behind his ranch house, Niall hunkered back on one boot heel, his opposite knee crushing the pine needles. That evening, the wind was snatching scarlet leaves from the cottonwoods and tumbling them, whirling them, around the simple marker. Merely his son's name and dates of birth and death were chiseled into the pink granite hewn from a local quarry. Nothing in the etched strokes on the granite could possibly indicate the heartache and tears and grief entombed in a living body.

Cupping his palm to block the wind, he struck the lucifer and lit the kindling. He watched the flickering flame lick the twigs, then blister the branches, and, gradually leap to the split logs.

For the second year now, he was observing Jamie's death—give or take a day, depending on the weather—in the way most familiar to him, given his gypsy heritage. Their tradition of mourning was a bizarre one, granted, leftover from the Middle Ages when all personal belongings of a gypsy were burned to prevent the spread of the plague.

The bonfire in memory of Jamie roared to a life of its own, its smoke wreathing Niall with its woodsy scent. He settled back on his haunches and blew his breath up his face in what was a half groan, half sigh.

After a moment, he stretched an arm to feel blindly for the article nearest him. Cold, hard metal poked his fingers. The rowels of a spur. He picked up the pair, fingering the worn leather strap of one. They had been Jamie's first pair and had lacked the adult's chap guards, but six-year-old Jamie hadn't cared. He had strutted about like a cock in the henyard. Niall flung the pair into the bonfire, pressing his lips into a firm seam that silenced his heart's scream.

His gaze not forsaking the eternal flame, his hand groped for another item and encountered the *Franklin Primer* and *First Reader,* its spine nearly peeled away. Without glancing through the thumb-worn pages, he knew he'd find Jamie's scribbling and doodles in the schoolbook's margins. Once again, mere markings and etchings and strokes that somehow contained a wealth of meaning and memories.

And all for what? Who would remember that there was this incredible boy who grew to be an extraordinary young man, once he and Rafaela were gone?

The bonfire's ghostly light illuminated the wraith-like apparition moving toward him . . . as if his yearning and his loneliness had summoned Rafaela. Spreading her skirts, she dropped down beside him, not touching him, and hugged her knees to her chest.

"How did you know . . . what I was doing?"

The firelight flickered over her vulnerable beauty, a beauty tinted with ineffable sadness. The crackling of the fire almost drowned out her soft response. "Do you not think I know every single item in Jamie's room, Niall? Last year, around the time of his . . . the anniversary of when he left us . . . his shaving mug, his whittling knife, and a pair of his suspenders went missing. I wasn't sure what to think. Then today, when I discovered more things missing, I understood. Your gypsy roots will never die."

But loved ones did. He swallowed hard. "I'd give the world to wrap Jamie in a bear hug one more time."

She leaned her head against his shoulder, surprising him. Since Jamie's death, she had seemed remote, detached from this world. "I know. It's never again to be."

He lapped his arm around her and pulled her to him. The way she nuzzled her face against the cradle of his neck and shoulder was the solace he had been seeking these last two years. He turned his own face up to the firmament. "We'll see him on the other side of the stars, me luv."

MATAMOROS, MEXICO
OCTOBER 1859

Liam sat across from the Earl of Grantham at one of the long boards of the Calle Real Cafe. At another board, a government official and two shopkeepers hunkered over their cups of Havana coffee.

The Coffeehouse's shaved wooden floors and wainscoted walls, decorated with exotic local taxidermy, was much the same as Liam remembered it in 1835, when he first arrived in Matamoros as an orphan—well, an orphan being passed off as Fiona Flanigan's son. A son who would never receive what should be rightfully his.

And for that reason, if no other, Liam frequented the Matamoros coffee house. Here, he plied sub rosa undertakings best negotiated away from the *nouveau riche* society of Brownsville, where he and his twins now lived since the year before last, when malaria killed off the sickly and forever complaining Dolores.

Even Brownsville was not all that safe. Earlier that year, the Mexican bandit Juan Cortina had captured the town for a while.

That afternoon, Rod and Sarita, going on thirteen, had accompanied Liam and were playing aboard his shallow drafter steamboat moored nearby at the Paso de la Anacuita dock. Better they play on the *Colonel Worthington* than eavesdrop on his dealings today with Geoffrey Brighton.

Not that Liam underestimated the balding dandy. The man was perceptive and was doubtless out to play both sides of the fence in order to sustain his frivolous life style.

Liam, too, was determined to sustain his own lavish life style. Slave trading was one of the means to that end.

Although slave trading was illegal in Texas, slaves who came with their owners from the older slave states were permitted. A loophole in Texas law allowed slavers to discharge slaves in New Orleans, the center of the Deep South trade, and bring them into Texas with false papers.

Using his steamboats to ferry the illegal African trade through Galveston and Corpus Christi was beginning to pay off big for Liam.

Blocking Paladín's bid for the San Antonio-Rio Grande Valley railroad had already paid off. Whatever it took, Liam planned to be the powerful Sherman locomotive barreling down on The Barony.

". . . by altering range records in the inventories of purchasing agents," Brighton went on, "Paladín and his investors will own fewer cattle than they suppose. Over the years, what I propose doing, merely through record keeping, can amount to enough to break The Barony."

"And your efforts would cost me? What this time?"

Initially, the bait that had lured Brighton to Texas was the opportunity for him to reap a tidy sum of money in exchange for keeping Liam abreast of The Barony Land and Cattle Company's range of business dealings. But, of course, the grasping Englishman was always on the hunt for more money.

Brighton's lips curved into a droll smile. "My dear chap, I assure you what I propose will benefit both your plans and mine. One day, in the near future, I shall return to Ireland and Grantham Manor with enough wealth garnered from my proposal to restore it to its proper grandeur—and you shall have your Barony Ranch."

He paused, and those little eyes met Liam's with an avariciousness that took even him by surprise. "At that time, I want your daughter's hand in marriage—uniting my title with your wealth."

He blinked, for once caught off guard by the man. "Sara is only thirteen."

Grantham smiled blithely. "I am willing to wait a few years."

"And if I refuse?"

"You lose all that you have worked for to claim The Barony." The earl smiled with a disarmingly damning simplicity. "My record keeping also includes a letter designated expressly for Paladín should I go missing."

AUSTIN
DECEMBER 1859

Austin's wooden wagon yards and saloons were gradually being replaced by solid masonry structures. Niall ambled catty-corner from the three-story domed and limestone Old Stone Capitol across the square to the General Land Office, an imposing stuccoed stone and brick building.

Houston, newly elected governor, in paying off an old debt to Alex, had arranged Niall's conference with the Land Office that morning. Wondering whatever had possessed him to agree to undertake this venture Alex proposed, it was with utmost reluctance Niall mounted the General Land Office's many steps to the Romanesque Revival entrance.

Alex must have had faith in Niall's gypsy's gift for gab. Karl would have been better at palavering, but Alex appeared to be using Karl's services less often these days.

"If ye climb in the saddle, be ready for the ride," had been the gypsy mandate of Niall's old man. Well, sure as there are trolls, he was in no way ready for this bronc ride.

Perhaps he was uneasy because he had already been to this *charreada* with a Land Commissioner twenty-five years earlier. That Land Commissioner, the late Cavett Magnum, had represented the Mexican province of Tejas y Coahuila

Magnum had previously been a crack Connecticut attorney and business associate of Rafaela's father. While in London on service for the United States government, Magnum had taken advantage of fourteen-year-old Rafaela's naivete and embezzled funds sent her from her father.

The cunning Magnum breathed no longer because of the Battle of San Jacinto, when Niall's lovely, aristocratic, and genteel wife had plugged the traitor to Texas between the eyes with a Springfield musket's .69-caliber lead ball.

So, what could Niall, acting on behalf of The Barony Ranch Partnership, expect today from this present land commissioner, representing the State of Texas?

Not much. Not much if Land Commissioner Holcomb's insalubrious mug was anything to go by.

At Niall's entrance, Holcomb and the handful of legislators rose from their seats at the long table. The grave looking men with long coats, striped trousers, eyeglasses that hung from black ribbons, and dangling watch fobs, eyed Niall's attire with disapproval.

He'd dressed in his customary tan woolen fringed shirt, denim pants, boots, and spurs, with a red bandana around his neck. Only at Rafaela's insistence had he surrendered up years ago his flat Paddy's cap for the brown wide-brim beaver hat to protect his face and ears against the fierce southwestern Texas sun.

He tossed that dirt-and-sweat-stained hat onto the long table and took an empty seat at its far end. "Morning, gentlemen." Carefully, he laid his revolver next to his hat. Another of his old man's mandates—"Don't pack hardware for bluff or ballast."

Well, it was up to him to bluff his way through this conference because The Barony was scraping the bottom of the barrel. It badly needed to diversify if it was to survive.

The Guadalupe-Hidalgo Treaty ending the Mexican-American War and its resulting Compromise of 1850 had reduced Texas's land holdings by more than a third and, also, ended The Barony Ranch Partnership's substantial revenue from the military's presence.

"Gentlemen, I am here on behalf of The Barony Ranch Partnership to save Texas."

Silence.

"How very magnanimous of you, Mr. Gorman," the stringent, cadaverous Holcomb remarked drily from the table's other end, "but I think the days of shoot first and talk later are long past. I would suggest diplomacy would better accomplish your agenda today."

Niall set his damp, locked palms, laced fingers clenched white, on the table. "Contrary to your statement, Land Commissioner Holcomb, both cease-fire and recess are over. The days of shooting are about to begin again. I am talking about the ongoing conflict generated between the states by the political powerbrokers in Washington."

Houston was doing all he could to keep Texas in the Union, but Texan Secessionist politicians railed against

Houston and threatened to have him impeached as governor.

A bored-looking, portly senator stared down over a bulbous, red-veined nose at Niall. "Am I to understand you waltzed in here with this preposterous offer—financing for The Barony Ranch Partnership in exchange for the General Land Office granting a charter and land sections for a railroad?"

He was wise enough to know that wagons were soon to be a thing of the past. If you couldn't beat 'em, join 'em, "Aye, ye are."

Another legislator removed his ribboned eyeglasses and studiously wiped them with a snowy handkerchief. "You are wasting your time and ours, Mr. Gorman. A railroad that crosses a desert to connect with some dusty pueblo on the Rio Grande?" He donned the eyeglasses and his hooded eyes were magnified with his contempt. "If there is indeed to be a war, the plantations of our Texas heartland want a railroad to freight its cotton to one of our *Gulf ports*. Not some camel caravan to Cairo or God knows wherever Laredo might be."

Niall leaned forward and smiled. A smile went a long way toward making *palabras* palpable. His old man would've said, "Talk low, talk slow, and don't talk too much."

"What's wanted isn't always what's needed."

He rose, blunt fingertips splayed on the highly polished table. "Gentlemen—should a war between the states come, you can bet your boots the North will blockade every Texas port on the Gulf. The Barony Ranch Partnership's railroad would provide Texas with an invaluable river port to a neutral Mexico—where the North could do nothing but twiddle its thumbs in the face of International Law."

That scurvy entrepreneur, Obregon, may have blocked The Barony's direct approach to the mouth of the Rio Grande, but that was not the only approach.

Niall picked up his hat and revolver. "Should you have any further questions, you can find me at the Swisher Hotel—but only until tomorrow morning."

SAN ANTONIO
DECEMBER 1860

This Christmas should have been another festive family affair, what with the wild turkey, ham, and oysters, along with stewed prunes, cranberries, and creamy butternut squash gracing the Gorman table. There was even a barrel of ice from New Orleans to chill the champagne.

But a lingering gray mist, much like the past week's inclement weather, hung over the entire household. Except this fog seemed to have prevailed for years rather than only one week. At times, it seemed thicker and Niall could pinpoint the reason neither for its existence, nor its random moments of thickening.

He should have felt elation that he had swung the railroad deal with the General Land Office. Alex certainly did. He and his family were celebrating Christmas at Niall's house, which made better sense, as both Austin Collegiate Female Institute and Baylor University at Independence, were closer to San Antonio than to San Patricio.

That nearly deserted colonial town and The Barony were another three days or more stagecoach ride from San Antonio, what with the mud-mired road that could sink a stage to its axles. Both Catarina and Kerry would be home from college for the holiday . . . and Jamie would never be home.

Certainly, even after five years, Jamie's death was a hole in Niall's heart that could never be plugged. Still, this particular sense of uneasiness amounted to some other unidentifiable source.

What was there to worry about? His transport business was stable. At fifty, he was hale and hearty. Catarina, though a handful, showed promise of her mother's brains and subtle beauty.

And her mother?

Niall, who believed in the gypsy mandate to fall in love only when one couldn't help it, had gone and done just that at his first sight of eighteen-year-old Rafaela Carrera. But she had been engaged to Alex, his best friend and a baron—and, worse, her refinement, her education, her breeding all warned him she was too good for the likes of himself. However, though it beggared his imagination, she had wanted and chosen him.

Over the nearly twenty-five years of their marriage, he had worked long and hard to provide her with all that he felt she deserved, to provide her with the luxuries that were a part of her former life. The finer things of life to which a baron—the polished Alex, Geoffrey, or even Karl—would more easily have accessed.

Niall glanced at the other end of the table. With pale brown hair invaded by silver, Rafaela had acquired few wrinkles, most at the corners of her eyes, but her dimples still deepened in response to his quirks of humor.

He was inordinately proud of his accomplished wife. She served as president of San Antonio's amateur theater group that performed at the Casino Club, where German fathers reserved memberships for their sons and formally introduced their daughters.

Along with the stuffy and pompous Sra. Esmerelda Rodriguez, descendant of one of the sixteen families who settled San Antonio in 1731, Rafaela also chaired the Debating Society and co-hosted the Annual Rowing Race on the San Antonio River.

That afternoon, conversation buzzed like a bee among the Christmas dinner guests, and Niall's reflective gaze moved from one to another.

Maria Elena, who had plumped with age, gently admonished her eighteen-year-old Max. "Mind your manners, *mijo*. They go a long way toward making anyone attractive."

He was fairer than his Hispanic mother, with summer-blond hair that more nearly resembled Karl's, although his had a reddish cast.

At that moment, Karl was trying to persuade his adopted son to attend college. "But I am not interested in studying law." Max frowned, dishing out a helping of coleslaw. "I want to see something of the world first."

Wade's fork hovered at his wide, grinning mouth. "You

can ride herd with me and see something—the tail end of a cow."

The lanky twenty-year-old had Alex's dark good looks. Niall could tell the young man was proud of his rugged occupation and independent lifestyle. Despite his parent's pleas, Wade had refused to take his education further than the first two years at St. Mary's Institute. At last, Alex had agreed to let him drive longhorns, under Diego's eagle eye, to nearby frontier forts and as far as the Brazos Indian Reservation in North Texas.

Tara shared her younger brother's dark good looks but, at eighteen, was still a string bean of a young woman. Stewing and silent, she moved the peach pickles around on her plate.

After Fiona had discovered Tara missing last month, she tracked her daughter to a cow camp in The Barony's southernmost section. Alex had informed his recalcitrant daughter that, as of January, she was being packed off to join Catarina at Austin Collegiate Female Institute.

Toward the middle of the table's length, Geoffrey, his beringed fingers flashing, was explaining something to Alex.

Alex listened, his features never an indication of his thoughts. Was the conception of failure or doubt or fear ever a part of the man? After their twenty-five years working side by side, Niall still knew so little about Alex. But he suspected if Alex indeed ever experienced fear, it might well be loss of face, which would seem to manifest for him as loss of property. Niall thought his friend believed that what he was *equated* with what he *possessed.*

Not the most appealing set of beliefs, but then that was Alex. He never had the close-knit family clan like the Irish Travelers with which Niall had been surrounded. Alex's origins as a second son, relegated from birth to second-class citizenship within his own family, might have made him strong because he felt he must be—yet kind to those who supported him and deadly to anyone who opposed him.

Niall's gaze drifted across the table's elaborate centerpiece of pine cones, red-berried holly, and lambent candles, to Karl. In a sense, the lawyer was responsible for the Christmas decorations.

The mistletoe and greenery that draped the arched doorways, and the garland festooned Yule tree in the courtyard, was a German tradition he had brought with him from the Old Country.

The German baron's reddish-blond hair had turned completely gray early on, but behind his spectacles, his eyes were just as vivid—and even more discerning. Yet Karl had lost . . . what? More than likely, it was what he had acquired. A soberness, a dour reserve as gray as his hair.

He was deep in conversation with Catarina. "What would you say, goddaughter, to an after dinner musical recital for us?"

Catarina's lashes lowered. She focused only on spearing a bite of mince pie. "I would rather not, Uncle Karl."

Her voice had lowered, but Niall hadn't missed her reply. What had happened to his impetuous and outspokenly brilliant daughter, who at eight could charm wallpaper off the wall, but who at eighteen had almost become a mute?

Rafaela assured him that it was merely a stage their daughter was going through and that her ardent nature would resurface.

But when?

Kerry cleared his throat and stood. He lifted his wine glass. "I propose a toast. The tea has been thrown overboard. South Carolina has initiated the revolution of 1860. To the South's confederacy."

"Not so fast on the draw, Kerry." The lines bracketing Alex's stern mouth deepened. "No secession has been officially declared."

"But if war between the states comes—and it will, Father—I am fighting for Texas."

Fiona did not touch her wine glass. "I understand ye are chafing to fight, son, but I want ye to finish yuir education. I may be a dedicated Texican, but I am no secessionist."

Kerry's eyes, green as the holly, were defiant. "I must volunteer, Mother." Silverware ceased to clink on china plates. All eyes were drawn to the young man with hair as fiery as his grit.

Niall's daughter astonished him by coming to her feet. Her glass uplifted, Catarina declared in opposition, "As Governor Houston said, 'A nation divided against itself cannot stand.' To the Union!"

Niall blinked at beholding his daughter's newly animated features. Her pale brown eyes fired darts of poisoned arrows at Kerry. Her naturally pink lips parted the way they used to do when, in breathless wonder, she observed a roly-poly or birthing mare or horned toad. All he could think was her latest stage might even be worse than her sullen one.

BRAZOS ISLAND
AUGUST 1862

Sweat combined with the Gulf humidity limed a salt trail across Kerry's upper lip. In long strides, he stalked across the denuded parade ground, where clumps of grass struggled to survive on its perimeter of hell-hot sand.

If there was a place in Texas where misery surpassed purgatory, that honor had to be awarded to Brazos Island on this sultry August afternoon. He wore a gray flannel shirt of the pullover type under his natty blue woolen jacket, which was worse than a repentant sinner's hair shirt.

With frustration, his ears tuned in to the jingle of spurs and the clank of sabers. Soldiers on their way to the enlisted men's mess hall—not into battle. With disgust, his nostrils flared at the smell of old leather and old horses. All too few and none of them his.

Back in April, after the opening Confederate bombardment on Ft. Sumter, Kerry had lined up to enlist. He had hoped to serve under Col. Rip Ford, a veteran captain of the Texas Rangers and close friend of Uncle Karl's. The colonel had acquired the nickname during the Mexican War, when he had composed the company's official death notices with "Rest in Peace" scrawled at the top.

Old Rip now commanded the Confederacy's Military District of the Rio Grande. Even at this moment, his men were seeing action. They battled Union invaders, Comanche warriors, and Mexican raiders led by Juan Cortina.

Lieutenant Kerry Paladín battled sand, seaweed, and boredom.

Leave it to his father's legendary expediency. Secretly, he had arranged for General Kirby Smith to assign Kerry to coast artillery duties, where his parents felt he should be safe enough during the remainder of the Civil War.

Brazos Island, a sandy strip four miles long east of Brownsville, served as a vital, if remote, area for the cotton trade. At its north end was an old mud fort with three wharves, four barracks, a hospital, thirty-two-pounder gun emplacements, numerous warehouse buildings, and a lighthouse.

That lighthouse's lantern beam the night before had propelled Kerry's steps toward his commander's office today.

Kerry had been pacing the beach last night, his high officer boots sinking into the sand. The smash of breakers against the shore muffled his boots' crunching. When the lantern beam swerved around once again to pierce the ghostly fog, Kerry realized with a gut-churning nausea that his life was replicating that beam's monotonous revolution—his life's lens cranked in motion by someone other than himself.

His father? The government? The military?

Its power source was beside the point.

His boots climbed the Post Headquarters wooden steps two at a time. Behind the front desk sat a young captain with whitish blond hair. Quickly, he returned Kerry's salute as Kerry strode past him. He rapped on the commandant's door and at the barked "Enter!" thrust it open.

Lt. Col. Hugh McLeod was a fat man with a bushy beard. He and Sam Houston were not what one would call drinking buddies. In fact, McLeod hated Houston. Worse, Kerry could not look to Houston for influential help.

Last March, all Texas government officers were asked to take a loyalty oath to the Confederate States of America. Governor Houston, warning of a Northern victory and the inevitable destruction of the South, refused to do so. He was the only southern governor to oppose secession, saying, "I refuse to take this oath. I love Texas too well to bring civil strife and bloodshed upon her."

Immediately, the office of the governor was declared vacant by the legislature and the lieutenant governor was sworn in as Houston's replacement.

Following the required formality of Kerry's salute, McLeod went back to the solitaire he was playing. "What?"

"Damn't, sir, I don't know about boats. I know about horses."

"Well, no Texican ever walks a yard if he can help it."

Kerry wanted to retort that Texicans had a predilection for cavalry service founded upon their peerless horsemanship, but he knew better than to gainsay his cantankerous commander. "I want to be transferred to the cavalry, sir."

The fat man's gaze caught Kerry as if from behind a gun sight. "You do, eh lieutenant? Well, I want a desk job in Austin."

"If you will grant me a two-week furlough, sir, within a week of that you will be taking tea at Smith's Hotel in Austin. Your nine of hearts goes over there, on the ten of spades, sir."

SAN ANTONIO

This was a drought year. From riding shotgun on one of the Gorman Transport packed stagecoaches, Kerry viewed the brush country—scorched, many of its streams and water holes sucked dry. Skeletons of cattle, sheep, and other unfortunate critters littered the San Patricio Trail from Brownsville all the way to San Antonio.

Only when the town's splashing fountains and shady cottonwoods came into view did the knotted muscles of Kerry's shoulders relax a bit. At last, he would have something he could wrangle with, whether it was the military's paperwork or his father. No one ever dared to buck the man. Maybe, at twenty-three, it was long past time Kerry did.

First, he was required to present his furlough papers at the Confederacy of Texas headquarters—the former San Antonio Arsenal.

Founded on the banks of the San Antonio River in

1859 to furnish arms and munitions to the frontier forts in Texas, the Federal post's twenty-one acres were now occupied by Confederate forces and the Fed's supplies had been confiscated for the South's war effort.

Stonemasons and carpenters were at work on the headquarters' fortifications and new building construction. Everywhere was evidence of the Arsenal's gearing up for the war undoubtedly coming Texas' way.

As was Kerry gearing up. He was dead set on becoming part of some distinguished mounted regiment of volunteers, like Terry's Texas Rangers. Privately, Kerry despised the draft laws. He believed that the good men had already volunteered. The exceptions that made for petty office holders, slave owners, and men wealthy enough to buy their way out of the war were damnably unjust.

A long strung-out column of rag-tag, ninety-day cavalry-men were creaking on their saddle leather back into the Arsenal's compound. Nevertheless, their off-key weary voices sang "I Wish I Was in Dixie's Land."

They all looked either too young or too old for the draft—a volunteer regiment of mostly baldheads and troopers who had yet to shave. Yet their ragged uniforms and spent mounts indicated quite clearly they were seasoned fighters. The regiment had no official designation, and its task was merely to patrol the West Texas border and desert against attacks by Indians, Mexicans, and Yanks.

He got no further than the headquarters' front counter, smelling resinous of fresh-sawed pine and fielded by a captain whom he recognized as a former Cotton Bureau man, when Kerry heard voluble arguing from a hallway.

"Goddamn it to hell, you lily-livered, blood-thirsty lard-asses! My men need rations and rest. Not another godurned hike back out to that sand-oven you all hereabouts call Rio Grande City."

Kerry knew only one man who was that free with his profanity, his money, and his pistol. The exact man Kerry wanted so much to serve under—Rip Ford. With his scraggly acorn-color beard, he looked to be in his late sixty's well past his actual forty-six.

He stomped past the counter, then stopped abruptly and swung around. "Kerry Paladín?" The short man shoved back his battered black cavalry fedora, its brim pinned up on **the** left side to the crown by the CSA emblem. "Well, I'll be damned for a scurvy landlubber."

"I should hope not, Rip." Kerry shifted his weight to one leg and tucked one thumb under his haversack sling, the other hand rested on the hilt of his saber. This was most likely the closest he would ever get to a mounted regiment, lackluster though it was. "What I am hoping is that you will approve my transfer to your outfit."

"A state militia?" Old Rip squinted up at him. "Daddy Paladín know about this?"

"Did you ask your father for permission to fight in the Texas Revolution for Independence?"

Rip spit tobacco juice on the floor. "My old man wasn't Baron Paladín."

"I'll take care of my father, if you'll take care of Col. McLeod for me. He's hankering for a paper-pushing job in that great shining town on seven hills, Austin."

"Hugh McLeod? I'll push that porker into the first cannon I can find and fire off his fat ass all the way to Richmond, Virginia, by God."

"Thank you, sir."

THE CASINO CLUB WAS chartered in 1857, with a membership of 106 men—all German Texicans. The names of Ulysses S. Grant and Robert E. Lee could be found scrawled among the long list of prior illustrious guests. The club occupied a goodly expanse on Market Street.

On its west side presided a bar with skat tables and a reading room. On the east side, a salon and lounge. In between the two, the club's center was dominated by a ballroom that could be converted into a theater with a stage and balcony.

It was that ballroom, gaily decorated with gray and red bunting, that had plagued Catarina for weeks. Its cotillion that night was her parents' last ditch effort to see their nineteen-year-old daughter happily affianced. At least, 'happily' was the word her mother had used.

'Happily' stuck in Catarina's throat and filmed her eyes the way poached prairie oysters did.

What kind of potential groom did her parents expect their daughter, and now their only child, to attract? No suitor could possibly be attracted to her compelling beauty, or rather, lack thereof. Every suitor would only be attracted to the prospects of her Gorman Transport fortune.

And did either of her parents truly exhibit 'happiness'

with each other? Loyalty. Devotion. Admiration. Yes, to all. But also to a boredom that went beyond tedious. It was as if a malaise of despondency occupied their home.

If she could muster through this last parade of Crusaders—Crusaders for a side she could not fully support—perhaps her parents would abandon their relentless Grail quest to see her married off. Happily.

Despite her black silk stockings that evening, she considered herself more a Bluestocking than a well-bred Dixie Belle. The epitome of females was to be homemaker and mother. Pretty and pure, hardy and hardworking, yet forever docile and submissive.

Well, docile and submissive had never been any part of her temperament. Besides, no jars of creams or potions or wide-brim straw hats to protect her skin could possibly make her into a ravishing beauty.

From behind flower-painted fans, the belles attending that night flirted either coyly or outrageously. The recipients of their flirtations were the many soldiers in attendance from the companies posted at the Arsenal, along with a few geezers too old to be drafted into military service and some far-too-young pimply-faced boys.

The flirtations were aptly adapted that evening for the cotillion—from the French word for petticoats that flashed along with pantalettes beneath hooped skirts, as the changing partners spun about. The German cotillion was one of several *contredanses* where the gathered participants introduced themselves.

A glum Catarina was facing many men, young and old,

who longed only and too eagerly to introduce themselves to her.

The heat from the candelabra combined with her heavy, rose taffeta ball gown felt stifling to her. From beneath the waxy candles, Catarina faced the false bravado of the mostly untried soldiers who importuned her. She stifled a yawn from behind her lacy fan.

That demure accessory was used to convey messages more useful than producing a breeze. A fan pressed to lips begged a kiss, lowering it meant friendship only, drawing it across the eyes expressed apology.

This last gesture she offered her crestfallen swains most often. One by one, with gentle refrains she sent away the men with their pomaded hair and cologne redolent of Araby's camels to beseech other partners.

The military band launched into The Lancers Quadrille. Relieved, she turned back to join the wallflowers and older adults who girded the wall. She had succeeded. The dance card suspended from wrist by a velvet ribbon was empty of names.

"Catarina?"

She halted, squeezed her lids closed, and sighed heavily. Then, opening her eyes, she screwed on an apologetic smile and pivoted. She was expecting to confront yet another vexatious prospect.

Before here stood a roguishly handsome redhead whose very presence was a blight on any pleasure she hoped to experience. Tall, with shoulders so wide they should have been patented, he doffed his steel gray slouch hat with its dark blue cord. He swept a bow as gallant as any swashbuckler, but his grin revealed its mockery. "My lady."

He wore his yellow cavalry sash knotted on his right hip, whereas all other states but Texas knotted theirs at the left. Her dismissive gaze took in the dark blue cording, signifying the Confederate navy and unfurling up legs that quite nearly reached the length of stilts. "Well, if it is not our latest and greatest—'Sinbad the Sailor.'"

She snapped shut her fan. How did this cad always manage to make her feel so inexplicably gauche? Growing up in Kerry's footsteps, she had been taunted and ignored by him. He was as much a rounder as his father had been.

At that moment, as her ire was beginning to reach its peak, he winked at her. She had all but forgotten the bonhomie ebullience he wielded so effortlessly.

"A sailor only until midnight—a deal I made with Colonel Ford today." His squared-off chin pointed at the Confederate Stars and Bars spangling one wall. "And I see you have become a patriotic rebel after all, Kiddy Kat."

"Do not call me that."

The music was loud, so they both were almost shouting. Without asking her permission for a dance, he took her gloved hand in his and pulled her into the closest square of dancing couples. She fumed. He was behaving like an autocratic brother.

His arm banded the back of her waist. "There." His sparkling grin was tinged with full-out deviltry. "Close enough we no longer have to holler at each other."

She tilted her chin aloofly. "Speaking of hearing, last I

heard, you killed a soldier in a boxing match held on a Rio Grande sand bar."

For the space of a lid-blink, she thought a haunted expression might have peeked from his hazel eyes. But just then, he led her into the square center, never missing a beat of the music's lively cues.

"So, does that mean you have been inquiring about me?"

Her gaze shot up to meet his. "No! Of course not."

She noticed his eyes lowering to take in the nearly transparent lawn fabric that barely disguised her decolletage. "Hmmm, you really *have* grown up, Kiddy Kat."

"*You* have not!"

The quadrille called for the requisite change of partners. She found herself partnered with an old man whose face had the texture of grapefruit rind.

When next Kerry joined her, he leaned towards her ear. "Tomorrow, I am on my way—first to The Barony, then to Rio Grande City. With any luck, the Cavalry of the West will be back in San Antonio before the end of the year. I plan to court you then. Meanwhile, do not give your heart to any of these peach-fuzzes or old fossils."

SAN PATRICIO TRAIL
APRIL 1863

Lady Luck had not been generous to Kerry. Ford's Cavalry of the West had spent the last seven months chasing dust storms, tumbleweed, and occasionally, the elusive Juan Cortina. Kerry found it difficult to dislike the vexatious Mexican, whose illustrious background happened to almost parallel that of Alex Paladín's.

Cortina's aristocratic mother was one of the heirs of a large land grant in the lower Rio Grande valley, including the area surrounding Brownsville. In the decade following the Mexican-American War and the Treaty of Guadalupe Hidalgo, Cortina began to hate with the fury of a hurricane the Brownsville judges and attorneys who colluded with unscrupulous land schemers.

He accused them of seizing land from Mexican-Texicans, unfamiliar with the American judicial system. In the years since, he had become a Robin Hood to many of the poorer Mexicans who lived along the Rio Grande.

However, his forays against American property and

citizens were scarcely a pesky horsefly as far as Rip Ford was concerned. Far more beleaguering to Old Rip was the extreme Confederate States of America's policy that was withholding supplies for his Cavalry of the West.

The regiment's method of sourcing a supply was itself thorny. Baled cotton was stored along the route from San Antonio to the Nueces River, where both the Wild Horse Desert and The Barony began. The cotton would be picked up and hauled south to the Rio Grande by Old Rip's dragoons, where it would be sold for cash his unit needed in order to purchase supplies.

At last, that week Lady Luck appeared to be taking a more positive turn for Lieutenant Kerry Paladín. He had been assigned the monthly duty of leading a platoon of forty-five horse soldiers plus their outriding scouts. The troopers would ride security for wagons that would collect the cotton bales to haul them on to Rio Grande City.

Kerry had counted on a leave by the end of last year to begin courting Cat and claim her as his bride. These military duties had postponed his plan. But now, this latest assignment would take him within miles of both The Barony at San Patricio—and Cat at San Antonio.

Cat.

Her name had been drumming a tattoo in his mind, a chorus lifting him through all the monotonous days and sleepless nights of the past seven months. How had her beauty escaped his notice all those years of growing up? It was as if Kiddy Kat had waved a magic wand over him during the last year or so.

Her boring pigtails had become luxuriant, cafe-au-lait tresses. Her ordinary-looking brown eyes had become a haunting shade of brown topaz. Somehow, her face, with its imperious youthful nose, had evolved into the frontispiece of an exotic beauty—declaring her boldness, confidence, yes, and her authority.

A quote from Poe haunted Kerry. "There is no exquisite beauty without some strangeness in the proportion."

Cat haunted him as well.

Would she wait for him, as he had told her to—-or, even now, was one of the Arsenal's slacker soldiers courting her?

Jealousy, a previously untested foe, had begun assaulting Kerry.

Reviewing his vivid childhood memories of her made the monotonous crunching of wagon wheels, the clinking of spurs, and the endless jingle of harness bearable. So much so that Kerry did not catch the sudden reflection of bright desert sunlight off the gun barrels aiming at his troopers. He did not observe the plume of black powder smoke, he did not hear the ping of the minie ball, and he did not feel its shattering effect until it was far too late.

RIO GRANDE CITY

President Lincoln labored under enormous pressure. Northeastern industrialists and pompous congressmen demanded he regain Texas, the almost wide-open back door to the Confederacy. If Texas could be cut off and captured, that would serve the North as a major source of cotton as well as a killing blow for the Confederacy. The Union, squeezing the South like a boa constrictor, would be able to deprive the South of its only significant source of hard currency.

With its loss of commerce with the Union, Brighton and Paladín's Barony Land and Cattle Company was barely surviving. Paladín had been selling off pockets of land and the ranch had lost cowboys conscripted for the war. However, his *Paladíneños* remained loyal, even with little or no pay forthcoming.

Paladín had banked on transporting Barony cattle via The Barony's San Antonio-Laredo Railroad, then shuttling them by steamboat downriver to the neutral port of Matamoros, Mexico. But the Civil War had been a death knell to the railroad's completion.

At Matamoros, the Confederacy had established a relationship with the British shipping firm of Fraser & Trenholm to buy and sell Confederate cotton. The Confederacy then used that currency to purchase British Enfield rifles and ammunition, uniforms, and other supplies to support its war effort. Fraser & Trenholm became, in effect, the Confederacy's international banker.

Geoffrey Brighton had arranged to market Barony cattle through Fraser & Trenholm, though at a much lower price than they would have commanded before the Civil War began. In Wade's dictionary, Brighton was a fop, but occasionally, he would manage to come through for The Barony with a boost that provided connections and resources.

Determined to close blockade-running trade, the Union had captured Galveston, the second largest city in Texas, then successfully blockaded Corpus Christi, and was now focusing its trade interrupting efforts further south, on Brownsville.

As a result, twenty-two-year-old Wade and his father's *Paladíneños* now drove Barony cattle overland to the closest river port, Rio Grande City. The town was a hundred miles from Laredo to the north and a hundred miles from the twin cities of Brownsville and Matamoros to the south, at the Gulf of Mexico.

Driving Barony cattle to Rio Grande City was less dangerous and much faster than driving them all the way to the twin Gulf ports. Consequently, the route was also more profitable.

On both sides of the Rio Grande, battles were being waged and intrigue abounded. Spies for the North shiftily eyed South Texican routines. Followers of Mexico's revolutionist, Benito Juarez, spied on the opposing Napoleon III's French Foreign Legion, now posted along the border.

Wade Paladín was competent at going up against the finest of the spies, though none of them ever figured that out. Even to the keenest observers, he was at best a scruffy cowhand, thus no threat to any of them.

Wade was a genuine cowboy through and through. His long, ambling, gait revealed to any observer that here was a man more accustomed to the saddle than to a stroll. Lean and lanky and a loner, he loved the freedom his trail driving life offered.

There were more than six times more cattle in the state of Texas than people. Cows didn't need coddling like people. Life required little of Wade except for soothing a bawling, restless sea of cattle, stringing out a herd to keep it from stampeding toward a water hole, or lassoing strays out of the treacherous spiny brush.

Where else did one see wild camels hoofing it across the sand dunes, an ocelot slinking through the chaparral, purple mountains sailing like ships on the horizon, and turquoise waters lapping white beaches—all within a couple hundred-miles radius?

However, Wade's free-roaming occupation also put him in an excellent position to pick up information—in Texas and Mexico. Both Uncle Karl, through his contacts with the chairman of the Senate Military Affairs Committee, and his father had persuaded Wade, rather than joining the Confederate army, to undertake a job with the Confederate Civil Service—that of undercover agent and arms procurer.

To spy, one needed to be good with detail, or so said Wade's father, who had served as an undercover agent for both Sam Houston and Andrew Jackson. And good with detail Wade was. Even as a boy, he had learned to denote turkey droppings and Indian pony hoof prints, to interpret spider web significance and weather warnings.

But that particular Tuesday morning, Wade was having problems that had nothing to do with his spying.

He sat at Rio Grande City's pharmacy-cum-soda fountain and drank his prerequisite two cups of coffee with sugar. Falcon's Pharmacy, at the intersection of Water Street and the boulevard-wide Britton Avenue, looked out over Davis Landing. It consisted of shipping offices, two docks, and warehouses filled with cotton and stock pens filled with cattle.

Cotton and gold were synonymous, with cattle trailing only by a little. Rio Grande City flourished as a cattle center, yet Barony cattle languished in its pens, awaiting boats to transport them to Matamoros.

The hitch was that Obregon Enterprises out of Matamoros controlled the steamboat fleets. It had landed the Confederate transportation contract from Brazos Santiago at the mouth of the Rio Grande, on the Brownsville side, all the way upriver to Ringgold Barracks at Rio Grande City—without making competitive bids or offering a surety bond. Obregon Enterprises indiscriminately, and without conviction or loyalties, hauled goods for the South and the North alike. And for both the Juáristas and their foes, the French. But apparently not for The Barony.

Wade wanted to find out why.

The night before, at the saloon on Fandango Plaza, he had overheard a drunk remark about one of the river pilots for Obregon Enterprises. Something about when ashore at Rio Grande City, the Obregon pilot headed straight for the pharmacy's soda fountain.

The clicking of castanets and gunfire tapping of heels in the saloon's background had drowned out the drunk's next laughing ribaldry and rib gouging. Nevertheless, Wade made up his mind to patronize the pharmacy the next morning.

He would have rather dropped by Ringgold Barracks, a half-mile away. Confederate troops under Rip Ford periodically occupied the abandoned fort and Wade had hoped to spend some time with Kerry, but his brother and Old Rip's cavalry must be off chasing the Mexican marauder Cortina once again.

Consequently, waiting to ambush the pilot of Obregon's *Shamrock,* which had just put in, Wade sat at one of the pharmacy's two long boards. A shambling geezer in spectacles and a battered derby, who could have easily been an intelligence gatherer for the Union's Pinkerton National Detective Agency——or a bum—sat at the other.

The tables were girded by twelve-foot-high walls. The back wall was lined from floor to ornate tin ceiling with dark-stained pine shelves. On those shelves sat medicine bottles and vials. From behind the counter, the white-haired, elderly apothecary filled these bottles and vials with laudanum, cocaine, quinine, arsenic, and other exotic concoctions, readily available from Mexico, some of which would later be shipped to the war front.

But which war front? The North? The Confederacy? The *Juaristas?* The French Foreign Legion?

Wade tucked away that bit of information.

The geezer had nodded off, his derby slipping down to his spectacles. Wade was huddled over his second cup of steaming coffee he had convinced the apothecary to part with when a girl sashayed through the door and past him. Beneath her half cape, she was trussed out in some sort of brown plaid frillery dress.

Her wide smile wrinkled her pert nose. "Morning, Oliver."

"Mornin', Miz Obregon. The usual?"

Wade's head jackknifed up.

"Oliver, now would I travel all this way only to miss out on all your fizzy, sugary carbonated water?"

As if she could feel Wade's burning gaze, she looked over her shoulder. Her nose wrinkled again, but this time he had the feeling it was at the sight of his rumpled, dirty black duster and days-old beard stubble.

He rose his lengthy frame and tipped the wide brim of his sweat-stained hat. "Miss Obregon?"

Her eyes, they might have been blue-green or hazel, he wasn't sure, narrowed in an oval face that could not have seen more than fourteen, maybe fifteen, years. "Do I know you?"

"You will."

"I doubt that." She turned back to old Oliver. He hee-hawed, sucking air through his false teeth.

"Would you risk being a Doubting Thomas?"

Her head swiveled back to him. From beneath her straw corded bonnet, blonde ringlets bounced on her small shoulders. Clearly, she had not expected a learned remark from one with his riff-raff appearance. Without taking her gaze off him, she turned to Oliver. "I shall take my soda water at this . . . this gentleman's table."

She settled her wide hoop skirts on the bench across from him, folded her gloved hands over the jade beaded reticule in her lap, and raised a brow as thick as an artist's brush. "Convince me."

"Of what?"

She lowered her voice. "That I want to know you better."

He stalled, taking a sip from the tin coffee cup. "I doubt that you would want to know me better, Miss Obregon. What I said was that you try to know me better."

Her head tilted to the side. She looked at him out of eyes that appeared wise beyond their years. "Why?"

He could tell he had lassoed her interest. "Because I want your steamboats to ship my cattle, and I won't give up until they do—or find out a damn good reason, pardon my cussing, ma'am, why they won't."

Her sable brows knitted. "Obregon Enterprises ships everything."

"Everything but Barony cattle."

"You are a Paladín?"

He nodded.

She waited for Oliver to put the glass of soda water before her, thanked him, then said in a most practical voice, as if talking to a child or servant. "Well, that explains it. My father would never do business with a Paladín."

So, Obregon was her father and not a brother or uncle—-or husband. He nudged aside his tin cup and, crossed arms propped on the table, leaned into her and stared with shotgun eyes. "Why?"

Unintimidated, she shrugged her shoulders. "Something to do with land that the elder Paladín cheated him out of when he was a kid."

Wade was not surprised. His father gave no quarter. Well, there were more ways to kill a cat than choke it with cream. "Can you introduce me to the *Shamrock's* pilot?"

Her lashes, as black as soot, blinked. She took a sip of the fizzy confection and rendered a fetching smile that must have been pleasure with her carbonated water. "Sarita Obregon."

"What?"

Her tongue stole out and licked the fizz from the twin peaks of her upper lip. "You asked for an introduction to the *Shamrock's* pilot. That I am—as well as its captain."

"You . . . you pilot the *Shamrock?*"

"I grew up on steamboats. And I am, indeed, licensed."

"You do this, alone . . . by yourself?

"Big Mick helps me. He's the boiler room engineer. And I run a crew of five. Mick should be here shortly. I sent him on to the custom house to make the duly report for Obregon Enterprises."

"You cannot be more than fifteen. Your father permits this?"

"Going on seventeen." She smiled jauntily. "What I do is inconsequential to my father, I'm afraid. It is my twin brother, Rod, who is the prisoner of Obregon Enterprises."

Wade, surrounded by family loyalty, could not comprehend such familial indifference. As if reading what was behind his dazed stare, she narrowed her eyes. "My mother died when I was quite young. Mick Mallory is my family."

"Then can I maybe work a deal between myself and you, excluding our feuding fathers?"

Once again, the perfectly delineated thick brow elevated. "A deal? Personal or business?"

This one was quick on the uptake. He rubbed his stubbled jaw. "Look, Miss Obregon, I am not accustomed to doing business with a woman, so you may need to go—"

"You do not like women?"

Her question was as rapid fire as a Gatling gun. "I love them." He decided not to mince words. "Just so you understand, Miss Obregon, I like fast horses, fast-burning liquor, and fast women. Obviously, you are not the latter. You are the kind I like to stay as far away from as I possibly can."

"What kind is that?" Her smile had shifted to the type a *femme fatale* most likely delivered up to some unsuspecting mark.

"Bluntly, the kind that wants both a ring on their finger and a ring in their man's nose." Even then, they were never satisfied. He had shared stale coffee and puking pulque with too many wranglers who had spent nights riding herd to keep cattle calm while their wives were off cheating.

She nodded like an old post squaw about to part a trader from his goods and this made him mightily uncomfortable.

"You understand, no deal with Obregon Enterprises goes down that my father does not find out about. As far as my doing business with you, my hands are tied. Still, I may be able to help you. Seek out Bias Uribe. He operates a fleet of keel boats with stern sails that haul cotton from Laredo to Matamoros."

Guarded, he took in this information with a skeptical raise to his brow, yet her tone was nothing but solicitous. So, why was it he felt like a callow, gullible male?

SAN ANTONIO

That spring, three buildings were under construction at the Arsenal—the magazine, the armorer's shop, and a hospital. The last edifice had only come about after relentless campaigning by the formidable Catarina Gorman.

Seated with all the majestic assurance of Queen Victoria amidst wadded paper, spittoons, and pencil shavings, Catarina had plagued old man Palmer, the editor of *The San Antonio Weekly*, until he ran editorials supporting the need for the hospital.

Using the tip of her parasol to punctuate her points, Catarina had cornered and lobbied nearby Austin bureaucrats to fund her project.

Taking tea with Esmeralda Rodriguez, one of San Antonio's elite, Catarina had maneuvered the old darlin' like a chess pawn until she had agreed to support a Descendants of Canary Island Settlers' benefit ball to raise money for the hospital construction.

Flirting outrageously with W. A. Menger, Catarina had charmed him into donating his new hotel's dazzling ballroom for the gala.

With the gala still two weeks away, she was putting in fifteen-hour days. Early one morning, she was working alongside the Sisters of San Fernando Cathedral at the makeshift hospital. The facility was little more than a Sibley tent attached to the crumbling adobe vestry of the old Cathedral.

Why was it, while attention was called to hospitals in Galveston, in Arkansas, and in Virginia, nothing was ever said or done for San Antonio's own sick and suffering soldiers right here at home? Why should they be kept in a hot, close, unhealthy place on one of the noisiest, dustiest, and most public streets in the city?

Meantime, situated on the Arsenal grounds was a fine building containing eighteen rooms so well adapted for hospital purposes—where the fevered brow of the sufferer could be fanned by cool invigorating breezes off the San Antonio River—and, by damn, if the building was not occupied as a private residence by an officer.

With war fronts far to the east and south, most of the vestry patients were confined because of thoughtless accidents. One soldier shot himself in the thigh as he was dismounting. The Arsenal's blacksmith pinched off his thumb when a chain snapped. Of course, there were the inevitable minor mishaps among San Antonio's civilian population.

The extremely high price and shortage of quinine rendered it almost impossible to acquire. Catarina found the best substitute for quinine, if indeed it was not equal to the drug itself, was obtained by removing the bark of the red dogwood, chopping its inner bark into fine pieces, covering it in a kettle of pure water, then boiling it to the consistency of molasses. After that, a little flour could be added that would render the remedy to the consistency of a pill.

Just before four o'clock, as she was leaving to prepare for another fundraising gala that night, soldiers carried in on stretchers the first two of a score of casualties. Initially, a curly-haired boy caught her eye—a thirteen-year- old, the litter bearer told her, who had been mustered into service with the Cavalry of the West. Grapeshot had collapsed his lung.

She dropped everything—her reticule, parasol, gloves— and rolled up her sleeves. She sent one of the nuns for Doc Bailey, but he was a booze hound. Who knew when he might show up? Frantically, she plunged a sponge beneath the kid's sticky, blood-coated jacket. Searching. His breathing might be rattled, but his heart was still beating. Faintly.

Thank you, God, thank you, thank you!

She turned to the second cot . . . and froze. Her breath vaporized. Covered to his collarbones by a faded sheet, Kerry lay there, his face the color of old teeth . . . where it wasn't scarlet with dried blood.

Swallowing, she drew back the sheet. A dizzying ringing sounded in her head. His left arm . . . it was attached below the shoulder only by some shredded flesh. The arm bone looked like a splintered lance. Fumbling, her hands shaking violently, she began what she knew with sickening certainty would be an exhaustive but losing battle.

For better or worse, Kerry Paladín had occupied her thoughts and memories as long as she could remember.

Indeed, her earliest memory, at three-years-old, was of him. It seemed her mother had insisted she let him ride her beloved pony. She had thrown a hissy fit. The irritating image of his cocky grin at that heartbreaking moment was burned into her brain.

And, burned into her heart, were the many times he had been there for her, her guardian angel. Like the time she had stepped barefoot into a patch of goat's head stickers. He had set her on his knee and patiently removed the burrs. He was in all the landmark moments in her life. And, damn the irony, at the ebb of his life, she was only realizing how much she had loved him all these years.

Now it was up to her to remove his pain. And, loving him as much as she did, she feared she did not have the wherewithal it was going to take—that perceptiveness and wisdom needed to navigate the complex and torturous paths his suffering would take.

She battled his fever, infection, and dehydration. Nearly forty-eight hours passed before he was clearheaded. It was just after dawn, when the nuns were performing their lauds. As if their soft intoning summoned his spirit, his eyes opened. His puzzled gaze roamed her face.

Her dolorous voice was as soft as those lauds. "Welcome back, my love."

She did not know how to tell him, what to say. She did not have to say anything. Abruptly, his head turned to the side of his pillow. His gaze shot to his injured shoulder. She watched as he flexed it, watched as his eyes slowly widened.

"Where's my goddamned arm, Catarina?"

She cleared her throat. "We had to amputate it, Kerry— or you would have died."

His jaw clenched. His eyes drilled into hers. "Maybe you should have let me."

Nine days later, she was still battling. No longer to save Kerry's arm but to wage war against his anguish, his anger, his apathy . . . and to rekindle his pluck, his boldness, that had forever enthralled her.

Outside the vestry window, flowers bloomed in profusion all around Alamo Plaza. Yet his russet head was turned away.

She knew he stared unseeing at the stucco wall's exposed bricks. "Your mother and father have come all this way. You have to see them."

"Maybe later." His eyes seemed like empty tree hollows. His usually riotous red hair was matted with sweat. His body, mere skin and bones, seemed as lifeless as a scarecrow.

"No, now, son," Alex Paladín commanded from behind Catarina.

She turned on the stool, looked up at the man who was still severely handsome despite his fifty-something years. He carried himself with the military bearing of an eighteen-year-old and his black eyes crackled with life force. Only his ace-of-spades black hair, highlighted at the temples with silver, gave even a hint to his age. The stringent lines that plunged from the ridges of his cheekbones to his mouth had been there as long as she could remember.

When he nodded at Catarina, she rose wearily to leave

them alone. "Fiona and Rafaela are getting bedding ready for the wagon. If you will collect my son's personal belongings, I would be most grateful."

"I am coming with you to The Barony."

"No!" Kerry rolled back to face them. His eyes were the shimmering green in a roaring fire's blazing center. "No. You. Are. Not!"

Hands clenched, she glared down at him. "Last summer, you told me to wait for you, that you would court me. I am holding you to that, Kerry Paladín."

"I changed my mind."

She chose a more direct attack. "Don't you think it's about time you stopped feeling sorry for yourself?"

He held up the bandaged stump—all that remained of his left arm. "Take a good look, Cat." His tone was shockingly harsh. "Do you think you could fall in love with that?"

"And you, Kerry, now you take a good look—outside the vestry window at that leafy cottonwood shading the courtyard. See all its knots and dead branches? Well, they are just like our bodies. You need to learn that beauty and imperfection go together wonderfully. I did—and so will you, I swear by God!"

THE BARONY
THANKSGIVING 1863

Tara's leather-gloved hands reined her piebald to the right to avoid a low-swooping mesquite limb. The scent of autumn nipped the air, and morning frost diamonded the corn tassels. "Wade taught me to lasso by using a big loop to rope fence posts. After weeks and weeks, I was ready for moving objects."

"I would bet cats, mongrels, roosters, hogs—anything afoot—were no longer safe from Tara the Terror."

She burst out laughing. She had forgotten how Max's dry humor could blindside her, leaving her helpless with girlish giggles. She could also tell him how she learned to throw a calf for branding, to cut cattle from the herd, and to make skillet-size discs of bread at a cow camp.

While Max was a good horseman, he was totally unfit for ranch life. They were both the same age, twenty-one. Preferring to stay at The Barony, she had received an education at home—a quite thorough education given by her mother.

And he had been sent away to Germany's Heidelberg University to study law, only now returning to Texas to work for his stepfather, the Baron Karl von Hesse-Lippe, whom he resembled somewhat. With his tall Nordic height and wealth of wheat-blond hair, Max didn't possess the Hispanic dark looks of his short, stout mother. He must have taken after his long-deceased, German father.

Still, Tara fancied Max looked more like the tintype she had seen of the Union's 'boy general,' twenty-four-year-old George Custer—whose long, wavy blond hair had a wildness and whose well-trimmed mustache added a somewhat skeptical appearance to the mouth.

But Max displayed none of Custer's braggadocio. Rather, Max's manner was a unique mixture of Western frankness and Spanish dignity. Tall and athletically graceful, he had an aquiline profile and a low-toned voice that suggested a deference oddly mixed with assurance.

As The Barony's *hacienda* was close to where the Gorman Stage and Transport passed through San Patricio, Tara had met many travelers whom The Barony entertained overnight—statesmen, couriers, officers on leave, merchants, and traders from all parts of the world. Yet Max was one of the most striking.

Although the three families—hers, Catarina's, and Max's—gathered at The Barony every year to celebrate the holidays, this was the first time she had seen her playmate and friend in four years. With his return, she felt a certain loss of camaraderie, a strange awkwardness she could not quite follow to its source. They should have been able to pick up where they had left off four years ago. He had changed, of course, but so had she. He said as much.

"You have grown up." He reined in near a motte of acacia and braced overlapped gloved palms on his saddle horn. "Tell me, Tara, why have you not married yet?"

She halted her piebald and looked at Max. "Our Dixie Belles would say because of the dearth of men in these trying times."

His light blue eyes held her gaze. "What would Tara Paladín say?"

She looked away, running her fingers through her piebald's glossy mane. "I would say I am not well disposed to being halter-broke." Her hand gestured in a head-to-toe sweep of herself—indicating her spurred boots with pants tucked inside, her linsey-woolsey shirt, and big, floppy hat. "Besides, do I look like a Dixie Belle? Fragile as porcelain? Is not that what our gallant Southern gentlemen prefer?"

"I cannot speak for any gallant Southern gentlemen—" He checked himself. "I will say that you wear a pair of pants like no woman I have ever seen."

Her eyes narrowed. "I am not certain that is a compliment."

Unexpectedly, his own crinkled at the corners with mirth. "You know, when I was away at school, my stepfather occasionally sent copies of the *San Antonio Express*. Are you by any chance the woman disguised in men's clothing, who gained admittance to the Sons of Malta lodge room a couple of years ago and passed all the degrees of initiation—until the time came for the worshipful commander to pin the emblem on the applicant's breast?"

Her mouth dropped open. "You saw that column? 'A Daughter Among the Sons?'"

His perfectly trimmed mustache lifted with his grin. "What I want to know is how did the commander discover your trick?"

Kneeing her mount forward, she hid the quick grin that sprang to her face. "I lay no claim to that charade. But I did hear that the female candidate was found unworthy to receive the emblem."

He rode up alongside her. His teeth gleamed. "I would think the affair caused considerable consternation."

From beneath the brim of her felt hat, she slid him an impish glance. "You cannot even begin to imagine."

WAS IT TRUE, THAT QUOTE that music hath charms to soothe a savage beast? God knew, a savage warred within his own breast. Perhaps that attributed to the imperative nudging that propelled Kerry's boot steps toward the drawing room. But was his harrowed heart seeking the solace of the drawing room's music or its musician?

He paused at the double doors, slightly ajar, and watched Catarinas skillful hands flow across the piano keys as she practiced for a recital following the Thanksgiving dinner that afternoon. Those same skillful hands had bandaged soldiers' wounds and administered medications prepared by herself . . . and now they lovingly cared for him in an attempt to meet all his needs. But, surely, they both had to know this was something at which she would fail.

When he joined her on the piano bench, she ceased playing and glanced up at him. "Join me in a duet?"

He had to admire her. She didn't flinch from the painfully obvious, as did so many others.

She offered him a warm smile. "I've found some sheet music scored for three hands."

His hand covered her stilled one, resting lightly on the keyboard. "I am not so much interested in the music score as I am in the duet." His palm turned damp and he could feel a muscle in his jaw twitching. "You're wanting—and deserve—marriage, Cat."

Her eyes searched his, seeking an answer that even he did not have. Her responding smile was tight. "Is this a proposal of marriage?"

"No. It is not." Every morning, she appeared at his bedroom door, there to help him shave and dress. She helped him saddle up the days they went riding. Her loving touch quietly, gently assured him in his moments of agitation and frustration. "I know you would never leave me. So, I am telling you I am releasing you from . . . from the understanding we had."

"And what you don't understand is that I am staying not out of some morbid duty but because I love you, Kerry Paladín. And the beautiful music we could make together comes from the heart, not the hands." Her haunting expression reflected an intimacy with both his anguish and hers. "What I need to know is if the feelings you once had for me are strong enough to continue . . . our understanding?"

He squeezed her hand. "My feelings have never changed. I have always loved you, Cat. Even when I didn't realize what those feelings were."

This had never been more true than now. Then why did he feel the bitter bile of self-doubt backing up in his throat?

WADE SETTLED BACK, STOVEPIPE legs sprawled under the long rosewood table, an elbow supported on one chair arm, chin propped on his fist. From beneath half-mast lids, his dark brown eyes scanned the table. Both roasted turkey and duck that he had shot graced its center, along with a plethora of side dishes. His mother, with old Winnie——nearly blind now—and the kitchen help, had spent days cooking and baking.

All the Paladíns, the Gormans, the von Hesse-Lippes, and even Geoffrey Brighton, were present for The Barony's traditional Thanksgiving dinner. The occasion had become a much easier affair to celebrate together than Christmas with all the attendant logistics it presented. President Lincoln had even proclaimed Thanksgiving a national holiday that very month.

Naturally, the conversations revolved around Lincoln and the latest news regarding the war. "I heard there have been draft riots in New York City." Niall emphasized his comment by spearing a slice of turkey.

"And bread riots in Richmond," Karl muttered darkly. "Can San Antonio be far behind?"

"We hear it whispered on every street-corner," Maria Elena put in, pausing to pass the gravy boat, "that a mob is organizing to go to the Market and get the vegetables and meat they need at their own prices—or hang every butcher on a hook in his own stall."

From there, the conversation turned to a recently invented submarine boat designed by Wilson & Richardson, meant to sink the Yankee blockaders at Texas ports. Then a new voice, Brighton's, mentioned the recent Union invasion of Brownsville.

Back from Brownsville just ahead of the invasion by sea two weeks before, the Englishman dolloped a generous portion of sweet potatoes on his plate. "I think the Union was anxious to show its presence along the border as a warning to the French to keep their armies well inside Mexico."

Rafaela patted her lips with her linen napkin. "Surely, the loss of Brownsville will disrupt Confederate trade drastically."

"Well, thanks to Wade's initiative, Barony cattle will find their way to market by way of Rio Grande City." Tara's dark brown eyes sparkled and Wade affected a negligent shrug at his sister's praise.

His gaze shifted speculatively to Max, sitting next to her, and wondered if the young man was the cause for her vivacity.

Brighton's puffy eyes narrowed on Wade. "How so?"

He said nothing, only took a sip from his wine glass.

"When Obregon Enterprises refused to ship Barony cattle on its steamboats," his father began with what sounded to Wade as close to bragging as his father ever managed, "Wade circumvented Obregon. Contracted to send them downriver via keelboats."

Karl, who had handled the legalities with Bias Uribe, smiled. "And I might add, Wade, you obtained a good deal on the shipping charges."

He wondered if Karl was aware of Sarita Obregon's part in mediating with Uribe for equitable charges. Wade's agreement with her called for her mediation in exchange, supposedly, for his teaching her to ride horseback when next they both put in at Rio Grande City.

Despite her nearly seventeen years, she exhibited all the feminine guile of a debutante. He knew exactly what she was after—and it wasn't riding lessons. He found perverse pleasure in meeting with her again, merely to thwart her ambitions to land him as her groom.

"I don't think I ever mentioned it, Father, but when in Rio Grande City, I learned that, apparently, the head of Obregon is a former acquaintance of yours."

His father cocked his dark head. "Really? I do not recollect ever meeting an Obregon."

"Seems Obregon believes you cheated him out of land or inheritance or something due him."

Wade's mother set down her wine glass. Her fingers flew to her four-leaf-clover pendant necklace—as they invariably did in times of fretting—as if it were a rosary. "What is this Obregon's name? His full name?"

He paused, then shrugged. "I can't recollect overhearing it, but it seems he is hell-bent on destroying you, Dad, and The Barony."

He caught the worried look on his mother's face. For the first time, he noticed how drained she looked. Preparation for the holiday dinner may have tired her, but she was accustomed to presiding over dinners at a moment's notice.

Over the last half year, he had been more worried about Kerry and how his older brother would adjust to the use of only one arm. Wade himself had yet to adjust to seeing the neatly folded empty coat sleeve pinned above where Kerry's elbow should have been. However, Kerry's initial depression and resentment appeared to ebb with each passing month.

Wade could attribute it to his brother's indomitable will, but one glance at Catarina sitting beside Kerry was evidence enough that another factor, equally as strong, had been at work.

Even now, she was unobtrusively cutting his portion of roast duck into bite-size pieces. Wade glanced back to his brother and caught Kerry's dark, fleeting look of frustration that Wade could only imagine must come from feeling inadequate or insufficient. At whom was Kerry's frustration directed? Himself or Catarina?

At that moment, Kerry chose to stand, his wine glass raised. "Niall, Rafaela, all of my life you have been like family. I am asking permission now to make your beautiful daughter, Catarina, my wife and hopefully start our own family."

AFTER THANKSGIVING DINNER, the men gathered in Paladín's office for their customary cigars. To Paladín, his favorite cigar—a Havana blend imported through Matamoros—tasted stale that evening. Like his business. Neither possessed their full flavor lately.

Mayhap it was that he sorely missed Sam Houston's wry humor and fearlessly honest comments at gatherings like this. The patriotic statesman had died back in July. Pneumonia, the newspapers said. Paladín suspected it was more likely grief. He surmised the wise old leader and invaluable friend had foreseen the disaster that would await his beloved Texas once the War Between the States ended. His dying words had been, "Texas, Margaret, Texas."

Or mayhap Paladín's malaise was due to his preoccupation with the Union cavalries out of Brownsville. They ranged north and west, raiding distant ranches, including the nearest to The Barony, the Kennedy Ranch, and taking livestock to feed Union ranks.

Then again, his malaise might also be due to his own overriding concern for his elder son that made everything else seem stale just now.

Kerry had been such a bright light of energy, like the violet glow of St. Elmo's Fire that danced between the tips of cattle horns on stormy nights. A good omen, like Fiona. Kerry had possessed his mother's vibrant life's light. But with the loss of his arm . . . .

Cigar tips flared in the candlelit office. Idle comments were being traded among the men, lazy and pleasantly full from the sumptuous dinner. From the drawing room came the piano music trilled by Catarina's gifted fingers. What was that minstrel song . . . Swanee River?

Paladín made up his mind. He laid the cigar in the pewter ashtray on his executive desk. Placing clasped hands, fingers interlocked, on its red leather writing top, he cleared his throat. "I think it is time for a changing of the guard."

All heads—Niall, Kerry, Geoffrey, Max, Karl, and Wade—swiveled toward him.

"There are still many things I want to do. I am interested in visiting the Shammar Emirate this coming summer. Their coveted Arabian stallions, bred with our mares, could make for a racehorse worthy of England's Ascot. Then, too, Fiona wants to return to Ireland—and County Kerry—for a visit. You can understand that ancestral draw, I would imagine, Brighton?"

Without waiting for the Englishman to respond, he continued. "Since this past summer, when Federal armies closed the Mississippi River to traffic, unbranded cattle have multiplied here in South Texas. These mavericks roam the ranges by the thousands, devouring the grasslands worse than any biblical plague."

He leveled his gaze upon Kerry. "More cattle than I want to wrangle with at my age. Son, I want you take over the reins of The Barony and its various subsidiaries."

Kerry blew a helix of smoke. He paused one beat too long. "Ford has written me that he could arrange an office job for me with the army at the Arsenal."

His son was stalling. Why? "This war won't last forever. Every man jack in this room knows the South is doomed.

And you would be doomed, sitting behind some god-damned desk day in and day out."

"Well, bugger it, then," Brighton began, but his next words were obliterated by the piercing scream reverberating through the house, raising the hair on Paladín's nape.

"ALEX?"

How long had he been sitting there, like that—face buried in his damp hands? He raised his head and looked over his shoulder.

Rafaela stood in her parlor doorway, one palm on its frame, the other holding a candle holder's brass drip pan. The candlewick's wavering light revealed worry in her tear-swollen eyes and the dark shadows beneath. "You've been here all night. Why don't you let me keep the wake while you get some rest?"

His gaze went back to the table, where the small body was laid out, surrounded by lighted tapers. Except for her face, the body was covered by a sheet. "No."

"I have refreshments prepared for the mourners. They should begin arriving by this afternoon, as word spreads."

"Turn them all away."

The parlor was as silent as a falling star. "Alex, damn it, there are others who loved Fiona, too. Think of Kerry and Tara and Wade. They have a right to be in here with their mother."

He sighed, tunneling his fingers through his rumpled hair. "Give me a little longer, Rafaela. If you please."

He wished he had had a little longer with Fiona—long

enough to tell her he loved her more than his own life. That she had been his life. His light. His laughter. His love. Instead, that thief Death had swiftly stolen his Fiona from him. Robbed her, it seemed, of her next heartbeat. She was too young for heart failure. All those years, he had thought they still had left . . . .

All right. He would do his duty by his beloved—give her the grand Irish wake she deserved. The clocks would be stopped, mirrors turned to the wall. There would be lots of food and plenty of drink to be consumed. People would come and socialize, drink copiously and remember her life.

Though none of them knew her life like he did.

Fiona, trapped in the confessional by him back when they met at his Presidio. Fiona staunchly firing the blunderbuss at his attacker there on its parapet. Fiona protecting her virtue by glibly declaring to him she had the French pox. Fiona, in childbirth, swearing like a soldier.

Fiona. Fiona. Fiona.

Even in death, she seemed to radiate her utterly unique beauty. Perhaps it was his tear-swamped eyes, but his lass's freckles, once as bright as halfpennies, seemed blanched. He blinked back tears, stood up, leaned over the table, and drew back the sheet.

In her clasped hands had been placed, as was the Irish custom, her rosary of crystal and onyx beads. Though it was not the expensive rosary between her hands his fingers caressed, but the ordinary four-leaf clover locket at her neck.

RIO GRANDE CITY
MARCH 1864

Since the Spanish colonial days of 1753, the warehouses and stock pens had been visible on the riverfront of Rio Grande City—founded as *Rancho Carnestolendas* and named for the carnival just before Lent.

That morning, the only thing visible was a man hanged from a hackberry tree where Main Street intersected with Britton Avenue. The tree, its limbs weighted down by raptors, herons, and red-billed pigeons, was a bird fancier's paradise.

Wade paused in his ambling stroll toward the riverfront, seeming to chew the fat with the carne vendor at the corner. From the serape-draped vendor, Wade learned the foul-smelling, bloated body swinging from the noose had been suspected of being a Unionist. Unionist or deserter, the consequences were the same.

Already downriver in Brownsville, where the Union Jack waved desultorily in place of the Bonnie Blue, hundreds of Texas's Unionist refugees had formed a chapter of the Union League of Texas.

The Confederacy's Secretary of War in Richmond, Virginia wanted Wade to keep a finger on the pulse of the vital international river border—from Brownsville to Laredo.

Wade figured it was his own erratic pulse that needed monitoring. A couple of times that past year, he had driven cattle to Rio Grande City to ship downriver on Bias Uribe's keel boats. He had also braved the dust storms and lice, thunderstorms and Comanche, to drive herds of swine and mustangs to Rio Grande City—all as pretexts to collect information on the Yank's activities and movements along the river.

Over those half dozen times, he had yet to chance across Sarita Obregon.

The death of his mother had curtailed his traveling for a while, but not his foolish distraction at the most unwelcome of times with thoughts of Sarita. Just two weeks ago, the mayor's daughter had taken him to task for his preoccupation while in the midst of a bed romp.

He had been cock-sure certain the daughter of his father's enemy had him earmarked for marriage. Yet, as many times as Bias confirmed her steamboat *Shamrock* had put in at Rio Grande City, she had made no effort to contact him or even to leave a message for him through Bias. Neither had he crossed her path at Falcon's Pharmacy. Grudgingly, Wade had to admit his male pride was pricked.

It had been a year of women throwing themselves into his arms at every opportunity. What with the loss of Texas' studs to the Confederate army, he had become prime horseflesh. Wives, widows, and debutantes casting sultry glances over rapidly swishing fans, but nary a word from Sarita Obregon. Perhaps she had married.

"Yi-yi-yi-yi." Bias rolled muddy-brown eyes. "The men, they pursue, *Señorita* Sarita—and her money—like coyotes after a jackrabbit." The pint-size Mexican and he were walking along unpaved Texas Street toward the pens where Barony cattle were waiting to be loaded onto Bias's keelboats.

Cotton, hides, furs, bear grease, tallow, beeswax, and wool were stored in nearby warehouses until steamboats arrived. From the carne vendor, Wade had learned that arms, ammunition, and medical supplies had been moved and stored one block over. Why?

Approaching the pens, Wade noticed a Goliath of a man with thinning auburn hair talking to one of Wade's Paladíneños near the pen's chute. The man straightened, his measured gaze assessing Wade from head to toe. He stuck out a ham hock of a hand.

Wade eyed the hand, then the ruddy face. "Yes?"

"By Sarita's description, you're none other than Wade Paladín—'a long, tall drink of a man. Dark and dangerous looking.'"

He shook the giant's hand, determined not to wince at the grip. "She mentioned you. Big Mick, is it?"

"Aye. The lass is at Falcon Pharmacy, partaking of her usual."

Wade waited for the rest of the message. Apparently

nothing more was to be forthcoming. He nodded. "Thanks."

Big Mick nodded too, then swung away toward the docks.

Wade finished his business with the smirking Bias, then turned reluctant footsteps toward the pharmacy and its soda fountain. For all his reveries about Sarita, he was about to cross that dreamy line into reality. His gut told him she would not be one of the chicas he could string along like he did cows at the watering hole. Sarita Obregon would be a 'now or never' girl.

Only, he was a 'never' man.

Damn it, she was even prettier than he had recollected. Blue-green eyes regarded him steadily above her soda. She was amazing. How she could be so dainty and feminine and yet captain a steamboat was beyond him. She sat down the half-filled glass.

"Good morning, Mr. Paladín."

He tipped the brim of his hat. "Morning."

She nodded at the bench opposite her.

He slid onto it, took off one cowhide glove, and stretched out his forefinger to wipe away the soda water foam that graced her cupid's-bow upper lip. Her eyes widened as large as pie pans.

"Never did particularly hanker after a woman with a mustache."

"Are you hankering after me, Mr. Paladín?"

Taking off his other glove, he tucked them both under his gun holster belt, then signaled Oliver the Apothecary for his customary cup of coffee with sugar. "Haven't made up my mind yet."

"Then let me help you."

He started grinning.

She did not. Primly, she held up kid-gloved fingers and ticked them off. "Number one, we are obviously both attracted to one another. Number two, we both are besieged by members of the opposite sex who would delight in helping us spend our inheritances. Number three, we both highly value being out from beneath patriarchal control, whether it be an Obregon or a Paladín at the helm. Number four, I have defied my father's dictum to marry that old dung heap Geoffrey Brighton and am going to run away."

Marry Geoffrey Brighton? What was this?

"Lastly—and most importantly—you have had one year to make up your mind about me. If you do not know by now, then I am not interested in—"

An ear-ringing *boom* vibrated the pharmacy walls.

Wade grabbed her upraised fingers and jerked her off the bench. The streets were filled with people running and yelling. He paused on the edge of the boardwalk and strained through the shroud of smoke to see the warehouses at the far end of Water Street. Black whorls billowed from one. Most likely the cotton warehouse.

Dodging the frenzied men and women who clogged the street, he hauled Sarita along with him. Her free hand was clutching her ridiculously frilly hat to keep it from flying off. He caught the bridle of a passing buggy. "What has happened?"

"The Yankee's are coming," the elderly driver gasped out. "The Confederates are putting the torch to everything. Best to git while the gittin's good!"

Before he could question the old man further, he cracked his whip over the nag, and the buggy shot forward.

Wade's first thought was to get Sarita to the *Shamrock* and safety with Big Mick, then make his way to Ringgold Barracks to see how he could help. But frenzied crowds whirled them about like debris in a dust devil.

From the opposite end of Water Street, soldiers wearing the yellow stripe of the Union cavalry were charging like cassocks down the street.

Everyone was anxious to reach the ancient town of Camargo on the Mexican side of the river, which was heavily garrisoned, guaranteeing safety from the attacking Yankees. But at the docks, he saw the hand-pulled ferry spilling over with people frantically boarding.

At the *Shamrock's* gangplank, three men had pulled guns and were forcing room for themselves to board.

Worse—upstream at Ringgold Barracks, Confederate soldiers scurried to dump the siege gun into the river. The Confederates were not even going to defend the city. Its citizens were on their own.

He shouldered through the melee of men and women who rushed past like stampeded cattle. Suddenly, thousands of pounds of Confederate gunpowder exploded in a great roar. The ground beneath his feet shook.

He looked over his shoulder as orange and red tongues

of flame leapt from the armaments warehouse. Firebrands showered down upon Rio Grande City roofs. The Confederate destruction of the warehouses had spread into the town, where looters were already shattering the window of a dry goods store.

With Sarita in tow, he whirled and changed course, shouldering out of the streaming mob, away from the conflagration, toward Texas Street and the cattle pens. Somewhere along the way, he lost his hat.

The crowd grew more sparse. Smoke filled the air, stinging his eyes. Swerving around a runaway wagon, he hauled Sarita through the maze of corrals. If she made even one protest about the manure piles, he swore he would throw her over his knee and whup her.

Next to them, an entire wall of the livery stable crumbled. Instinctively, he enfolded her in the concave of his body to shield her from the falling timbers. Sparks showered them.

"My skirts!" She staggered to her knees to slap at the fiery ripple consuming her circus-tent hems.

He reached around her to swat down at the flames. They were traveling too fast. In one sweeping yank, he tore away her overskirts. The hoop skirt resisted him. Seconds whizzed by before he wrestled her free of it. With her clad only in her hat, shirtwaist, pantalettes, and ankle boots, he tugged her forward toward the distant *remuda* of the *Paladíneños* horses and chuck wagon.

There was no telling where his *Paladíneños* were—most likely struggling into their pants, chaps, and boots in one of the town's myriad bordellos. Wasting not another moment, he encircled Sarita's waist with his hands and hoisted her into the chuck wagon. She flailed backwards in the narrow row created by chests on either side, and he scrambled in to brace closed their wobbly doors and drawers.

A mistake, because his spur caught on her pantalettes. He stumbled, landing atop her. Her breath whooshed out. Then they were staring into each other's eyes. While outside the chuckwagon, forces battled and fires raged, the pounding of their own hearts with the fury of their escape was the only sound within.

Her lips, as pink as a west Texas sunrise, parted in a perfect 'O.'

Hell, there was only one thing to do. He kissed her. The kiss was meant to be planted as solidly, as swiftly, and as indifferently as he would a branding iron to a heifer. But at the response of her soft lips moving beneath his, it was his flesh that sizzled. Stunned, his head jerked back. He frowned down at her. "Hell's fires!"

In the dimness, her eyes gleamed with a light of their own. "So, you felt it, too."

"The only thing I'm feeling is the need to skedaddle before the fires burn us to a crisp."

Her smile was tender, like that of a teacher to a struggling pupil. "It's too late for that."

His eyes fastened on those parted, plump, and moist lips. Reluctantly, he conceded to her statement. As he slanted his mouth across hers, this time in a lingering foray of every aspect of her mouth, he was dimly aware that his bachelor status was as threatened as the Confederacy.

When at last he released her, her breath released in a whoosh. "Oh my!"

"Well, well, well," was all he could manage. He could have been kicked by one of the chuckwagon's six mules. Or all of them. He raised on one forearm to look down at the intractable young woman.

Her arms wedged their way up between the drawers on either side of their trapped bodies to wrap around his neck. Her lips puckered to blow the swath of his hair falling diagonally across his eye. She was smiling serenely. "I fear I have compromised you, Wade Paladín. You will simply have to elope with me."

By godawlmighty, no way he was fixin' to let that happen. No way was he going to be castrated.

SAN ANTONIO
JUNE 1864

Only since Queen Victoria's marriage to Albert of Saxe-Coburg had white become a popular choice for a wedding gown—and a symbol of virginity.

It was the virginity part that concerned Catarina as she prepared for the opulent wedding ceremony at San Antonio's majestic old Cathedral of San Fernando. What if her marriage to Kerry was never consummated?

Perhaps that was why she had gone against tradition—why she had advanced their wedding date well before the year-long wait dictated as an appropriate grieving period for a family member's death, that of his beloved mother.

The repercussions of the Civil War had banished such proprieties. A loved one might not return from the war front. Or might return with changed feelings, or changed bodies. Or both.

And Kerry was changed. No longer did she glimpse that roguish smile that was charming and disarming, that cocksure attitude that had the power to snare all females, that exhilaration that animated his face and brightened his gloriously green eyes.

At one time, that enthusiasm had been part and parcel of his devotion to The Barony. Recently, it seemed aimed more at his devotion to Texas. He had mentioned offhandedly an interest in teaching political philosophy at St. Mary's Institute. That enthusiasm had at one time also encompassed her. Now, she was not so sure.

Her mother must have sensed her disquiet. Rafaela paused in adjusting the magnificent lace veil that was supposed to enwrap the bride like a precious present. "Are you having second thoughts, Catarina?" Those amber eyes searched her own. "Have your feelings for Kerry changed?"

"No. No, it's not that." She bit her lip. How to express in finite words what she could only sense was going through the complex mind of the man she had adored since childhood? "I fear Kerry's body may have healed, but I am not sure if his mind has, momma. Or if it will ever heal. With an arm gone, what if he feels that part of his manhood is gone as well?"

Rafaela clasped her shoulders, draped in Brussels lace. "Now, you will listen to me, Catarina. Do you understand that you may have to help him regain his confidence in his masculinity tonight and during the nights to come? Do you understand what I'm saying?"

Topics such as the intimacies that transpired between a male and female were never discussed between her mother and her. As if her mother and father never engaged in such activity, although Catarina knew better. Occasionally she overheard smothered noises that sounded like rasps of rhapsody.

A knock at her bedroom door spared her mortified response. Her mother opened it only a smidgen, and Catarina heard her future father-in-law's rough textured voice. ". . . moment to bestow . . . my son's bride . . ."

"Come on in, Alex." Her mother's tone was unmistakably compassionate as she opened the door wide. "It's only Kerry who must be kept from seeing the bride."

Seven months of grief and drink and insomnia had ravaged the roue's distinguished good looks. Days' old beard shadowed Paladín's hollow cheeks. Eyes that looked like smashed milk glass with red ink funneled into the cracks gazed back at her. His black dress coat was as rumpled as his thick, silver-threaded hair.

He bowed deeply and extended a small, square velvet box. "A wedding gift, Catarina."

She looked questioningly from the box to him.

"Fiona would have wanted you to have it."

Tentatively, she pried open the lid. She recognized Fiona's good luck charm, her four leaf clover pendant. Her mother inhaled a small but audible gasp.

"I ordered it made into a brooch for you." His voice was a whiskey gravel.

She looked up at him. "Wouldn't it by rights belong to Tara?"

"You know Tara, Catarina. She puts no value on jewelry."

Catarina closed the box and stood on tiptoe to kiss his scruffy cheek. "I'll treasure this, sir, but I can think of a perfect place it belongs and it's not with me. That is, if it is all right with you?"

He cast her a puzzled frown, then shrugged those uncommonly wide shoulders. "Nothing is right with me anymore." He turned back to the open doorway. "Do as you will."

WITH OLD WORLD GRACE AND smoothness, Alex tipped his top hat to the white-aproned waitress. Rosy cheeked, she grinned winsomely at him. She could be no older than her mid-twenties. At fifty-seven, he felt centuries older.

Passing her his hat, he bypassed the bar to take a seat at a table in the rear of Menger's dining salon, where the chandelier's lights faded away. The restaurant, said to equal New York's Delmonico's in elegance, was nearly empty that late in the evening.

From the adjoining ballroom could be heard the festive noises of Kerry's wedding reception that was winding down. Music that made Alex wistful. Laughter that made him lonely.

The young woman eyed him speculatively. "Our cook is gone, but I'd be glad to get you coffee . . . or something else."

His stringent mouth silenced his groan. The wench was young enough to be his daughter. After half a year without Fiona's knowing ways with loving, his body might be clamoring for release, but his heart was nailed tighter than a coffin. "Make it bourbon. A double."

The reception's gaiety, the required civility with guests, set him on edge. The last thing he wanted was the dreary exchange of sentiments, observations, opinions. . . and most of all, the nauseating, awkward condolences.

The waitress returned with his bourbon. Instead of leaving, she stood there, fussing with hair that had untidily escaped her white lace cap. "You look glum, sir."

He ground his teeth. "Do say." He took a swallow. Good, the bourbon had a bite.

Still, the young woman hovered and he was too weary to shoo her away. "What with the war, Uncle Bill has turned over most of the rooms upstairs to military personnel, but still . . . ."

"You're old man Menger's niece?"

She dimpled '*Ja.*. We're short of staff these days, so I help out." She looked down, rubbed her palms, then peered up at him through blonde lashes. "And I could help in other ways, Mr. Paladín."

So, she knew who he was. His heavy-lidded eyes regarded her. Why not? His cock ached. Like a phantom limb. His flesh yearned for human touch.

By choice, his life had been a solitary journey but for two females who had breached his defenses. Early on, the beguiling Frenchwoman Thérèse Del Valle and then the Irish lass Fiona Flanagan. And it was the latter that he did not know how he could do this life without.

He tossed down the rest of his drink and stood. "My apologies, but familial obligations beckon in the ballroom."

STANDING MIDWAY UP THE Menger Hotel's staircase, Catarina posed at the wrought-iron balustrade and tossed over her left shoulder the bouquet of freshly picked wildflowers.

Below, the female wedding guests scrambled to catch it. It bobbled along several upstretched fingertips, then plummeted toward the outskirts of the melee. She giggled at Tara's startled expression as her hands shot out to save the bouquet from being trampled. At her side, Max's mustache curved with his smile of wry amusement.

Maybe Fate did play a role in one's life. Maybe life didn't happen as willy-nilly as one would think. All along, some inexplicable feeling—intuition?—had whispered insistently that she and Kerry were fated to be together, even those times she had riled and ranted against the preposterous idea.

But had Fate, also, destined for Kerry a way of life to be so bereft of fulfilling his yearnings and dreams? A way of life, she knew, that now made him feel half a man?

At the back of the room, she caught her father's encouraging nod. It was time. She looked up at Kerry and smiled. "Shall we retire?"

As he bent to kiss her temple, she smelled the fragrant nosegay pinned to his lapel. Cheers and applause erupted below them. "I believe they're ready for us to. Let's hope they're not planning to fete us next with a chivaree."

She groaned. "Dear Lord, spare us that."

As he grasped her elbow, leading her up the remaining stairs, she desperately prayed the Lord spare her beloved the humiliation she knew he experienced daily . . . and for that night most of all. She knew she would be walking on eggshells. Careful. Careful.

Though barely five-years old, the elegant hotel had recently shut its doors to accommodate both military staff and wounded soldiers trickling in, but the Menger family had generously provided its guest suite for the newly wedded couple.

In that bedroom, she turned to Kerry as he closed the door on the rest of the world. Putting all thought behind her, she held out a gloved hand to him.

He took it, turned the inside of her wrist up, and kissed the bare skin exposed by the glove's embroidered oval cutout. A delicious shiver eddied through her. Deftly, he peeled off that long glove, then began to remove the other.

She had to smile. "I remember the time you pushed me in the tree swing that hung over the river. I had to be all of seven-years old and frightfully scared. I started to fall, and you grabbed my jacket. I slid right out it like this glove and plopped into the water."

He shrugged out of his claret frockcoat, dropping it

carelessly on the tufted loveseat, and turned down the lamp's wick. "If I remember correctly, you crawled up that muddy bank, holding aloft a crayfish like a prize." His eyes never leaving her face, he stripped off his white tie, then unbuttoned his white vest. "Come here, Cat."

She bit her lower lip. "I'm a little scared now."

His expression was solemn in the lamplight. "So am I, Kiddy Kat."

Her heart full of her love, she went to stand before him. He winked, as if to reassure her, and she knew he needed reassurance as well. Then he turned her, so that her back was to him and began to undress her, the fingers of one hand mechanically working at her Basque fastenings.

"Things will never be quite the same between us. Will they, Kerry? They'll change."

The gown rustled to the floor around her ankles. "They already have."

She stepped out of it, toeing off her low-strapped pumps. She flashed him over her shoulder a smile she hoped was not tremulous. Her undergarments drifted behind her as she crossed to their marriage bed. In their wake, he trailed her.

She understood he needed her vivaciousness, her spirited wit he often acclaimed, to override the inadequacy that now plagued him. And she needed him. She whispered as much, as he moved up over her and, with relief, she saw the tension ease from his face.

His kiss that began as tenderly as their recent vows gradually turned urgent, and her lips parted at the insistent nudging pressure of his, welcoming this new part of him to explore her . . . and welcoming this new and intriguing experience. She felt her untutored body responding rapidly to the rapture of his kiss. Her skin flushing, her heart thudding, her feminine parts moistening.

Why had they waited so long?

Shockingly, her hips shifted, pressed that mounded part of her upward against that hard erection evidencing his own desire. Her fingers anchored in the russet hair that framed his face. To her astonishment, she also heard herself, as if in a distance, sighing her pleasure.

His hand cupped her neck, slid along the curve of her shoulder, and palmed her breast. At her surprised gasp, he stiffened. Between the thicket of her lashes, she saw the utter anguish the dim lamplight could not hide.

Immediately, his countenance turned taunting. "Your passion delights me, Cat. But is it that of the shy maiden or the dutiful wife?"

"What?"

He pushed off her, bracing his weight on his forearm. "Your passion—is it feigned to conceal the repulsion you find in the reddened, shriveled skin puckered at my stump?"

Her hands shot up to frame his face. "Stop that right now, Kerry. Stop this ugly talk."

"Yes. What an ugly sound that word makes. Stump." He rolled from atop her. "Your fingers are chilly, my love."

"Kerry." Her voice was barely above a susurration. "I just have not had the experience of—"

"Making love to a one-armed man?" He forced a

lightness and turned away from her to lay facing the wall.

"No! That's not what I was going to say."

His voice cracked and words poured out in a raw whisper. "I assure you, the technique is no different."

THE BARONY RANCH
JULY 1864

"You remind me of dad, the way you pace," Wade said.

Tara swung back to face him, sprawled in the armchair opposite their father's expansive desk. Her brother looked tired. But what could one expect?

Following Kerry's wedding, Wade had spent a week on the trail to Laredo and then a hard, quick turn-around, arriving only this morning. Which was so unlike her brother, who with his devil-may-care attitude usually took his own sweet time.

"I swear, Wade, I don't know what I am going to do with father. He glowers, he snaps, he drinks too much, and he refuses to attend to Barony business." She thrust out her palms, her long fingers spread in a helpless gesture at the mound of papers tossed haphazardly on the desktop. "It's been almost eight months and still he pines. I can run our ranch activities, but all the complexities of its various enterprises . . . ." She left off and massaged her throbbing temples.

"Send to San Antonio for Karl—have him explain the ins and outs to you."

"I have. He's expected today or tomorrow." Her voice lowered. "But, seriously, Wade, I was hoping Kerry would want to take up the slack. And this latest insistence of Brighton's—hells bells, I don't know why father didn't just send you instead of Kerry with Brighton. Not that father is paying any attention."

Wade stretched out his stilt-long legs, his spurred boots crossed, and intertwined his fingers over the buckle of his mangy chaps. "Most likely because I was off in Laredo with the—"

"That's what I mean. You were so close to Rio Grande City, why didn't—"

Her brother jerked up straight and shoved back his low-crowned, wide-brim hat. "Rio Grande City? When?"

"When what?"

"Damn it, Tara, when did Brighton leave with Kerry for Rio Grande City?"

"Why, the day before yester . . . no, yesterday. Seems Brighton thinks Barony Land and Cattle could go over old man Obregon's head and secure a freighting contract with his son, Roderick, who agreed to meet them there. I don't think father gives a farthing right now about The Barony or what—"

Wade shot to his feet and headed for the door.

"Where are you going?"

He shot a glance over his shoulder. "Rio Grande City."

"Why?"

"'Pears Brighton's tendin' to marry Roderick's twin sister, Sarita Obregon."

Her brow furrowed. "What has that to do with you?"

Frustration etched his biscuit-brown, sculpted face.

"Hell if I know, sis."

Her eyes narrowed. "You need a better reason than that. She's the daughter of The Barony's arch rival."

He huffed a sigh. "How's 'bout 'cause I took one look at Sarita Obregon, and I was plumb fractured."

THE DOOR TO PALADÍN'S OFFICE was slightly ajar. Max nudged it farther. Late afternoon sunlight filtered through the office's slatted shutters to fall on Tara, sitting behind her father's mahogany desk.

Elbows propped on its red leather writing surface, she rubbed her temples, as if she would rub out whatever panicky feeling it was that gnawed at her. That squared off chin of hers was dropped against her chest, so that her single long braid draped over one shoulder like a thick bell cord of sable velvet.

The Kashmir carpet muted his footsteps. "Tara?" He placed the bound record books, folders, and ledgers on the desk.

Her head jerked up. "Oh, Max." He was gratified by the pleasure in her voice. "What are you doing here?'

"Father pulled me off another case and sent me in his place. Seems his services are as much in demand by the Confederacy boys in Austin as those of Col. Ford's. What's going on, Tara? You look beat. And that's not like you."

"What is like me?"

"Passion. Persistence."

"I don't think I have it in me anymore." She buried her head into the cradle of her arms, folded on the desktop.

"Sure you do." Much of The Barony's continued existence during the past year, when other ranches failed, had more to do with Tara's good 'ranch' sense than her father's visionary resourcefulness.

"I'm just so tired."

The wild spirit that he so admired in this woman would rally. Her indomitable energy was as much a part of her as her openhanded generosity and overbearing opinions. She was gloriously human—flawed and fabulous.

He came around the desk. Without heeding propriety, which he rarely did anyway, he placed his hands on her shoulders and began to massage the taut, tense muscles there.

"Ummm." Her warmed-honey voice welled up from her folded arms. "That feels so good, Max."

Instantly, his hands ceased their kneading. He could sense that powerful arousal that happened often when near her. But for all her strength and grit, Tara was woefully and abysmally ignorant when it came to matters of human sexuality.

Around her, he might as well be a steer—and everyone knew those neutered bulls wound up as barbecue. No, his throbbing desire would have to be assuaged, instead, the day after tomorrow by the luscious and obliging young sister of that Austin railroad lobbyist.

But, Christ's thorns, he would sell his soul to be the one to awaken Tara to the sensual side of her femininity and its power. Tutoring and gentling her would be a demanding but pleasurable task that would take, at least, a lifetime.

At his sudden stillness, she looked up over her shoulder at him with that innate direct and uncompromising gaze so characteristic of her. "What?"

"Nothing. We just have a lot to do and I need to get back to Austin."

"How long will you be here?"

He dragged up the armchair next to hers, flicked out his coattails, and, shoulder to shoulder with her, flipped open the first ledger. "As long as you need me—until you get a grasp of the financial and legal aspects of The Barony Partnership and all that it entails."

With store-bought ink not to be had, the ledger entries, scrawled with ink made from indigo roots and purple pokeberries, were at times nearly indecipherable. "Now, look, Tara, your expenditures here last month for the Merino sheep came at a—"

She raised her hand and shook one long finger at him. "You listen to me, Max von Hesse-Lippe, I am here to tell you that the beef industry will collapse on the stock market in the not too distant future. Diversifying by investing in the sheep—"

He caught her hand. "Tara, Tara—I am in agreement with you. You bought at a perfect time."

Her eyes, so brown they were almost black, lit up like highly polished ebony. "I'm building a hide and tallow works two miles north of the rancho. And next I want hogs, Max. Hogs in the thousands."

He began laughing.

"What?" she asked again.

"Only that I find you utterly entertaining." He smiled, still holding her delicate hand.

"Is that good . . . or bad?"

His thumb massaged the ridges of her knuckles. "It's good, Tara." His voice was huskier than he would have wanted. "Very good."

Her gaze roamed over his face, as though trying to find and identify some pesky feeling she could not quite fathom, then settled on his mouth. He held his breath, waiting to see what she would do.

She was a smart woman—and so unpredictable because she could instantly switch thinking like a man to that of thinking like a woman more quickly than a Chinese tallying on an abacus. And he never knew which side would take precedence. Or if both male and female mentalities would surface simultaneously, which sorely confounded his attorney's precise and analytical mindset.

"You want to kiss me, don't you." It was a statement.

He inhaled slowly. "Yes. For some time now, I have wanted to."

Her thick dark brown brows almost met over the bridge of her patrician nose. "Then why have you not? Kissed me, that is."

He still had hold of her hand. He leaned ever so slightly closer. Their faces were mere inches apart. "I didn't want to lose the vital friendship that I have carefully nourished over the years with you."

"Then it is only friendship you feel? You want to kiss me, as friends do?"

His free hand slipped up to cup the back of her neck. "Friends kiss on the cheek, Tara."

He brushed his lips over hers, waiting for resistance, and when none came, firmly kissed her until their lips blended. When her lips parted at the sweep of his tongue tip, he was wise enough to draw away. "Does that feel like the kiss of a friend?"

She shook her head. Confusion and wariness battled chemistry for predominance in her expression.

"Would you like to explore the possibilities of the kiss further?" He waited and could feel the painful burgeoning at his crotch and the agonizing trip-beat of his heart. He could see she was gathering her wits about her.

"This is something I will have to give some thought to."

He sighed but smiled. That was so like her. "I am willing to wait, Tara." She was not yet ready, despite her body's urging.

RIO GRANDE CITY

Moderate rain fell most of the day as Kerry, with Brighton, cantered along the muddy Military Road, or the Cotton Road as it was now called, that paralleled the Rio Grande.

Fortunately, Old Rip's command had won several sharp skirmishes with the Federals, pursuing and forcing them to retreat from town after town back down the Rio Grande, until they occupied only Brazos Santiago at its mouth.

Kerry missed that part of his life—the enormous energy surge that came during battle. He definitely didn't miss the heat, boredom, mosquitos, or the skimpy rations. No, it was the energy pumping through him, that feeling of time standing still, of details being sharper when he looked Death in the eye.

Returning home to The Barony, to his family, to Catarina . . . finding himself with a stump for an arm . . . to say that period had been an extremely confusing experience was an understatement. Confusion interspersed with numbness—and dullness. The anticipation and excitement of uniting with Catarina, where their hearts beat faster, had been muted by his ultimate and overwhelming feeling of emptiness.

He supposed he and Catarina only needed time to adjust to his . . . impairment. And what if she never did? What if his wife found him measuring up to less than she had longed for in a husband? Night after night, he knew she lay next to him, waiting. Her relief that he did not reach for her in the darkness was so palpable, how could he not be aware of it?

Their wedding night had been a disaster of monstrous proportions. How long before his injured masculine pride and mercurial temperament goaded him into making her his wife in all ways—or driving her away? She was his lone bright star that he could see from a million miles off. Did either of them deserve this?

Three weeks had passed since the wedding night and he felt like he and Catarina were locked in an eternal impasse. He knew she was desperate to please him—and that made it even worse. For that very reason, he had persuaded his father to send him along with Brighton to negotiate an under- the-table contract with Rodrick Obregon.

With Rio Grande City freed of Yankee occupation and once again open for business, teamsters cursed, burros brayed, and oxen bawled as cotton wagons congested its damp streets. All this commotion converged on the riverfront at Water Street, where hand-pulled ferries and puffing steamboats carried cargo across to Camargo on the river's other side, in Mexico.

About a block west of the landing, Kerry and Brighton checked into the Yzaguirre-Longoria House, an inn for passengers debarking from the riverboats. Arched arcades formed shaded transitional spaces leading from the domestic areas into secluded gardens of courtyards and patios.

Kerry thought how delighted Catarina would be with its beauty . . . and how revulsed she would be with his next destination—a seedy saloon off Fandango Plaza, whose adobe walls reeked of urine where drunken patrons had splattered them.

Why Rodrigo chose to conduct business that drizzly afternoon in a cantina that smelled like a stinking morgue puzzled Kerry. Brighton swore it was the safest site, as Guillermo Obregon's spies would not likely suspect either his son or a Paladín to be patronizing a place that afforded all sorts of nefarious activities.

"There the chap is." Brighton pointed his gold-knobbed walking stick toward the smoky saloon's far right corner.

Beyond the tables of drunken carousers, Kerry saw only a strolling musician in a sugarloaf *sombrero*. The paunchy man stood in front of a table and tipped back his cornet to launch into a wailing rendition of *'La Paloma.'* The brassy music deafened the sibilant drone of the rainfall outside.

Then Kerry caught the negligent wave of a hand from somewhere behind the table. The cornet player's music ceased abruptly and he faded into the crowd. A man seated at the table stared back at Kerry.

Rodrigo Obregon was not what Kerry had expected of

the heir of the implacable enemy of the Paladíns. Eyes the shade of pale green limes looked out of an angelic face framed by curly buff-colored hair. Despite the humid heat, he wore a black velvet suit, corded with gold trimming, and a ruffled shirt under a scarlet waistcoat. He looked as at ease as a king presiding over his court.

Brighton made the introductions with a jaunty flourish. "The scions of Texas's most illustrious families. Roderick Obregon, I present Kerry Paladín."

Obregon indicated the three other chairs at the table. "Have a seat, please." Angling his body so that his knotted sleeve was out of view, Kerry chose the chair directly across from the young man, whom Kerry judged to be a little younger than he.

Roderick signaled to a waiter wearing a food-stained apron. "What will you have, Mr. Paladín?"

He had a predilection for a New Orleans Santini but doubted the saloon, barely one step above a communal outhouse, had the requisite ingredients. "Bourbon." His father's penchant.

Kerry clapped onto the ear of the vacant chair next to him his rain-damp Confederate hat, its broad brim pinned up on the left side with his mother's four-leaf-clover brooch—Catarina's wedding gift to him. "Now, your good luck charm to keep you safe for me," she had told him.

Brighton slid into the other empty chair. "That demon rum will do for me."

Roderick placed the order, languidly leaning back in his chair. "It would seem you and I have a similar interest, Mr.

Paladín."

"Kerry will do."

"Kerry. And I go by Rod."

"That interest would be?"

"You and I both desire to circumvent my father."

"I am well aware of why The Barony wants to circumvent your father. He refuses to transport our cattle. Just why do you wish to circumvent your father?"

Rod waited until the waiter arrived with the tray of drinks and left them before replying. "My father refuses to let me make even the most minor decisions in Obregon Enterprises."

"That's where we both profit," Brighton interjected, grabbing for his tankard of rum.

Kerry's bourbon tasted watered, but then what could one expect from this privy-cum-cantina? "Exactly how do we both profit?"

The man with the seraph's face sipped at his gin and tonic. "My newly acquired company transports your cattle."

He shifted his body to fully face the man now. "You are a fool if you truly believe your father knows nothing about this acquisition."

A facial muscle twitched in Rod's face. "French troops of Mexico's emperor control Matamoros. My steamboat is a French registry. With the Unionists forced from Texas, all but Brazos Santiago, my father has by necessity aligned with the Confederates, who, as you well know, have welcomed the French troops with abrazos at every turn of the corner. The registry would not be questioned."

He took another sip. It tasted putrid. "And exactly why would you want to align with a Paladín when your father refuses?"

Rod's smile was celestial. "I would think that would be obvious. My father can buy anyone but a Paladín. I need your business."

Leaning forward, Rod began laying out over the next hour his plan and terms, which appeared to Kerry both justified and generous. Beware of Greeks bearing gifts drifted in the back of his mind hazily. Maybe it was the cheap rot gut he was drinking.

At some point, Brighton pushed back from the table. "Gentlemen, I am afraid I must take my leave. I have a wedding to attend tonight."

"Oh?" Kerry inquired, puzzled. He could not recall Brighton mentioning any such plans. "Whose?"

"My own."

"What? Who is the fortunate bride?" His tongue, thick and fuzzy, struggled to form the words he felt were slogged by more than mere firewater.

Brighton glanced at Rod. "His twin sister. Miss Sarita Obregon."

Kerry thought he had heard the name before but couldn't recall where or when.

"Shall we drink to that?" Rod raised his glass. "And to the partnership between us, Kerry?"

"I would want to review a contract first." At least, that was what he thought he said, but had his words seemed slurred?

"Of course, I have one here."

He blinked several times to refocus his hazy vision as a brown-eyed, dusky beauty brought another round of drinks. A few moments later, he realized Brighton had departed, and she now occupied his vacated chair.

Magdalena was her name. Voluptuous, swaying globes, inviting a man's touch, nearly tumbled from her low-cut flounced blouse. As Rod went over the contract's fine print with him, Magdalena's fingers stroked his taut thigh under the table. Lightly, up and down, ever closer to his crotch.

After a long period of quiescence, a mighty yearning was rebirthing in him. His manhood stirred at the pressure of her warm fingers. He struggled with rational thought, knowing too well he was about to damn all he valued, all he held dear.

AS USUAL, SARITA TOOK HER evening meals with the *Shamrock's* crew in its dining saloon, where she also caught up on duties previously performed by the steamboat's clerk. She had discharged the old man at the Roma layover for drunkenness. She noted that too often the ink on the clerk's ledger was more red than black. Alas, good hands were hard to come by these years.

Between bites of fried catfish, she organized freight bills, kept track of waybills, and handled payroll.

Big Mick was reporting to the wharf master of Rio Grande City's custom house before overseeing the loading and unloading of cargo. Then it would be back to the Pilot House for her.

Normally, even though she had full license to work the river day and night, she did not like to operate her sidewheeler at night unless the moon was bright. There was too much danger in navigating in the dark, especially in low water. Snags, sandbars, and driftwood waited to wreck and flounder her beloved *Shamrock*.

But since last March's debacle, she made certain her time in port at Rio Grande City was a quick turnaround. She had no desire to run into Wade Paladín and make a jackass of herself again, even if it meant foregoing her cherished fountain soda. She had no desire to revisit the weeks and weeks of disappointment and heartache after the scoundrel's disappearance following her mortifying declaration.

Thinking back to that afternoon of the Union invasion of Rio Grande City—and she often did—she fully perceived Wade was no scoundrel. He had made no commitment. He had merely listened and watched, then quietly and coolly saw her back into Big Mick's safe keeping before hightailing it out of Rio Grande City.

Reviewing what had taken place, she realized she was too forthright for him to bear. Never having had an interest in a man, she did not know how to act otherwise. Without a mother to instruct her in the guiles of a woman—the flirtatious remarks, the coy glances, the demure helplessness, she could only observe other females and practice their wiles, which was enough to make her gag. That period of theatrical performance lasted for about a summer.

Since then, she had tried to be true to herself. She was a female doing a male's job, which meant being direct and plain spoken while maintaining the refined female attributes with which she entered this world. But obviously, that had gained her naught but rejection from the only man who had ever fascinated her.

Could be she had simply picked the wrong man? After all, without a father's love to guide her through the maze of male selection, what chance had she? With nary a hug nor an approving word from her father, how could she navigate the mating process successfully?

True, she had Big Mick faithfully dogging her every step, but his big paw alighting on her shoulder when she felt low or lonely was not quite the same. For her, the word 'home' conjured up the woody smell of the heated boiler room, Big Mick's trousers bagging at the knees, the mighty sound of the water sloshing over the *Shamrock*'s paddles, and the familiar blasts of the landing whistle.

"Captain Sarita?"

She looked up from the ledger. One of the deckhands, cap in hand, stood respectfully before her. "Yes, Pete?"

The Negro bobbed his head, but she didn't miss the anxious look in his eyes. "Your father awaits you in the captain's quarters."

Now this was a turn of events. She swallowed. Her father's appearance could not bode well.

More than her father awaited her in the cramped captain's quarters on the Texas deck. Within a pool of light cast by the gently swinging lantern, she beheld her father, that bloated peacock Lord Brighton, and another man she vaguely remembered—old Oliver Morton, one of the Obregon Enterprises steamboat captains.

The hook-nosed man was fingering her brassbound telescope on the bolted-down chart table. Her father was perusing a chart of the Rio Grande's shoal areas, channel islands, reefs, and chutes. Lord Brighton, hands clasped behind his back, was staring out the oblong, dust-filmed window into the night.

He swung around as she closed the door behind her, a too-bright smile on his pasty face. Morton, an uneasy look about his stern features, returned her telescope to the desk. Her father looked up from her note-scribbled chart.

"It is outdated." He eyed her as he nudged the scrolled ends across the table with his knuckles.

"Yes." She clasped her trembling hands, out of sight, behind her striped merino skirts. "After this week's rain, Father, the river changed its course again, and there are now twin reefs just below Laredo."

Although not even of average height, her father's looks were above average. Even at forty, he still had an abundance of thick, blond corkscrew curls and the erect carriage that indicated good health. Only the deep furrows of bitter discontent that grooved either side of his mouth and bisected the bridge of his nose marred his looks, though he still managed to intimidate her and probably always would.

"You are far from Brownsville, Father. Do I assume your presence aboard the *Shamrock* today is for business?"

Surely not pleasure, for her father found pleasure only in increasing his wealth. He was the proverbial king, sitting in his counting house, surrounded by his precious money.

"I have waited long enough and am tired of yuir shillyshallying, Sarita. 'Tis time ye were wedded."

Her stomach dropped away—that same kind of feeling she had when negotiating rapids. Her clasped hands tightened into a clench. "I told you. I have no interest in marrying."

Her father's pewter-gray eyes slitted. "That's not what I be hearing. I hear tales that make me blood run cold. That ye are cozying up to Paladín's youngest son. A common cowboy—and the son of the bloody thief who stole yuir inheritance!"

Now *her* blood ran cold.

How could her father have known? Had Big Mick betrayed her? Oh, dear God, surely not!

"I've brought along Captain Morton to perform the ceremony."

Morton had the good grace to look abashed before glancing away.

Lord Brighton, on the other hand, appeared jovial. "Do not let the difference in our years, Miss Obregon, detract from what promises to be an excellent union. As Lady Grantham, you will have Grantham Manor's vast estate in Ireland to preside over."

She could scarcely believe her father was going through with what had seemed in the past more suggestion than intention—that she wed Lord Brighton!

Her eyes fired volleys at her father. "I have no desire to reside in Ireland—and least of all to marry this—" she flicked her fingers at Lord Brighton, "—this creature who makes my skin crawl."

"Your desire is irrelevant to me."

"I can well imagine what is in this for you, Father—some sort of escalation in your financial well-being, doubtlessly." She flung a disgusted glance at Lord Brighton. "But what's in it for him?"

Brighton's overblown features took on an indignant look. "Why, with a wife of stature to grace Grantham Manor . . . ."

"Oh, please. Spare me the banalities."

His blubbery lips stretched into a hard line. "Have it as you will. You need breed only once, provide me an heir, and you are allowed your freedom there—and I mine."

"Then I suggest you find yourself a titled maid who would welcome your advances and you hers," she shot back. "But I most certainly do not entertain such an—"

Her fusillade faltered. The realization hit her. Her crewmen's whispers of Brighton and Bagdad, Matamoros's port that rivaled the sordid places of the earth. The Englishman needed her. He needed her to provide the façade of a normal English male . . . when there was nothing normal about his own sexual predilections—young boys. And he needed an heir.

"Think long and hard about it, Sarita," her father warned. "Tell me, do ye have another choice? The bloody *Shamrock* belongs to me, for all that ye think of her as yuirs."

"Why . . . I . . . I shall—"

"What? Run away to Mexico and live as a *puta?*"

She drew herself up. "I know steamboats. I can hire—"

"I control the Rio Grande. And any Union steamboat outfit would scoff at such a preposterous idea. Ye have no means to provide for yuirself. Ye are still under me authority. Now I recommend ye use some common sense. Let's proceed with the ceremony. Morton?"

The captain stepped forward, withdrawing a small Bible from his coat pocket. She stepped back, coming up against the cabin door.

"Think about it." The persuasiveness in her father's voice not completely hiding his determination. "Ye will lead a life of grandeur in Ireland. Once ye provide an heir for Brighton, ye are free to do what ye want. Buy yuir own steamboat—hell, a bloody fleet of them—and sail them up the bonny River Shannon if you must."

So that was what it came down to—being bred like a mare. Other young women submitted to arranged marriages with little or no qualms. But, she could not. Not, at least, to Lord Brighton. "And if I refuse?"

"I will bloody well see ye dead first before I would let ye marry a Paladín." Her father patted the bulge in his waistcoat pocket

There was no doubt a derringer there, but she was not absolutely certain her father would use it. She believed there existed within him, if not fatherly love for his daughter, then some spark of goodness, of decency, of selflessness. Or, at least, she wanted to believe that.

"I. Will. Not. Do. It." To her, her words sounded breathless, whispered, spaced with infinity between each.

Morton cleared his throat.

"I think ye will." Her father's eyes narrowed. "I can have ye confined here until ye realize the value in marrying Brighton."

Frantic, she stalled. "You do not have witnesses."

"Oh, but I do. Big Mick should be arriving any minute with the other." As if on cue, the cabin door was rapped twice. "Enter."

She whirled. Big Mick filled the doorway. His right eye was rapidly swelling and already a bruising blue. One beefy arm supported a badly battered and slumping Wade. Blood dripped from his nose to dribble on his weathered leather vest.

"He swallowed it. Hook, line, and sinker." Big Mick said.

"No!" She pushed past Morton to wedge herself as a buffer between Big Mick and Wade.

"Apparently, not without a fight, Big Mick," Lord Brighton drawled, "if your right eye is any indication."

She reached up and cradled Wade's craggy, bloodied face between her palms. He was breathing rapidly, shallowly. Reproachfully, she glared up over her shoulder at Big Mick. "How could you? You knew I cared about this man!"

The giant met her condemning stare with a shrug. She could not believe it. All these years, she had thought him devoted to her. His betrayal hurt even more than her father's indifference.

She skewered eyes glassy with unshed tears back toward her father. "Wade Paladín has nothing to do with my refusal to marry Lord—" Her flurry of words fell away when she spotted the derringer in her father's hand.

"Nothing would give me greater pleasure than to give Paladín's younger son another navel and dump his body overboard as food for the river's bottom scavengers."

She believed he would do that. The only reason her father had not killed Wade was probably the pleasure he always took in watching his foes suffer.

"I told ye, Sarita, I do be thinking ye will agree to this marriage with Lord Brighton. Do it, and yuir young lad here will wake tomorrow morning in some whorehouse not too much worse for the wear than he is now."

Her mind darted about for an alternative . . . and found none. She swallowed hard at the prospect of her life stretching abysmally before her as Brighton's wife. Her chin pointed toward Morton. "Then let's get on with—"

"I beg to disagree."

Her head swiveled, and she saw Wade drawing a pistol from beneath his leather vest.

"Your daughter is not marrying Brighton."

Her father cocked his pistol and she moved to fling herself at her father—simultaneously with the explosive report of a pistol.

"DO YOU—SARITA OBREGON—take this man as your lawfully wedded husband?"

"I do."

"Do you—Wade Paladín—take this woman as your lawfully wedded wife?"

What a wedding this was. Pistol in hand, Wade glanced from the captain, frowning down his hooked nose and waiting impatiently for Wade's response, to Sarita's furious father and the fuming Brighton, to the sprawled corpse of the mammoth who had valiantly intercepted Obregon's bullet meant for himself. And, at last, to Sarita. Her chin was held high, but it trembled.

"I have to ask this, Sarita. You are sure this is what you want? You don't have to marry this duded-up dandy." He jutted his bruised jaw toward Brighton. "I'll see to that. But you don't have to marry me either."

Her eyes were two lit fuses. "Just answer Morton."

For the life of him, he couldn't visualize himself settling down. Still, he sure as hell didn't want anyone else to have this tiny pack of dynamite. He wanted her in his arms, in his bed. Damn't, she was already a burr in his heart. "The answer's yes. Now get on with the marryin', Morton."

"Then, by virtue of the authority vested in me by the sovereign state of Texas, I hereby pronounce you man and wife. God help you both."

Sarita cleared her throat and glanced askance at Wade. "Uhh . . . a ring?"

Ring? Like a tumbleweed, his mind rolled this way and that and bumped up against the wall of logic. Grinning, he reached into one of his vest pockets and drew forth the cigar, crushed in the tussle with Big Mick. Solemnly, he drew off the cigar band and, taking her left hand, slid the makeshift wedding band onto her third finger.

She stared up at him with awe and his heart swelled.

Obregon's palm swiped at the desk's telescope, hurtling it against the cabin's paneled wall. "Ye and yuir family will rue this day, Wade Paladín. I swear by God."

He was anxious to hightail it. Still holding her clammy little hand, he turned his gaze on the three men. "Big Mick here needs a burial. He being a riverman, I respectfully suggest you deep six him in the Rio Grande. Meanwhile, my wife and I have many miles to cover, and we'll just say our *adioses* and hit the trail."

With Obregon likely to set henchmen on Wade's heels, he made a stampede of a journey back, riding double with Sarita held before him. But he only got midway to The Barony when he had to call a halt the second day to conserve his horse before it stoved in.

A mott of *huisaches* offered shade from the searing sunlight. Snagging the horse blanket and dismounting, he reached up to his nearly comatose bride. "Sarita?"

Lids closed, she didn't even glance down at him. He noted that, without the protection of a bonnet, her face was sunburned.

He tugged gently at her waist and she toppled into his arms. Flapping wide the blanket with one hand, he lowered her on it. "You're tuckered out, gal, but you've born up right well." The approval in his voice at what she had endured surprised him.

She didn't bother to answer. Just lay there, paralyzed.

He went back to the lathered horse for his canteen and, since he was missing his hat to serve as a container, trickled a little water into his palm, which the horse robustly lapped. Returning to kneel beside her, he dribbled water into her mouth.

She coughed and sputtered, a moan escaping between her blistered lips. "Just leave me be to die."

"Nope." He removed one of her kid boots, then the other. "Not ready to be a widower yet."

She dozed off again. He peeled off her cotton stockings and tossed them. Any other time, he would have lingered over the sight of those trim ankles, beautifully formed knees, and shapely thighs, marveling at the boon that had come his way.

He lifted one of her limp legs. She groaned rebelliously with the sharp spasm of pain. "Can't move."

"I'm fixin' to take care of that."

He set to work restoring circulation to her legs. Vigorously, he massaged first the arches of each foot, digging in with his thumb and knuckles. He worked his way up to the cramped muscles of her calves, then used his entire hand to grip and knead the flesh of each thigh. He was not sure if her responsive noises were ones of protest or pleasure.

He flopped her over onto her stomach, flipped up her skirts, and tugged down her pantalettes. Ignoring her mumbled protest of outrage, his searching fingers dug into the more sensitive muscles of her wonderfully rounded rump. Her groan turned grateful, then she fell asleep on him.

Still concerned about forthcoming retribution from her father, he allowed her a half hour of rest, then, with the blanket binding her to him, he set off once more. The next night, his horse hobbled through The Barony's arched wrought-iron gates. Well after midnight, he staggered into the *hacienda,* cradling a somnolent Sarita against his chest. A bewildered Catarina, candle in hand, greeted him in the sala.

"My bride," he said by way of introduction, "our foe's lovely daughter, Sarita Obregon."

Catarina stood on tiptoe to peck his cheek, then with a "tsk-tsk," shook her head. "Only you, Wade. Tomorrow is soon enough to share this stunning surprise with your father. Meanwhile, your red eyes and drooping lids tell me you need sleep."

"Ahh, yes, the bridal chamber." However, the bridal chamber had been his bedroom since Kerry had been given one of his own. Still wearing his dusty clothes and boots, Wade fell, exhausted, onto his bed with an arm flung around Sarita.

It was still there fifteen hours later. Only, when his lids peeled open, she was facing him now and gazing adoringly up at him . . . and her fingers were deftly loosening the silver-star buttons of his navy bib shirt.

He could not refute this affinity between them—how she saw into him. No matter, she was still an Obregon, a female bent on breaking him to saddle. What the hell had he gone and done?

THE BARONY
NOVEMBER 1864

"*Sacre bleu!*" The forty-year-old, twice-widowed and childless, Thérèse del Valle Engler raised perfectly arched brows over her warm brown eyes and placed gloved hands upon her twenty-two-inch corseted waist.

From the central courtyard, she surveyed the two-story hacienda that looked to her as decimated as any Georgia plantation home unfortunate enough to be in the path of Sherman's Union army.

The Barony's inhabitants were almost as depleted, according to Niall.

True, the hacienda's neglected, barren garden could be restored with careful nurturing. Equally true, a good polishing with beeswax would restore the interior banisters, mantles, and furniture to a lovely finish. After that, shutters could be thrown wide, drapes cleaned, and carpets beaten free of dust to restore freshness to The Barony's stuffy rooms.

But how to restore the inhabitants, robbed by emotional

decay of their previous vitality?

Tara lacked guidance in connecting with her femininity. Kerry had lost the Paladín's traditional over-confidence. Wade was hopelessly befuddled. As for Alex, the true love of Thérèse's life, he was mired in one *magnifique* blue funk.

As a young French girl, she had been married off to a dour, high-ranking Mexican officer introduced to her while she was attending Ursuline Academy in New Orleans. An innocent—well, not exactly, as she had been expelled from the academy for a season for confessing to several of her more notorious escapades—but an innocent nevertheless, she had fallen in love instantly with his uniform and was married to him in six months' time.

She had grieved even less than that after he was killed in action during the strife of Mexico's civil war of 1834. The following year, she dedicated her youthful widowhood in Matamoros to one long glorious celebration of life.

"An adventurous vixen," Alex had called her then. They had been well matched in their mutual pursuit of pleasure and passion. But Alex's personal *diable* had been tamed by that winsome *jeune fille,* Fiona Flanigan.

Then, of all people, Presbyterian parson Daniel Engler's untapped passions had stormed Thérèse's battlements of frivolity, taking her by surprise with devout explanations that convinced her to wed once again—something she had theretofore denounced vigorously. But she had fallen head over teakettle for the reverend and his raw energy.

Misfortune stole Daniel from her much as ill health had taken Fiona from Alex. Life still thrummed in both of them, of course. Ignoring his truer instincts, that obstinate Alex was choosing to wallow in his misery, as life passed him by. *Incroyable!*

It was a deeply troubled Niall, with his execrable handwriting that took her forever to decipher, who convinced her to pay an early visit for Thanksgiving to his partner and their mutual friend.

Thérèse, a grieving Alex and his family need comforting. You knew Alex as he was—an intolerable, arrogant, and inflexible pain in the arse. I sorely miss that man. Help me to bring him back to us all.

"*Eh, bien!*" It would appear she must take matters into her own hands. With a toss of her head, ostrich plumes of her wide-brimmed hat fluttering, she gathered her duster and copious crinoline skirts, careful to keep them from snagging on the fountain's surround of broken bricks. Eagerly escaping the morning's nippy weather, she pointed her slippers toward the grand sala.

Catarina met her at the foot of the stairs. The young woman possessed her mother's classic features—features that now lacked their pre-marital vibrancy. "I had Diego's son, Pepe, put your trunk in one of the guest bedrooms upstairs, Thérèse. The last room on the right."

"*Merci,* Catarina. I would like to freshen up first and change out of my traveling clothes."

The young woman paused, her hand on the newel post. Her voice lowered. "I apologize for your reception here— or its lack. If this were my house, I could have taken charge more easily. You know, try to regain some semblance of order. But as it is . . . without Fiona . . . and with Kerry and I moving out after the first of the year . . . well, I am sure you can understand. I just did not feel it was my place to make—"

"You and Kerry are moving?"

"To San Antonio. He has taken a teaching position with St. Mary's Institute. We have been here since Fiona's death. Kerry did not feel he could leave his father alone before this."

"Does Alex know about this? That Kerry will not be managing The Barony?"

Catarina's gaze skittered toward the corner kiva fireplace, where fragrant piñon was burning, then her eyes lowered to the Talavera tiles. "Kerry was planning to tell Alex after the holiday."

"*Sacrebleu!*" she muttered again. "We have Thanksgiving dinner in three days to get through first. Find me an apron and I shall need a bottle of your best wine. Make that two. Two bottles, *ma cherie.*"

Catarina's spiked lashes blinked. "You mean two bottles of wine for your French cooking?"

"*Non.* For our Alex."

WITH A MOODY WADE dispatched to bag ducks or turkeys or else to wring some chicken necks for the upcoming Thanksgiving dinner, Thérèse turned her attention to The Barony kitchen—and its help.

For her, the Thanksgiving dinner preparation required little more forethought or effort than a snap of her beringed fingers—celery remoulade, potato galette, oyster dressing, roasted radishes with sea salt, herbed *haricots verts*, and maybe a curried rabbit. These Americans knew nothing about la bonne cuisine, that fine art of cooking.

It was the kitchen help that required more of her focus. Doddering Winnie was nearing eighty and her sight was lamentable. Nevertheless, Thérèse tactfully deferred to her that morning whenever she could. Winnie knew where pans and pots could be found. Thérèse sent old Frederick to collect fresh eggs and hustled Pepe off to milk a cow.

With Winnie and Frederick both mollified and occupied, Thérèse switched her attention to The Barony women—Tara, Catarina, and Sarita. All three strong-willed women.

Merci a le bon Dieu. Like sisters, they lovingly got along well with one another. Well, for the most part, at least. She put each of them to work. Hands were fluttering. Kettles were set to boiling. Flour dust flurried in the air.

Thérèse assigned the recently-married Sarita to creating an intense French chocolate custard with nibs. From the little Catarina had shared with her, Sarita was mourning the loss of a man named Big Mick, a sort of surrogate father. "You will add the chocolate to that three-quarters cup of creme, Sarita. And when you are finished, pipe the custard into shot glasses."

Sarita's pert nose wrinkled and her lips parted in dismay. "Shot glasses?"

"*Oui, mon peu crepe.* Shot glasses." She kissed her gathered fingertips. "I would so love to serve this treat with a sweet Banyuls wine from the Languedoc. With its hint of chocolate and overtones of raspberry, what could be a sweeter partner for a chocolate dessert?"

She intercepted the uncertain glances exchanged by the three women. Her knowing smile crimped dimples.

"Catarina, after you have cubed the pumpkin, you will want to add the cilantro, shallots, and lime juice to the chicken stock as the base for our pumpkin soup."

Catarina, the eldest and most mature of the three young women, tilted her lovely head, so reminiscent of her mother's own aristocratic gesture. Thérèse did not miss the young woman's preoccupation, undoubtedly the result of concern for her own and Kerry's future—or was it something else?

"I was thinking more along the lines of pumpkin pie, Thérèse, not pumpkin soup."

"You realize, *mon enfant,* that contrasts add piquancy— what you Americans call the spice of life, *non?*"

Tara wiped the flour dust smudging her straight nose with the back of her arm. The young woman not only knew little about the art of cooking, but even less about the art of flirting. Her thick dark brows knitted. "These apples are rather tart. You are sure you want me to make—what is it— a lavender-apple *torte?*"

"*Mais oui,* Tara. Slice the apples very thin. We will arrange the slices in spiraling layers, sprinkled with chopped pecans, grated orange peel, cloves, and cinnamon. Presentation is everything in the culinary arts, non?"

It was a beginning. Thérèse could only trust that these

three *jeunes femmes* could begin to intuit the lessons in womanhood she meant to impart, as well.

However, there still remained Alex with whom she must begin her next restoration effort.

LATER THAT AFTERNOON, nearing dusk, Thérèse's fingers paused on the doorknob. She suspected Alex was sequestering himself for the coming Thanksgiving holidays in his office, where he was either sleeping or more likely than not, drinking. Not even Tara dared enter.

Thérèse wished Niall were here now to back her up . . . or Rafaela to offer her sister-like solace, but the couple were not expected to arrive for the festivities until later, along with the von Hesse-Lippes.

Drawing a breath, her ribs barely expanding the tightly laced bone stays supporting her bosom, she eased open his door. The room was sallow in its semi-darkness. Alex's high-back chair was turned away from his desk toward the window, its shuttered slats closed against the gathering darkness.

Entering, she left the door slightly ajar so the aromas of cinnamon, apples, and oranges wafted through.

"What do you want?"

From behind, she bent to slip her arms around his shoulders, palms resting on the ruffled shirt that was open at his throat. A jolting whiff of whiskey reached her nostrils. "I want my old Alex back. *Ce diable,* who loved and laughed at life." She longed to feel his indomitable energy enfolding her.

"He is dead, Thérèse."

He did not seem surprised by her presence at The Barony. "No. He is alive. Fiona died exactly one year ago last Thanksgiving. Now it is time for your mourning year to end, Alex."

Beneath her palms, she felt his chest muscles hardening into iron. "How *dare* you. You cannot possibly know what it is like to love and then lose—"

"My own Daniel died ten months ago. A simple accident—knocked from his horse when riding through a low, overhanging grove of mesquite. But, of course, you were too busy with your own self-pity to notice the news of his death. Or that others might be suffering as well. Like your own daughter and sons."

"Damn you to hell, Thérèse!"

She did not remove her arms from about him. "Damned I most likely am, *mon chere*. But until I meet my perdition, I intend to make the most of what time I have left here on Earth." She moved around and knelt in front of him. "Now, no more silliness. Just lean your grizzled head over and kiss me."

Before he could recover from his surprise, her tapering fingers framed his angular, beard-stubbled face and drew it down until his taut lips encountered hers. At their contact, she could feel the shock running through him. He stiffened, stony as a statue. Adamantly, her lips grazed his, back and forth. She felt him easing slightly, so she decided to seize the opportunity, nibbling his lower lip playfully.

"Damn you," he growled again, but his arms wrapped

around her and he pulled her up between his thighs, crushing her against him. His long fingers tunneled through her upswept hair to cradle the back of her head, loosening the wooden pins anchored there. Slanting his head over hers, his mouth ravaged her lips, crushing them, surely bruising them.

She could feel her heart thud wildly. Hear her blood thundering in her ears. Stunned, she most certainly was, by all the conflicting emotions racing through her. At her age, she had not expected this. She still loved Daniel. He had been her safe harbor, where her heart had found peace. Even contentment. But Alex was a wild adventure on the high seas . . . with a few respites beside some exotic tropical lagoon.

At last, when he released her and raised his head to stare down at her, she saw something like the old mockery in his eyes. "How brave you are . . . always have been. And today, you dare enter the domicile of this raging beast?"

"A wounded beast. But then, are not all of us?"

His head bent over hers. As she yielded to the dominance in his kiss, she had to wonder if she was also yielding her own admittedly willful ways to this self-centered, challenging rogue.

THANKSGIVING MORNING, SARITA located Wade on the back patio near the pump, where he shaved every morning, blazing heat or frosty wind, when he was not away on business. He shaved trail-drive style, without a mirror. She stood beneath the colonnaded arch, watching, as he crooked his mouth to one side to stretch smooth the skin between his high-planed cheekbone and boxy jaw.

"Here, let me." She crossed to him and smiled tentatively. Despite four months of living at The Barony, she remained unaccustomed to the way her pulse pounded upon seeing him, to how she felt so gauche and unsure of herself—of her own worth, which at The Barony amounted to not much.

Here, she who was accustomed to being in command, was little better than a chunk of driftwood. But at least she was now safe from her own father. For the moment. She did not even want to ponder what form his vengeful wrath would take at being thwarted in his pursuit of another source of lucrative revenue—and a strike at his time-immemorial foe.

Wade hiked a brow and shot her a rakish grin before passing the razor to her. His grin did not hide his own uncertainty about this new state of matrimony. "Dare I hope for too much—that you won't take the opportunity to slit a Paladín throat?"

Her wry smile faded quickly. "Lucky me that it is not my face that needs shaving, or your father would take the opportunity to slit an Obregon throat." His head jerked to attention and he stared at her as if she had grown antlers. "Dad would never hurt you, Sarita."

With inordinate attention, she stropped the razor on the wide leather strap affixed to the pump handle. "No, but it is obvious he is not exactly happy that I am here." She and Wade were little better off than Romeo and Juliet.

"Dad is not happy with much of anyone or anything these days."

"Tilt your head." She stood on tiptoe and began stroking a path through his morning scruff. "You know your father will never bless our marriage, Wade."

"Give Dad time," he mumbled between tight lips, neck arched to accept the blade she was wielding. "He will come to accept you as my wife."

She suspected Wade himself was having some trouble accepting her as his wife. With an inner conflict he had waged over almost a year, he had been forced to the reluctant realization that he stood to lose her if he did not take action, even if he had a deep-seated aversion to marriage.

It was obvious to Sarita that he did not want her half as much as she wanted him.

THE BARONY
THANKSGIVING DAY 1864

"We have to be realistic," Niall drew a Havana cigar from the humidor before passing it around. "The Confederacy's days are numbered—and after that, our soldiers will return to a disastrous economy."

From the chair behind his desk, Alex watched Karl take a cigar and hand off the humidor. Word was that back in Germany, Karl had been a crack shot, but here he was that rarest of Texicans—he did not pack a pistol. He had once told Alex that he had seen far too much violence back in his homeland and would not be a part of it here in his new home.

Karl bit off the end of his cigar. "Texas legislators need to start preparing for the inevitable."

"Be prepared for a surge in Federal troops posted to Texas." Max took his time choosing one of the cigars. "And with emancipation, you better believe the labor system will undermine the economic power of those who dominated our slave-driven society before the war. Alex, you will want to prepare—to ascertain the Barony Partnership is not among the undermined."

Wade leaned forward to light his cigar from the candle on Alex's desk. "The Barony can prepare now—at this very moment."

"How so?" Alex dragged his reverie away from the splendid Thanksgiving dinner and the animated Frenchwoman who threatened the life he had created for himself with all its fine points and its flaws.

"The Union markets will be wide open when the war ends. With our upbreeding of the white-faced cattle and Brahmas, and getting rid of the longhorns, it has put us in a position to provide good table beef for the whole nation. After the war is when we start driving our cattle north through Indian country to the northern railheads. Meanwhile, Dad, we begin to set up our connections in Kansas City, Omaha, Chicago."

At twenty-four, Wade was finally coming into his authority—that time when a man thinks he understands life, that he has its vagaries hammered out. Or maybe Wade's recent marriage hog-tied and dragged him in that foolhardy direction. "What do you think it would take to outfit a trail-drive that went so far?"

Wade blew a puff of smoke, considering. "Oh, with Diego as trail boss, a dozen or so cowboys, a cook, and a couple of horse wranglers, we could trail 2,500 cattle in three months' time with some luck."

"You would have to figure on netting sixty to seventy-five cents a head to cover the outlay," Kerry added.

"What about that contract with Roderick?" Niall crossed his silver-spurred boots at the ankles.

"A ruse." Kerry shook his head.

Alex did not miss the anger that flushed his older son's face—or was it something more than anger? Had something else transpired in Rio Grande City besides the brawl over Kerry's refusal to sign the contract?

"Despite Brighton's optimistic urging for us to meet with Rod, the contract was one-sided. As drunk as I was, I figured out that much. The fracas with Rod that followed . . . well, needless to say I came up on the short-end of it. A blackened eye before Rod backed off."

"What kind of man attacks a—" Karl began, then sighed, "Did Brighton make any effort at all to assist you?"

"What do you think, Karl? The Englishman's a scurvy son of a bitch. He had already hightailed it."

Alex felt a flush of anger suffuse his own cheeks. Anger at himself for being so selfishly wrapped up in his wretchedness this past year that he had failed not only to take care of Barony affairs lately but also to protect his family. Kerry should not have been there alone. Damn it, he should not have been there in the first place. Later, he would take his son to task for just that carelessness.

"Ever since that night, I have noticed that Brighton has stayed on the go." Kerry's gaze focused on the cigar he rolled between his thumb and forefinger. "Apparently giving his abrazos to potential marks as far from The Barony as he can get."

"Obviously, Brighton was double-dealing with this

Obregon *hombre,"* Wade muttered. "I should have finished the slimy snake off back there in the *Shamrock's* cabin."

Alex swished the brandy in his sniffer, half-watching the amber liquid swirling. It would seem he had underestimated the bastard altogether—a near fatal blunder. But his mounting anger was not directed so much at Obregon, whom he would from now on keep a closer eye. At that moment, it was all he could do not to hurl his glass into the fireplace.

"And the contract with Bias Uribe?" Karl turned to his adopted son. "Is the ink still good?"

Max sighed and steepled his elegant fingers, cigar anchored between. "The ink will hold. The question is will Uribe, if Obregon pressures him?" He nodded at Wade. "With both you and Kerry in Rio Grande City at the same time—well, it is a one-horse town. Brighton parleyed with you both that night. You may be right, Kerry. Brighton could be an agent provocateur. Obregon is no fool. He has to have some inkling of the deal we negotiated with Uribe."

"Christ almighty!" Alex exploded and slammed down his fist on the desk. "It is bad enough that both my sons have lost either their mind, their bollocks, or both! You, Wade—marrying and bringing home the daughter of the very man hellbent on destroying The Barony—Guillermo Obregon! And, damn it, Kerry, how do you expect to keep The Barony running with both of you off gallivanting in Rio Grande City at the same time?"

Kerry shot to his feet and flung his cigar against the wood-paneled wall. "I don't! You have always expected it. Expected that I would run The Barony." His fiery expression raked the room's startled occupants, pausing on Niall, before returning to Alex. "I have accepted a teacher position. I will start after the first of the year, but Catarina and I can leave now, if that is what you prefer."

"'What I prefer' is that you begin to act like a man!"

"Alex!" A muscle in Niall's face began to twitch.

"We will be gone by the morning, sir!"

Wade levered himself out from the leather chair with his customary loose-limbed grace. "I think it's time this tumbleweed started tumbling." His teeth clamped around his gnawed cigar, he said from the side of his mouth, "Sarita and I will be on our way, too."

THE CANDLE BURNED LOW on its brass holder. Alex's cigar had burned out . . . and so had he. Yes, burned all the way out.

Abruptly, he snapped his cigar butt between the fingers of one hand, much like Fiona used to when cracking an egg. Tobacco flakes fluttered around him. His family—all of them—were disintegrating. First Fiona, now Kerry and Wade.

Granted, he had shut himself off from the world for a year, but Kerry and Wade were adults and had obligations, just as he had at their age. They were partly responsible, were they not?

Of the lot, he was angriest at Fiona. Though, for the hell of him, he could not exactly say why. Not from any sensible point of view, leastwise.

The Barony guests had all retired for the night, while he

remained behind his desk. For thirty years he had fought. Fought for Texas. For Fiona. For The Barony. For his family. Now this . . . this emptiness. Thirty years wasted. All for naught.

His office door creaked and a narrow bar of candlelight stole across the tiles. Then a slip of a shadow moving across the floor drifted toward him. He looked up. Thérèse was wearing a dressing wrapper of green silk that whispered with each step. Her exquisite features were taut—lips compressed, winged brows drawn close together.

His eyes narrowed. One more arrival coming into his office to rebuke his morbidity. "What?" What he really wanted to say was, *Et tu, Brute?*

Her tapering fingers smoothed back the swath of disheveled salt-and- pepper hair that had fallen across his forehead. "It is difficult to create the life you want, *mon amour*, and then to control it. *Non?*"

"Ask Sam Houston. He created a nation. While I have created only an anarchy. An anarchy of children who are unappreciative, self-centered."

He caught the lift of one brow and the tiny crimp of smile she strove to repress. A smile that said expressively, *And you are not?*

She wedged her slender body between him and his desk. Nestling like a cat onto his lap, she looped one arm around his shoulders. She smelled of some delicate fragrance. Orange blossoms . . . jasmine, maybe. He neither knew nor cared what.

"Kerry and Wade behave with the impetuosity of youth.

But you are a man seasoned by life. Once, you were as impetuous as they."

When he began to gainsay her, she laid a finger on his lips and laughed lightly. *'Non.* I remember all too well how reckless and impulsive you were twenty-five years ago. Now that you are older, can you not choose to overlook your own sons' callowness?"

His jaws clenched. "Overlook, perhaps. But beg them to stay? Never."

'Mais oui, you are quite correct about that, Alex. This next generation, it must break away and strike out on its own. Still, at least, could you possibly strive to keep open your lines of communication with them? Now, come give me a kiss."

"TAKE GOOD CARE OF THE place, sis." Kerry's mouth set in a grim line, he clasped Tara's shoulder and kissed her on the forehead.

Tara looked down, anywhere but at the others. She found the farewells awkward and strained—too much like her father's own unyielding features. All three families stood beneath the hacienda portico, each of their stiffened postures indicating how uncomfortable the moment had become. Waiting coaches and wagons backed up onto the caliche drive, with both Diego and Pepe, loading luggage.

At Karl's side, Maria Elena fidgeted with the buttons on her gloves. Rafaela fidgeted with the frogs of her cloak, Catarina fidgeted with the ribbons of her bonnet, and Thérèse fidgeted with her lavender infused handkerchief.

Niall gave her father the abrazo, one arm over the shoulders, the other around the back, then their positions reversed.

Alex turned to a very stiff Kerry and said in that gruff voice unique to him, *"Vaya con Dios."*

Then he pivoted to Wade, lounging against one of the portico's stucco pillars, arms folded, boots crossed. Next to him, little Sarita watched, her thickly lashed eyes absorbing the drama that was an integral part of what 'family' entailed—with its Gordian knots of the heart. "Son, our gate is always open to you."

Wade straightened, draped his arm over Sarita's shawl-covered shoulders. "We best be moseying along, Dad."

Karl clapped a hand on Max's endless length of shoulder. "When do you expect to get the Partnership accounts wrapped up?"

"Within the week, Father." Beneath Max's well-trimmed mustache, his mouth stretched into a dry smile. "Then I promise, I shall be back to our San Antonio grindstone."

IT WAS NOT WRAPPING UP the Partnership accounts that Tara found Max laboring over later that day, but chopping wood from the mesquite-infested Nueces River bottom. "There you are."

"You were looking for me?" He braced his weight on the axe haft. Despite the crisp and chilly afternoon still hazed with Indian summer, sweat dampened his chamois shirt where it clung to his rib cage. The cuffs were rolled to mid-forearm, revealing the light blond hair matted there.

She was accustomed to seeing him dressed finely in tails and waistcoat or formal equestrian garb, so this side of Max threw her off kilter.

She straddled and sat atop the stack of firewood he had split, the fragrant smell of fresh-chopped wood enveloped her. "The hacienda—it seems so empty, what with everyone gone. Now, only father. And Thérèse, but I don't know how long she will be staying." She looked up at him. He stood watching her. "And you. You don't have to leave so soon, do you, Max?"

His head canted, his longish curls tumbling beside one shoulder. Her fingers longed to tug on one of those curls until it was straight, the way she used to do as a girl, and then watch it spring back into place. "Once I have finished reviewing the accounts, why should I stay?"

Her brow furrowed. "Well . . . I miss the way it used to be, when you would visit."

He laid aside the axe and swung one long leg over the firewood stack to sit facing her. "And what way was that?"

She looked down. Peripherally, she noted the mud on her hobnailed boots. Her fingers worried the cut wood's rough bark. From the hen yard, a rooster crowed. Then she looked up and fiercely met his gaze. "Before you kissed me."

He nodded, his own gaze pensive. "That is why I am out here—working off for a while what might be termed . . . excessive energy . . . that needs to be focused elsewhere. Other than where it seems to be drifting."

Her mouth skewed. Her words tumbled out as crisp as

the air. "Where is it drifting?"

"Well, certainly not on *Blackstone's Commentaries* or *Coke on Littleton*. Which reminds me. I need to finish up the partnership legalities here so I can get back to San Antonio for an upcoming trial."

He shoved upright. Her fingers latched onto his forearm. At the tingling sensation, she immediately released her grasp. "Wait."

He arched one questioning brow.

"I don't know rightly what to think these days, Max."

He settled back in place opposite her. "Think about what . . . exactly?" "About us. About our relationship." Her gaze drifted from his to settle upon his lips. "About that kiss."

"And? What did you think?"

She rolled her shoulders. "I suppose it was a coin toss."

His mouth stretched into a rueful grimace. "A coin toss?" His hand stole up to tuck a stray swatch of hair behind her ear and lingered just below her lobe. "Sweetheart, if a kiss does not make one's knees buckle, then it and its giver should be rapidly dismissed."

"I didn't like how the kiss changed our relationship . . . but I liked how it made me feel."

Slowly, his fingers traced down the cords of her neck, made prominent by the tension she was feeling. "How did that kiss change our relationship?" His black velvety voice lowered.

"It lost its . . . easiness."

"And how did the kiss make you feel?"

"Lightheaded. Tingly. Breathless."

He nodded. Smiled. "What if I told you that the more we kiss, the better our relationship might be?"

"Might? What if our relationship gets worse?" She realized then, thanks to his attorney's probing ways, gentle though it seemed, she could now pinpoint what worried her most, the fear of losing that closeness she and Max already had. That, and the fact Max had doubtless met dozens of elegant, fascinating females while studying in Europe.

When his fingertip drifted lower to trace the bow of her collarbone, she shivered. "I figured you as a risk-taker, Tara."

She stared, lost in the depths of his pale blue irises, rimmed by black. "Yes," was all that her breath and tongue could manage in the way of consent.

He stood again and his hands slid beneath her armpits to pull her to her feet and off the stacked wood. Her eyes widened. "My father. Thérèse."

"Trust me. They are doing precisely what I intend." His arms encircled her waist and back, drawing her against him. "Close your eyes, Tara."

She did. The kiss he gave her this time did, indeed, make her knees buckle. She clutched his shoulders.

She heard him laugh softly. His warm breath fanned her face. "I do believe our relationship will be improving greatly."

SAN ANTONIO
JANUARY 1865

The bitter wind whistled around Kerry and Catarina. Huddled, they stood staring at the small stucco house off Flores Street. A denuded cottonwood stood in the grassless yard. The house, surely as old as the Alamo, was located near the Spanish Governor's Palace. More importantly, it was within walking distance of St. Mary's Institute, where he would begin teaching next week.

She tucked her arm into the crook of his elbow and turned her face up to his. "Can we afford to rent it, Kerry?"

He knew she was attempting to keep the eagerness from her voice. They had been staying with Uncle Niall and Aunt Rafaela for the past two months, since Kerry had walked out on his father.

Catarina's parents had been careful to give them their space and privacy. What with the additions over the years to the Gorman ranch house, space was not an issue. And as for privacy, well, intimacy was not an issue either.

Six months of marriage, and his and Cat's intimacy was

limited to that of the best of friends . . . solely. They both went out of their way to ensure the beloved was the recipient of cordiality and good will. And nothing unpleasant was ever discussed. Not politics, nor the war, nor sexual desires and needs.

"Yes, the administration agreed to give me a salary advance." Most likely, even though its personnel resources were stretched to the limit, what with the war, the Institute wanted to keep him. "Shall we check it out?"

"Oh, yes!"

Smiling, he let her tug him forward. Closing the metal-studded wooden door behind them, he welcomed the protection from the cold the old house offered, but its interior was stark and unsightly.

Peeling pea-green wall plaster exposed splotches of the mudbrick adobes here and there. The sala's small, wrought-iron chandelier dangled lopsided from one broken chain. Wintry light filtered through a window casement to fall on brown floor tiles that were cracked and missing in places.

He trailed her into the kitchen. Tucked within the cast iron oven, missing its door, was a rat's nest. The flue lay crumped to one side. He rubbed the back of his neck. Cat deserved better. The impoverished conditions imposed by his position as a mere college professor limited prospects of this.

He felt guilty. He could better provide for her had he stepped into second-in-command at The Barony under his father. Of course, he had heard not a word from his old man.

From another room came Cat's excited voice. "Kerry, come look."

Her reticule and pelisse gently swishing with the sway of her hoop skirt, she was whirling to scan the small cob-webbed room that once must have been a tool shed and was now an add-on. "This would be perfect for a child's room." At the strange inflection in her tone, his eyes narrowed on her.

Beneath her beribboned bonnet, her own sparkled with invitation.

So, at last the gauntlet was being thrown down. "Cat, that would mean I . . . we . . . would have to have relations."

She crossed to where he stood rooted. Her kid gloved hand reached up to align his jaw where his sideburn stopped. "Right here, right now, would be a splendid place to start a child."

"What if . . . ."

Her hand had deserted his face to slip between the folds of his caped overcoat. "My love, you lost your arm, not your cock."

Her brassy words, backed by her bold touch, he instantly grew hard and heavy. Then she shocked him. She dropped to her knees, her arms wrapped around his thighs, and she pressed her face against his crotch to nuzzle him in deep, noisy inhalations. Her fingers loosed his trousers' buttoned flap.

"Oh, God, Cat!" With no regard for preliminaries, he was pressing her back onto that cracked tile floor, thrusting up her skirts, his knee wedging between her thighs.

When he buried inside her, she gasped and momentarily stiffened. Then, her arms encircled his shoulders. His desperate growl was echoed by her urgent moaning.

Time after time, he plunged into her. Encumbered by his overcoat, his body was a roaring furnace. Sweat dripped from his face, but she seemed not to notice. Her own face was a rictus of unbearable rapture. Her fingers dug into his knotting muscles and she rocked her hips in furious timing with his. "Yes, my love. *Yes!*"

Too soon, he was exploding inside her with a force unlike anything he had experienced in his previous sexual liaisons with other women. And he sensed it had little to do with his lengthy celibacy.

When he recovered his breath, he was at once, ashamed. Ashamed of his rapaciousness. Ashamed that he could be so self-absorbed that he considered nothing else but satisfying his driving lust . . . and ashamed that he could be completely oblivious to the woman beneath him, this woman he loved.

He shifted his weight off her. "My God, Cat. I'm so sorry."

Tears were in her eyes, but her smile was wide. "My God, Kerry. I'm so happy." Later, on the drive back to the Gorman ranch, she snuggled close to him. He smiled and counted himself the most fortunate of men to have her, of all women, as his wife.

He reflected on the past six months of their marriage. Whether he was bathing, shaving, or dressing, he was rarely out of her sight. Oh, he understood her strategy. She was not there to assist him. She was present so he could not hide his dismemberment from her, so nothing could stand between them.

Except something did . . . something that would remain forever his one ugly secret.

HOUSTON
FEBRUARY

Babylon on the Bayou—that was what the Port of Houston was called.

The shanty town and humble docks—at the confluence of Buffalo Bayou and White Oak Bayou, a natural turning basin—were built among a profusion of bars and brothels, not to mention a profusion of ideas, dreams, risks, and schemes.

Sarita Paladín's scheme was merely one of many.

Wade had to admit that the Port's two-story Kennedy Bakery and Bar had the best beef stew he had ever greased his chin with. And it was cheap, too. However, he would need his usual second cup of coffee with two lumps of sugar before he could process his bride's scheme. His coffee, made from chicory owing to the wartime shortage of the brew, was not all that bad.

Sarita's scheme was.

Their journey to Houston on the Buffalo Bayou, Brazos & Colorado Railroad had been bad enough—a bone-rattling, sooty experience—not to mention having to obtain a pass from the Provost Marshal to travel and then being inquisitioned by Johnny Reb guards with bayoneted rifles at the depots.

And now this rawboned idea of hers—expecting him, a two-bit cowboy, to build a thriving business operating steamboats between New Orleans and Galveston, the second largest town in Texas after San Antonio. Still, the bay area was the farthest from Brownsville—and her father—as he could safely get Sarita for the time being. Until he figured out a way to best Guillermo Obregon.

She leaned forward from across the small table they shared. Its wax candle sputtered. "I'm telling you, Wade," she slapped him with that impudent smile, "if I know anything, it's steamboats. With Galveston as a seaport, it is the perfect location for the base of our operations. Why, it has two national banks, the Medical College, a Catholic college and orphanage, an opera house, two theaters, and three concert halls!"

With her smallish bosom propped up to global proportions by the whaleboned constraint below her décolletage, it was difficult for him to concentrate at all about her plan. Damn it, the girl had a way of engaging both his mind and his body.

"Okay, with what little money we have between us— and the luck of the Irish—we may just barely cover the cost of acquiring some dilapidated, retired steamboat. But I want you to think about this, Sarita. The Port of Houston has cheaper prices, abundant fresh water, and is more protected from the direct brunt of Gulf storms. What's more, I heard tell nine railroads converge here."

"And I am telling you the Port of Houston—and its

little ditch of Buffalo Bayou that it calls a shipping channel—is seventy-miles from the Gulf, Wade! Seventy needless miles!"

He signaled for his second cup of coffee. Hell, he realized he was going to need the extra fortification.

The wintry light coming from a small window, as well as the hearth's flickering fire and the dim chandelier hanging from the center of the ceiling, illuminated the giant of a stooped Black man with kinky graying hair shuffling toward them.

Immediately, Wade was reminded of Big Mick, and he winced unconsciously. The Irishman had taken the bullet himself to spare Sarita's life—and his.

He sighed. It seemed he and Sarita were almost invariably at odds with each other. Neither was completely comfortable yet with the peculiar traits of the other. Just what had his cock gotten him into? "Honey, I don't know beans about navigation, much less freighting. Cotton, lumber, iron . . . ." He shook his head. "All I know is cows."

"Yes, suh?" The Negro wiped his huge hands on his apron.

Wade slouched dejectedly in his chair. "Another cup of coffee."

"Cows."

Startled, Wade looked up—and up. "What?"

"Cows," the Black man repeated, his wide nose flaring with his audacity. "The Allen Ranch, on the south side of the Bayou—'bout eight miles from here—it has cows it wants to ship."

Sarita turned, looked up over her shoulder at him. "To where?"

The big man, blacker than coal, shrugged his sloping broad shoulders. "N'awlins, ma'am. Then on to Cuba."

Wade straightened in his chair. "How do you know this?"

"My son, Billy, works the Allen Ranch corn fields. And Esther, my wife, she works in Master Sam Allen's house. He bought my family's papers, suh. We'd worked the Oakland sugar plantation, twenty miles from here, out in Sugar Land. 'Fore that, I worked the docks in N'awlins."

Sarita stared at him. Puzzled, for certain. "Then, why are you here—at the Port of Houston?"

"Got too old to chop any mo' cane, ma'am. Master at Oakland sold my papers to Kennedy Bakery and Bar—and sold my family's to Master Allen."

As The Barony, with its loyal *Paladíneños,* had no need for slaves, Wade was on unfamiliar footing with this Negro. "Why would the rancher agree to ship with me?" Especially, when I don't even have a vessel!

"'Cause you would give Master Allen exclusive rights to ship his cattle, so's he could corner the market."

Maybe his mother's unerring instinct for a good thing was not wasted on him. It had gotten him Sarita, hadn't it? He rose to his feet. "What is your name?"

"Tom. Thomas Wheelwright, suh."

"Wade Paladín's mine. If I buy your papers, Tom—if I set you free—will you help me get the Paladín Steamboat

Company up and running?" He did not look to see how Sarita took this. He knew it was a harebrained offer. Here he and Sarita were without even a place to live.

"Set me fr . . . free?"

"Yes—and your wife and son, once we have earned enough." He stuck out his hand. "A deal?"

The slave looked from Wade to his outstretched hand with suspicion-narrowed lids, then with a more measuring gaze back to Wade once more. Tears glistened in the man's red-rimmed eyes. He extended his trembling big hand to grasp Wade's. "You won't never be sorry, suh."

Wade's eyes skittered toward Sarita, wondering how she had taken his newest half-baked notion. She couldn't exactly be dancing on sunshine. After all, he'd rode roughshod over her plans. Would she be the one to be sorry—sorry she had wedded him after all?

THE BARONY
JUNE 1865

"S'il te plais, cherie, you must hold still! Now tilt your head this way. Your hair, it is a calamity!"

Tara rolled her eyes but complied. Thérèse wielded the heated curling iron as determinedly as Tara did a branding iron. "You know I have no interest in attending the *Fiesta,* Thérèse. Besides, Father is *El Patron* of The Barony. Not me."

"All Paladíns are The Barony, *ma chere fille.* "

La Fiesta de San Juan Batista was a night-long celebration, in which the Mexican ranch hands and their families danced, sang, and feasted on June twenty-fourth, the longest night of the year. Traditionally, *El Patron* appeared during the festivity to offer them his blessing at the *Paladíneños* compound, *La Baroncita,* with its feudal-style collection of jacales.

In prior years, Tara had loved the merriment and the majesty of its pageantry. But this year, she did not feel much like attending or celebrating. All pleasure had been leached from her life. She had not seen Max since she had let him kiss her. Let him kiss her several times. Let him hold her and touch her in wondrous ways. Her lips, her neck, just below her ear, the inside of her elbow, the hollow of her palm.

'A brazen wench,' Winnie would call her if she had known about it. Thérèse, if she knew, would undoubtedly kiss her lips to her gathered fingertips, pronouncing her *"Une magnifique jeune femme!"*

Tara did not feel so *magnifique.* She felt . . . used. Used and tossed aside like a piece of wadded parchment. Yes, Max most certainly excelled at his profession. As an attorney, he had a way with words . . . and a way with her. He stole her kisses—and then stole away himself.

When the ranch bell began to clang, Thérèse left off with her hairstyling. Going to the bedroom's thrown wide shutters, she leaned out and called down to Pepe. "What is all that commotion?"

The clanging stopped and Tara heard Pepe call back, "Visitors, Señora Thérèse. Los Señores von Hesse-Lippe."

"Quick. Finish curling my hair. Ringlets in front of my

ears—small curls like yours. And I changed my mind. I will wear a dress to the fiesta tonight. That pink gingham you pulled out of the clothespress."

Thérèse put her hands on her hips and arched a perfect brow. "So, that's how it is."

Tara ignored her and hurried through the rest of her dressing, flew down the stairs, then paused, hand on the doorknob of her father's office. First, to draw a calming breath, then, she straightened her carriage, as Thérèse all too often suggested. *Stand up straight, cherie, and give a man something to adore.*

When Tara entered, both Uncle Karl and Max stood. Something they never before had bothered to do with her. Hats in hand, the two were dressed impeccably in waistcoat and tails.

In his own customary black attire, her father remained seated behind that enormous desk of his. His lids narrowed as he surveyed her. "Glad you're here, Tara. Apparently, there is news from the outside world."

She glanced at Uncle Karl and then, more reluctantly, at Max. Her heart might have been thudding after racing to get ready, but now it was pounding like a kettle drum. Damn, he had not turned into a troll, as she had hoped. He was every bit as handsome as she had dreaded.

His eyes coursed over her as he raised a questioning brow. When he offered no comment about her 'transfor-mation,' she was grateful he had spared her the embarrass-ment. "Well, Tara, we come bringing bad tidings."

"Is something wrong with Aunt Maria Elena?" Her

body tensed again. The Hispanic woman's mother-hen-hovering could be annoying, but Tara valued the woman's bluntness.

"No, she is quite well," Uncle Karl said.

Max pulled out his chair for her. With inordinate attention to arranging her maddening hoop skirt, she settled on the chair's edge, only then glancing up at him at her side, then to her father and Uncle Karl. "Then what is it?"

"To begin with," Uncle Karl exhaled a heavy sigh, "three weeks ago, General Gordon Granger and his Federal troops landed at Galveston with the news that Lee had surrendered. The South has been defeated."

"No!" Bitter dejection deflated her earlier euphoria. The news was difficult to assimilate, all that it implied and all that it did not—that of a vague and very uneasy future.

Uncle Karl continued. "Our General Kirby Smith has since surrendered all Confederate forces west of the Mississippi and set sail from Galveston to avoid treason charges against him by the U.S."

At this news, she relaxed somewhat. Now she was on more familiar ground and could go into her own take-charge mode. "We were expecting this." She looked at each of the other three. "The cattle market will be ready to boom. It's not too late in the year to drive a herd up through Fort Worth to Abilene. With Diego along, I can take—"

"It's no use, Tara." Max's voice was flat.

She looked up at him. "I can handle myself on the trail, Max. I have been doing—"

"That is not the issue," her father cut in. He tapped a small pile of unfolded papers on the red-leather desktop. "Max has discovered that Obregon Enterprise has wrested control of thirty percent of The Barony Land and Cattle Company."

"That can't be!"

"Unfortunately, it is true," Uncle Karl sighed. "I have already passed the news on to Niall. It appears Guillermo Obregon has secretly been acquiring your father's land over the years."

"How?" she asked of him. "How did he? How could he do this?"

"Through a trail of paperwork laid by our 'partner' Lord Brighton."

A fury built up in her like steam in a kettle. "That blood-sucking, piss-pot of a thief!" The only valve for steam was the knowledge that her family still owned by far the controlling stock, with Kerry as the eldest, the largest shareholder.

"Furthermore," Max picked up where his father left off, "Brighton also altered range records by creating discrepancies in the inventories of purchasing agents. Uncle Alex and Uncle Niall actually own far fewer cattle than our records declare."

"Apparently, it would seem," her father mused, "that I will be needing a second so I can issue a dueling challenge to Brighton."

"Under the complex etiquette of dueling," Uncle Karl wiped his spectacles with a linen handkerchief, "Brighton could refuse to receive your demand. And if Brighton does not acknowledge its receipt, you cannot fight him."

"Damn the etiquette," her father growled. "Before I am finished with Brighton, I will write my challenge in the blood of his heart."

"I WOULD NOT WORRY ABOUT your father fighting a duel," Max reassured Tara. "Geoffrey Brighton realizes his days in Texas are numbered. He is not that much of a fool. I would imagine right now he is fleeing with his funds on the same vessel as our illustrious General Kirby Smith."

Her strong features a study in preoccupation, Tara walked beside him—or rather, she was leading the way in the gloaming through a grove of pecan trees banking the gurgling Nueces. He and Tara were more or less headed in the direction of the *Paladíneños* compound to attend its *Fiesta de San Juan Batista*.

Everyone else—her father, Uncle Karl, Thérèse, and the house servants—had already gone ahead. Tara, it seemed to him, had stalled, even taking a roundabout path to the cluster of jacales. Yet her stride had accelerated now to a brisk pace, despite her limb-hampering skirts.

He had always been attracted—even as a youth—to who Tara was. Obstinate, intelligent, daring . . . and caring. But now, he was acting like an untried youth again over what Tara was—a sensuous, beguiling female. He had not fully realized these attributes until she appeared in Uncle Alex's study in a dress that so dramatically emphasized her femininity and her hair swept up in charming ringlets that softened her squarish features.

Suddenly, she whirled toward him, taffeta skirts swirling enticingly about her ankles. "Are you interested in me or not, Max von Hesse-Lippe?"

He had also forgotten her lack of artifice that he found so attractive. He balled his hands on his hips. "What is this about, Tara?"

She mimicked his fists-on-hips gesture, her stubborn chin outthrust. "We kissed—a lot—last Thanksgiving. Then nothing. Either you want me or you do not. There is no middle ground."

He tilted back his head, half-noticing the twinkling of the stars through the canopy of leaves. From the jacales, out of sight beyond the trees, filtered the lighthearted laughter of the revelers, the arousing aroma of roasting chiles, tamales, and peppers, and the heat of a thrumming guitar.

His own blood was heated from want of Tara. After a moment, he looked at her with an expression that offered no quarter. "Tara, there is a fine and very breachable line between mere kissing . . . and all the many ramifications it can inevitably bring about."

"Spoken like a true lawyer. You dolt, do you think I do not know that? I am neither asking you nor wanting to be hobbled by marriage, like some giddy filly. I am asking you to share with me, to experience the consequences, or ramifications as you put it, of my fulfillment of womanhood, as I choose to word it."

He expelled a frustrated breath. "Do not play with me the cat if you intend to become the mouse."

"You know me better than that, Max. At least, I hope you do. I don't play sneaky games because I don't know how."

He nodded. "No, you do not." His fists dropped from his hips. He stepped closer, so he had only to incline his head and claim her lips if he wished.

She held her ground. Her rich, coffee-colored eyes stared up at him, daring him.

He clasped her bared shoulders loosely, half-hoping she would bolt. His fingers detected her tremor at his touch. "Do you know how some people in Mexico celebrate St. John's Eve come midnight, my love—once the festivities are over and the revelers have all departed?"

Slowly, she shook her head. Her lips, untainted by any false coloring, parted in contemplation.

"They head to the closest body of water they can find—the ocean, a lake, a river—and they strip themselves of their clothes and fall backwards into the water three times. This is done to cleanse the body from bad luck—and to give them good fortune for the ensuing year."

His lips curled at the widening of her eyes. He nodded toward the Nueces, its ripples glinting in the moonlight. "What do you think about that tradition?"

Her eyes twinkled. "Why, Max, I think I can truly say that this year has been one of incredibly bad luck."

Max held out his hand and she placed her sweaty palm in his. He knew she wanted to discover that aspect of what it meant to be fully a woman but was unsure if she was prepared for what would be an irrevocably newfound relationship with him.

Never taking his eyes from her, he gently tugged her down the slope to the river's rocky ledge. Grasping her shoulders, he turned her back to the Nueces. "I suggest we create a variance of the St. John's Eve tradition." First, her slouch hat went sailing, then his felt bowler. "That we undress one another before jumping into the river, naked as the day we were born." His fingers went to the top snap button of her muslin shirt.

Despite her resolve, she flinched. He dipped his head, his lips moving softly but firmly over hers to allay her disquiet, while his fingers continued in their quest to bare her. He would encounter no forbidding steel bone corset, but a simple linen chemise that did nothing to conceal the sudden hardening of her nipples beneath.

His lips deserted hers and her eyes flew open to find him kneeling to draw off her boots. Her fingers dug into his shoulders for support as she stood on first one stockinged foot, then the other. Next, he was gliding down the trousers he had loosened. She stiffened at this intimacy that next divested her of all but her stockings and chemise.

When he stood, he gave her that double-dog-dare-you smirk of their childhood. "Well?"

He saw her shiver, but she returned his smirk. "What's good for the goose is good for the gander."

Amused, he watched her disrobe his outer clothing. Eventually there remained only the button fly of his drawers—and the obvious jutting of flesh beneath them. At least there was that reward of her sharply indrawn breath when her knuckles brushed the flesh of his stomach's taut muscles. Her long fingers fumbled, then froze. His own nudged hers away to pop free the button.

She bit her lip. "Max . . . I . . . I don't know . . . I didn't know . . . ."

"Ssshh." He grabbed her upper arms, pulling her up to him, and slammed his mouth over hers.

She responded to his mouth's hungry demand. Somehow, while exchanging those fierce and frantic kisses, they tore away the remainder of their clothes . . . and, laughing, tumbled into the cold, hip-high water.

He emerged first and vigorously shook his forehead and jaw free of his dripping, long golden locks. She surfaced close to him, and her flailing hands shoved back from her face her mop of thick, tangled hair.

He locked his hands on her goose-bumped hips and pulled her against him. She tensed. He captured her wrist, drawing her fingers to the hard knot of his groin. Her fingers found him. His response was half groan, half growl. "And turnabout is fair play."

Clearly, she was not prepared for the fingers that slipped between her thighs to stroke her insistently. She buckled with obvious pleasure in his arm, supporting her waist. She clutched at his shoulders, and he chuckled. "I think it's time we set about making our good fortune for the ensuing year, don't you?"

Her answering sigh was as soft as the soughing of the wind in the trees. And later, her outcry was as exultant as the cougar's scream.

AUSTIN
AUGUST 1866

El Camino Real was a centuries-old artery defining travel between San Antonio and Austin. The Gorman Transport coach, drawn by six thoroughbreds, was quite plush with its morocco-bound cushions and its padded ornamental panels.

Kerry and Catarina's families' firm might own Gorman Transport coaches, the only worthy conveyances in that area, but Kerry refused to take that advantage and travel free. No, they paid the same fee as the coach's other passengers.

Although there was relatively little concern anymore about Kiowa or Comanche scalping parties so close to the Austin outskirts, lawlessness nevertheless abounded—angry returning Confederate veterans, foraging farmers who had lost their land, and violent bands taking advantage of social collapse under the mostly outrageous new laws that had arrived in Texas, along with the Unionist reconstruction period following the Civil War's conclusion.

So, after seemingly lengthy hours traveling the Royal Highway, Kerry welcomed the sight of the Neill-Cochran house through the gathering darkness. Its six towering Doric porch columns defined the height of the two-story Greek Revival mansion.

Descending from the coach, he turned to assist Catarina. There was something to be said for having just one arm—this flaw gave him permission to encircle her slip of a waist and cradle her against him in what would appear an unseemly fashion for men with two functioning arms. He took the opportunity to cup the side of one breast covertly before releasing her to stand on her own.

Pale brown eyes flashed his way. "Sir, must you take such unseemly advantage of a helpless female?" Her husky voice was low enough that their fellow passengers could not overhear.

He cocked her a randy grin. "Female, that you most certainly are. But helpless? Cleopatra could take lessons from you, Cat."

His wife was certainly as seductive as Cleopatra—as he had come to learn over the three years of their marriage—and just as capable of employing guile. She never offered him even a hint of the pity over his missing arm—pity that might have emasculated him.

Behind them, General Sheridan, after traveling all the way from New Orleans, descended from the coach. He was shockingly short, barely five-foot-five, with dispropor-tionately long arms. He had told them on this, the final leg of his journey, that he was being sent to Austin as the state's newly appointed military governor in the next term.

Noted for his hard, disciplinarian measures—and for his retort that if he owned Texas and Hell, he would rent out Texas and live in Hell—his appointment was not a good sign for an early Texas recovery.

"Well, well." Sheridan scoped the blaze of house lights. "Just in time for the party. The Grand Old Party."

"Hardly a party, General," Kerry put in. The house had previously served as a school for the blind and, after that, as a military hospital. It now served as interim residence for the outgoing Provisional Governor for Texas, Andrew Hamilton. "Instead, I think Governor Hamilton has in mind something along the line of noses to the grindstone."

The provisional governor had invited Kerry to attend the meeting being held to implement the latest Unionist reconstruction policies. As Kerry understood it, his part this week, as a professor, was to study how best to use Congress's Morrill Act most expeditiously as a guideline for establishing the state's first public institution of higher learning.

While Hamilton advocated harsh measures under the radical Republican Reconstruction, he had been a longtime admirer and friend of the late Sam Houston, also a staunch Unionist. Kerry figured his own close ties with Sam was the sole reason he, a non-partisan, had been included on the list of distinguished legislators and military leaders invited that week—among them, General Custer.

The legendary Boy General was finishing his assignment in Texas—preventing Confederate retrenchment in Mexico under its French Emperor. Wearing his customary red handkerchief around his neck, he was a compelling personality, and his good looks reminded Kerry somewhat of an older Max.

Yet Kerry found it difficult to like Custer, if only because he had violated the rules of war and executed some Confederate prisoners interned at Front Royal, Virginia.

That evening, it was not Custer's compelling personality that charmed the crowd but Kerry's very own Catarina. She moved graciously among the guests, responded with wit, and listened with authentic interest.

Kerry had not fully appreciated when he had married her how wonderfully complex was the wife he had acquired. Her mismatched features, the too-wide mouth and impressive nose that had vied for dominance in her face, had finally attained a uniquely lovely collaboration.

Later, while conversing with Custer and his opinionated wife Libby, the stout Hamilton had drawn Kerry aside from Cat and the couple. Not quite at Kerry's six-feet-two inches, Hamilton had to stretch to loop an arm across Kerry's shoulders.

"Son, I have in mind for you more than just laying the groundwork for our state's first public institution of higher education. I want you to consider an appointment as our Secretary of State. I can swing your nomination before I leave office."

Kerry felt his head swiveling like a hootie owl's. "Secretary of State? Why, Governor, I have no political affiliation, much less any experience."

"Which is one reason I want you for this appointment. Your views are not influenced nor distorted by a party affiliation. Regardless, you are committed to Texas."

"Committed to Texas, yes sir—but not to your Radical Republicans. I mean no disrespect, Governor. As it is," Kerry shook his head, "I see looming for our Texas a potential disaster at the hands of the carpetbaggers. They are bent on destruction not on 'reconstruction.' Rather than curbing Texas like some magnificent stallion, I would choose to invest in it all the grandeur that should be its destiny."

"That is precisely why, Governor," Cat came up to slip her arm through Kerry's and delivering first him, then Hamilton, her most radiant smile, "my husband will one day be more than mere Secretary of State—he will be governor of our grand state."

THE BARONY
FEBRUARY 1867

At the stables, Diego held two saddled and restive horses he had prepared for Alex and Niall. Great frosty vapors streamed from the mounts' nostrils.

Alex was bundled in a leather duster and red woolen scarf, his Stetson pulled low against the frigid air. He swung easily but somewhat stiffly onto his mount, a gray Arabian, foal of the war mare from the Shammar Emirate he had bought several years ago.

Niall mounted the other, a shorter hot-blooded quarter horse. It fell in behind the Arabian as Alex kneed his steed past the carriage house, corn crib, and smokehouse, beyond the blacksmith shop, and, at last, out onto the open range.

For some time, the two rode, with only the creak of their saddles to interrupt the solace of winter's silence—a welcome respite from the frenetic activities over the past few days at the hacienda.

It had been a bedlam with the arrival of Rafaela, Niall, Karl, Maria Elena, and Max for the Valentine celebration

Thérèse had prepared. "Your Dixie beaux and belles are satisfied with a few miserable lines, neatly written upon fine parchment," she had admonished him, "but there is oh so much more to the art of romantic pursuit."

Alex suspected she was matchmaking, her Cupid's arrow aimed at Max and Tara, which, to Alex, was a perplexing and superfluous pursuit that skirted the more direct matters of the heart. But, then, Thérèse was like that—enigmatically passionate about whatever she chose to do.

Ostensibly, he and Niall were out to inspect the strays Diego, Tara, and a few of the *Paladíneños* had recently rounded up. The cows wore the brand he had bought and registered, the triple loop of the combined B and P, representing Barony and Paladín.

But this outing also allowed Alex to work out some kinks—induced by the winter constraints that had kept him office-bound—from both his body and his mind.

"I sold our controlling stock in the stagecoach company—and the ferry." Niall's disappointment hung heavy in his usually mellifluous accent. "That should keep us going until we can recover from the war—and from that pissant Guillermo Obregon."

Alex leaned forward in the saddle, bracing against the frigid, stinging gusts. "Good. Here's what I want you to do next. Sell off the wagon yard too."

Niall hauled up on his quarter horse's reins. "You can't be serious, Alex. That company is sound and doing bloody well. 'Tis the only enterprise we have that is still thriving."

After Alex halted his own mount, he glanced over his

shoulder at the Irish Traveler. "I'm deadly serious, Niall."

Hunched against the blustery cold, gloved hands braced on his saddle horn, Niall looked out across the motley tree belt and chaparral, then dragged his eyes back toward Alex. "My old man used to say, 'Never miss an opportunity to shut up,' but my two cents is that you have gone and lost your bloody mind."

He sighed. How many times had his spunky Fiona, hands on her hips, used the same phrase?

"Listen to me, Niall. We are going right back into the railroad business. Full throttle. We're going to build an extension from San Antonio to join up with the Houston & Texas Central Railroad. Our grand early days of the ferry, wagon, and stagecoach are quickly fading into history." He allowed himself a predatory smile. "And so will steamboats. Within only a few years, I will be in the strong position to drive Obregon right out of business until that crooked genius has to revert back to us all the lands he stole."

The wind was whistling so strongly around them that Alex almost did not hear Niall's next words. "And Wade and his wife—your own daughter-in-law, Sarita? What about their steam boating business? What will happen to it . . . and to them?"

"You know I will help Wade, if he asks me."

Niall looked down, shook his head, then looked up once more at Alex. "My old man would say that holding a grudge is like drinking poison and expecting the other person to die."

Alex glowered at Niall. Even so, riding back to the

hacienda, Alex weighed Niall's advice because he trusted implicitly its source. He knew fences should be mended, but Kerry and Wade's desertion continued to gnaw at him.

Betrayals in his youth—his own brother's squandering of the family fortunes . . . his mother abandoning the family for her lover . . . his father's total indifference to the existence of his second son, with all his attention centered only on the firstborn—all those sins in their fashion led to his Maypole-thin height those early years, which was a barely defined hint of the bruised heart inside him.

If he were honest with himself, he could now see how his brother's happy-go-lucky irresponsibility was his means of survival in a strife-torn house. He could also almost acknowledge how his father's philandering and vicious verbal attacks may have driven away his mother.

Oh, how Niall would appreciate the dictum that "the apple never fell far from the tree."

What had happened to Fiona's own dictum—that "family was everything?"

Another source he trusted was Thérèse, so once back at the hacienda he went looking for her. With her worldly wise way of approaching life's vicissitudes, she would know what he should do now. She was a font of sanity and she understood him. What with all the loyalties around him shifting like earth tremors, it was a boon that at least she would side with him.

He found her in the guest bedroom. Although she slept with him in his bed every night, she retained the guest bedroom she had occupied since coming to the hacienda three years ago. He stopped cold in the doorway.

She was kneeling before her trunk, packing. Her voluminous skirts spread out around her like mauve flower petals.

From where he stood, his eyes could not help delving into her daring and delicious décolletage. "What are you doing?"

With her bewitching smile, she looked up at him but continued to fold the purple cashmere shawl she held. "Why, packing, *mon cher*. Rafaela said I could ride with them after the party as far as San Patricio, and from there I can catch the next stage bound for Brownsville."

His black brows furrowed into a deep-set intractable line. "You never said anything to me about leaving."

She laughed lightly. "I was unaware I must ask your permission."

"You know damn well that is not what I mean."

She laid the folded shawl inside the trunk with the other items she had begun to pack. Then, hands folded easily atop one another in her lap, she stared up at him calmly. "And exactly what is it you do mean, Alex?"

He paused. Bracing his hands low on his hips, he stared at his dusty boots, then back to her. She was watching him with her expressive, so exotic eyes. "Well, I mean . . . are you not happy here, Thérèse ?"

"*Mais oui, bien sur*. Still, I have my own house in Brownsville, do I not? And servants and friends there. Why, it has been three years since I have seen our mutual friends, Charlotte and Moses. I have stayed here far too long."

"But you would leave without even a . . . a proper goodbye?" Thérèse and her damnably capricious ways.

She shrugged. *"Eh bien.* You know how I detest au revoirs. Sometimes one does not meet another again, is it not so?"

"And I hate adieus." He realized he was growling and amended in a more moderate tone, "Uhh, final farewells."

She held up beringed hands. "Then help me rise and give me one of your best au revoirs, the kind exchanged only between lovers."

He pulled her to her feet and, grasping those soft, bared shoulders, pulled her against him to stare down into eyes that had offered him a wealth of soulful meaning. But how to interpret what he saw there Was she doing her own matchmaking, only between them now, instead?

Was she hoping to wring a proposal of marriage from him? They were both well beyond that youthful rite of springtime joys. They had both already been married, she twice. There no longer seemed a plausible need for their recognition and legalization as a couple. Neither of them had ever given a fig for public opinion.

"I do not want you to leave. I want you to stay here with me—as my lover." It had truly not occurred to him until the words were out of his mouth.

"Forever?"

He nodded warily.

She placed her forefinger on the cleft in his chin. "That seems to me more than mere cohabitation you describe, *mon amour.* That seems to me to be a state of matrimony. Is that what you wish from me?"

His grip clenched. Releasing her, he spread his palms wide. "First Niall, now you, cornering me."

She raised a brow. "Perhaps you need to think on that, non?" Turning away, she dropped back onto her knees and resumed packing.

He pivoted and stormed to the door. In his office, he grabbed a cigar from the humidor and poured a tumbler of Scotch whiskey. Christ's thorns! Once she made up her mind to leave, he knew she would not give him so much as a single inch. He took a swallow from the tumbler, inhaled deeply on his cigar . . . then began to pace.

He and she were cut from the same cloth. Stubborn. They both wanted each other. But like Colonel Travis at the goldarned Alamo siege, she had drawn an indelible line in the sand. He hurled the tumbler against the paneled wall. Glass shattered. Whiskey splattered. Next, he hurled his cigar.

Back to her bedroom he stormed and threw open the door. "Damn it! I want you, and I will take you any way I must. Even if that means we marry."

Still packing, she sat among her puddle of skirts and looked at him, her smile gentle. "But, *mon amour,* it is not I who mentioned marriage. Non, it is not marriage I seek."

Females! Their reasoning faculties were beyond his comprehension. "Well, what the hell is it you want, then?"

An indulgent smile dimpled her cheeks. "Alex, your passionate Latin heritage may boil in your blood, but your Englishman's cold rationale blinds you to the obvious."

His felt his brows yanked upward. "And what might that be?"

"Oh, Alex, with all your wit and wisdom, what a dullard you can sometimes be! A woman wishes to be courted. Forever." Head tilted gloriously, he noted, she eyed him with all the beguilement ever summoned by a *femme fatale*. "At the moment, a few words of love from you to me would do for a start."

Chuckling, he shook his head. Then, with a little wincing of his joint, he dropped to one knee before her and lifted her hand. Soft and so elegantly shaped. He captured it between his much larger hands and looked her straight in the eyes, although his vision was severely tempted to stray toward her delectable cleavage.

"Know this, Thérèse. I love you madly. Beyond reasoning. Obviously, I have gone mad. You know I am a difficult man—and at this moment, I am going to be even more difficult by demanding that you marry me. I only pray that I do not follow in the footsteps of your two earlier husbands and predecease you posthaste."

With a dusky chuckle, she slipped her arms up over his shoulders, her fingers cradling the back of his head, tunneling through his over-longish hair, now shot completely through with silver. "I never agreed to marry you, you arrogant man." She drew him down to kiss his lips.

Some nether regions of his Englishman's brain warned him that Thérèse's feminine wiles had outgunned him, but, bloody hell, he simply did not care about any of that hogwash. He now believed in his true heart of hearts that his too-clever Frenchwoman was totally irresistible.

RAFAELA ADDED HER BRONZE LACE *mantilla* to the hastily collected wedding ensemble. Alex had given them only two days' notice to summon a *padre* from San Patricio and prepare the now-combined Valentine festivities with the newly announced wedding.

She adjusted the lacy scarf over Thérèse's upswept curls, anchored by the blue-lacquered hair comb Maria Elena had proffered. "Something old, something new, something borrowed, something blue," Rafaela recited, as if chanting some age-old goddess blessing.

"I doubt I have anything you would want to wear," Tara told Thérèse and held up a silver coin, "but in keeping with the superstitious rhyme, I have this sixpence for your shoe."

Thérèse offered her most enchanting smile, easily encompassing all three of her bridal attendants. "Prosperity! *Oui, en effet*—a token all of us could surely use right now."

Rafaela stepped back to admire their handiwork. "You are simply beautiful, my dear."

Hands on hips, dark eyes twinkling, Thérèse twirled. Her cream-and-brown-striped silk skirts swirled around her pantalettes. Pirouette complete, she flung up her long-gloved arms. "*Voilà!* Third time is a charm, *non?* This one will not die on me. Unless, it is from *le petit mort.*"

"You are truly incorrigible, *querida.* "Rafaela smiled.

To her left, Maria Elena clapped pudgy palms together. "You are bubbly, like champagne. And you will certainly intoxicate your groom tonight."

Rafaela thought how good Maria Elena was. Worldly wise, but always seeing the best in people. She had created a comfortable home for Karl, with few demands on him. He had become an old workhorse wearing blinders, seemingly focusing on little else but his law practice.

Downstairs, the gentlemen waited. Descending the staircase behind the three women, Rafaela noticed Alex's expression as he beheld Thérèse. Adoration softened his harsh features. Rafaela's glance slid on past him to Karl, who wore the same expression—only it was not directed at Thérèse, nor Maria Elena or Tara—but toward herself.

Hastily, she glanced away. His enduring love had weathered through all these years—through childbirth, weddings, deaths.

But he himself had not weathered quite as well. Where Niall's carriage was erect and confident, Karl's tall frame was stooped ever-so-slightly, that condition that would obviously worsen with the years. Where Niall's tousled brown hair was thick and threaded with little gray, Karl's reddish-blond locks had whitened early on and now receded from his brow. His spectacles tended to distort his intense blue eyes, their regard she invariably found so compass-sionate, comforting, and understanding.

She joined Niall. He grinned at her and winked. "Ye be the best of the breed, me love," he whispered in that voice that gentled females as easily as it did horses. He draped her fur-trimmed paletot over her shoulders and covertly nuzzled her neck. As he had gentled her, she thought.

If only Catarina and Kerry could be here. Kerry's

estrangement from all things related to his father and The Barony Partnership had put a strain even on Niall and herself.

If only Alex would forgive her and Karl's awful moment of indiscretion.

If only Niall would never hear of it.

IN THE SILENCE OF February's wintery afternoon, Tara followed her father, Thérèse, and the wedding guests up the slight incline to the bluff and the enormous live oak, where in 1767 a Paladín had first stood and surveyed his royal Spanish land grant.

A rotund padre stood now beneath the oak, awaiting the wedding party.

At her side, Max strode, seemingly lost in thought. The two of them had not been alone the entire five days of the St. Valentine's Day celebration Thérèse had staged—and Tara suspected Max had maneuvered it that way.

Her voice low, she spoke what was on her mind. "Are you regretting last June . . . what happened between us? Obviously, I am not with child."

He looked at her now, only a glance that encompassed her pancake-flat stomach, then looked away. "No. I am not regretting what happened. And I knew I had not gotten you with child."

"How?"

He managed a wry half-smile. "I begged Thérèse to tell me because I knew you never would."

"This . . . this Valentine's party . . . . Was it a ploy of

hers to get us together?"

"That would not surprise me."

Her next question was a struggle to get out. "Did I . . . . Then was it a disappointment? What happened that night?"

"Hardly." He kept his gaze pinned to the couples walking ahead of them. "I find you utterly fascinating, Tara. You are as at home in denims as you are in lace. A combination of silk and steel. You are confident and competent at whatever you set your mind to. And totally unpredictable."

"Then what is it, Max?"

As they walked, his gloved hand encompassed hers. "I will admit, Tara, that I have had other . . . liaisons . . . since you and I coupled." He turned to look at her now, his blue eyes as clouded as the weather.

She pulled on his hand, forcing him to pause, and swung round to face him. Her heart was pounding against her ribcage. Her next words seemed mere puffs of vapor amid the frosty air. "Max, I will never compete with those other women. I cannot change who I am."

"In truth, I found those other women failed to hold my interest at all." Confusion puckered her thick brows. "Then what the hell is it?"

He cradled her face between his palms. "It is I who cannot change, sweetheart. And I cannot compete with The Barony. That is your true love."

"I don't love The Barony, I *am* The Barony. With all its liabilities and assets. But it is you I love."

He raised a brow. "Enough to leave The Barony?

Forever?"

She was silent as his hands fell away. "I think your hesitation answers my question."

She caught the velvet lapels of his Chesterfield coat. "Now you listen to me, Max von Hesse-Lippe. That was not a hesitation. That was me, taking stock of myself. And of you. I was ferreting out any possible regret I might have by leaving with you. Because if there are any, I want to find out now, not later."

From half-masted lids, he was watching her closely. "And?"

"The question is . . . would you still—" she had almost said 'love,' but he had yet to say he loved her. "Would I still be the girl you want if I were to leave here . . . and try to become a part of your life? With its glitter and its glamour?" She could feel her bile rising. "And all its hollowness?"

He sighed, and his sadness was as cold as the evening. "Well, sweetheart, as I once heard your very own mother declare, a woman wants to be wanted, but a man needs to be needed." He leaned his forehead against hers. "So, I think your response answers my question. You don't really need me."

GALVESTON BAY
JULY 1869

Tom and Billy's black chests glistened with sweat in the unholy orange-red light of the *Bayou Queen's* boiler room. They were shoveling pitch and pine knots into her furnace in rapid succession.

The race was on. The red steamer, the *Henry Hudson,* of New York's well respected Morgan Lines, was a sure bet to win. It and a third steamboat of nearly five hundred tons, the *Osprey,* were running nip and tuck.

In cities along the Mississippi—New Orleans, Memphis, Saint Louis—interest in steamboat racing was enormous. Vast bets were staked. Professional gamblers had a field day betting on races.

Steamboat racing was well known as a criminally irresponsible pursuit. Despite that, it remained a constant among Buffalo Bayou river folk. The racing reputation of a new boat or her master could be made, even if that meant inspectors revoking a captain's or owner's license—or worse, risking dismemberment or death from a boiler explosion.

Because of that, Wade, dressed only in shirt sleeves, his collar wide open, had descended to the boiler room and was eyeing the gauge-cocks registering how many pounds of steam to the square inch were driving his boat.

The *Bayou Queen* had not a prayer of winning, but race she must if he hoped to make a name for the Paladín Navigation Company and to raise the *Bayou Queen's* visibility—and, even more important, nail the federal mail contract between Galveston and Houston with the letters USM emblazoned on the *Bayou Queen's* paddlewheel boxes.

Riverboats jostled for that contract, their resulting income adding significantly to a boat's profitability. And the Paladín Navigation Company's profit ratio was sucking swamp, despite its contract to ship Allen Ranch cattle.

Whether Paladín Navigation secured the federal mail contract or not, speed was important, because with so many packets plying the Buffalo Bayou route these days, the first racer to reach Houston from Galveston got a lion's share of both freight and passengers. At this time, the Morgan Lines dominated the steamboat trade.

Four years ago, he and Sarita had purchased the *Bayou Queen*, an antiquated antebellum steamboat used later as a gunboat during the War Between the States. Her main deck, fitted with flimsy lightweight metal plating, had earned the name Tinclad in mocking homage to the Civil War ironclads.

All their savings had gone into the purchase of the 254-ton steamboat—and the purchase of Tom, Esther, and their son, Billy, once the property of Sam Allen. A purchase Wade and Sarita could ill afford and a foolish one, as well, because they had set the Wheelwrights free only a few months before word of the war's end reached Texas—and as a consequence, he and Sarita had no reserves to acquire a home of their own.

So sleep they must, as did the Wheelwright family, in cabin rooms normally reserved for SS *Bayou Queen's* paying passengers.

The Wheelwrights more than made up for their purchase price in their loyalty and in Billy's knowledge not only of cattle but steamboats. It had been commonplace for riverside slaveowners to hire out their slaves to work on the river as deckhands for the prevailing rate of $480 per year paid to the slaveowner.

After the war, emancipated slaves had been turned loose to wander about the country. Destitute, they still grappled for a living as best they could. Twenty-year-old Billy had helped build up the *Bayou Queens* crew of former slaves to a total of eleven.

In between helping his father stuff the fireboxes with fuel, Billy wrestled with the gauge-cocks and safety valves. He paused to wipe the sweat blinding his eyes with the back of his arm.

"Billy, is the water supply shut off from the boilers?"

He nodded.

"Tom, how's the wood?"

"Pine's half gone, Mister Wade. Some cypress left."

Wade had learned quickly about steamboats. He had

been forced to if he and Sarita were ever going to make a go of it. What surprised him was the appreciation he was developing for steam boating. The ocean was as limitless as the prairies, and the excitement in racing was greater. A horse-race was mighty tame and drab by comparison. But then, nobody was ever killed in horseracing, leastways he could recall.

He started back up the ladder to the pilothouse. He had left Sarita at its helm. She might have an instinct for the vagaries of Galveston Bay, San Jacinto Bay, and Buffalo Bayou, but her small frame lacked the strength to control the eight-foot wheel in the sharp maneuvering tactics required for racing.

At the ear-shattering blast from above and the violent rocking of the steamboat, he scrambled up the remaining steps. On deck, smoke billowed. But from where? Fear for Sarita shot through him. Taking the next flight of steps three at a time, he made for the pilothouse.

Her bright, flower-patterned dress seemed the only color in the small room. She was hauling on the wildly gyrating wheel, its spokes spinning to port so fast it looked like a roulette wheel. He reached around her and grabbed it, wrangling to bring it under control.

"Oh, Wade, thank God!"

He felt her small body in front of his shuddering. Ahead and off to the left, through the whirling clouds of smoke, flames leaped fifty feet or more from what had been the *Henry Hudson.* Obviously, her boiler had burst. Its explosion had destroyed the hurricane deck above and blown passengers and crew into the lapping waves.

Just beyond the disaster, the packet *Osprey* was nevertheless proceeding full steam ahead, past the Red Fish Bar lighthouse, toward the mouth of Buffalo Bayou.

Bodies littered the whitecaps like corks. For most of those, it was too late. No point in remaining in the vicinity. Besides, if he did, the Paladín Navigation Company pilot could be charged for behaving with criminal recklessness in racing. Its license would be revoked. He and Sarita would then be destitute.

Still . . . . He inclined his head alongside hers. "You with me on this?" He really didn't have to ask her. She had stuck with him through all his reckless and impulsive moments. She knew him so well.

She nodded.

He swung away and crossed to the speaking-tube. "Stand by. We're shutting down the engines."

FORT WORTH
MAY 1871

After weeks of monotonous trail dust, dull food, and abstinence of all kinds, Tara paid her crew—most of them *Paladíneños,* but also a few Mexican *vaqueros,* freed black men, and decommissioned cavalrymen, desperate for jobs after the economy's collapse following the War Between the States.

She turned the randy, brawling cowmen loose in Hell's Half Acre, a district south of Fort Worth's courthouse and known all over the west for its salacious entertainment.

Then she went in search of a bath to wash the dust caked on her body and in her hair.

Fort Worth was the last major stop for rest and supplies. Beyond Fort Worth, she would have to deal with crossing the Red River into Indian Territory. She already had a lot to deal with, she brooded, easing into Daggett Hotel's steamy tin hip-bathtub.

The Barony cattle were infested with ticks. A rattler had bitten Diego on the thumb, and she had been forced to amputate it with the help of Johnny Scraneky—who was something else to deal with. Somehow, the peach-fuzzed kid had managed to make it through the war unscathed but had fallen a victim to Cupid's arrow. He imagined himself in love with her.

Then there was the thunderstorm that had stampeded the bawling cattle. Not only had she lost nine cows, but she had also lost three precious days trying to round up the strays.

Her father would not be pleased about that. But then, he had not been pleased about her determination to lead the trail drive as far as Saint Louis. In fact, he had been enraged—if for no other reason than the Kiowa and Comanche massacre of the Warren wagon train west of Fort Worth only three weeks earlier—and had forbidden her to go ahead with her plan to lead the trail drive.

Only, she had slipped away from the ranch before he realized it and could no longer stop her.

And if all that were not enough to deal with, there was the news Uncle Karl had personally delivered just before she skedaddled from the ranch. The hide and tallow factory she was building—its note she had personally signed—had been called . . . by none other than Guillermo Obregon. A stepped-on rattler had nothing on that shitty bastard.

But what she could not deal with, what had spurred her to make the dangerous trail drive in the first place, was the other news Uncle Karl had brought with him.

Max had gone and gotten himself engaged.

Furiously, she scrubbed her face with a threadbare washcloth, wiping away not only grime and dust but big, snotty tears.

HOUSTON
JUNE 1872

This time of year, Sarita delighted in standing on the holystoned white deck, letting the leaves of overhanging trees slip through her fingers as the *Bayou Queen* cruised the Buffalo Bayou. In her opinion, it far exceeded the mighty Rio Grande.

Profusions of seventy-five-foot-high magnolias, fragrant with blossoms, lined the shores—along with moss-draped Spanish oaks, towering pines, wild grapes, trumpet vines, and passionflowers. Beaver and turtles paused to watch the steamboat's passing. White herons, cranes, and thousands of ducks plied the gently moving water she had once scorned as just a muddy ditch.

Her bucolic reverie was quickly vanquished by a humming swarm of mosquitoes, and she started slapping.

"You swat one mosquito," a male voice teased behind

her, "and you invite a score to show up for its memorial."

She turned to find Bram Winthrop standing so close she could smell his pomade—and the spirits on his breath. He was a good-looking, well-dressed young man with a devastating smile and curly ash-brown hair already receding at his temples. Word along the river had it that he was quite the libertine that Wade's father must have been before Fiona, then Thérèse, had civilized Alex—or at least tried to.

Word also had it Bram was a Republican appointee by day, a Ku Klux Klan member by night, and a professional gambler in between. On the runs between Houston and Galveston, he would play Three Card Monte. Like many of the gamblers who plied their craft on the Houston-Galveston route, Bram took advantage of cigars and champagne in buckets of ice offered by competing river packets.

She feigned a smile. He was a paying customer—a slightly inebriated customer—and then there were wharfage fees to keep in mind. They had skyrocketed. "Mosquitoes are only one of the risks you take when you run the river, sir."

His smile was daunting. "Such as?"

Damn his cavalier ass. He was seeing how far he could push her. "Such as alligators."

He rested a hand on the brightly-painted bulwark. His long fingers, perfect for the gambler's sleight-of-hand artiste, were near enough that they fingered the lace flounces of her yellow gingham daydress.

No matter what kind of man's work had been required

of her when running the river, she had striven to dress prettily. And after six years as Wade's wife, she still strove to look her best. He might not have Bram's charisma, but he had something better—at least for her. He was pure, sensual male. And his bedside manners were not too bad either. Considering the amount of time devoted to their bed, she was mildly surprised she had yet to conceive.

"I would imagine you get bored, Mrs. Paladín, restricted as you are on the steamboat."

He continued to finger a flounce of her dress. Houston's San Jacinto Street wharf was around the next couple of bends—an excuse for her to escape. "If you'll excuse me, we'll soon be docking."

"There you are, Miz Sarita," came Tom's bellowy voice. "Esther will be ready when you are."

With relief, she looked at Tom, who had come up behind Bram. "Thank you, Tom. I'm coming."

Still, when she went to step away, Bram did not relinquish his hold on the gingham fabric. Startled, her gaze flew up to his. He smiled. "So, how do you occupy your time when not confined to your quarters?"

The question was by implication completely impertinent, and her mouth dropped open.

Tom reached around Bram and jerked the flounce loose. "Your dress seems to be snagged on a splinter, Miz Sarita."

Tom's move and his comment was so unexpected, Bram did not seem to have time to react. She swung away before a confrontation could occur, but she did not miss the rage that emblazoned Bram's face at Tom's impertinence.

As she passed by Bram, she focused inordinate attention on Tom. "Would you ask Esther to meet me on the wharf after we have unloaded?"

She did not tell Wade about Bram. Wade was like his father when it came to guarding his possessions—deadly.

Almost two hours later, after settling the passenger and freight ladings, she joined Esther, a gray-haired Negress with high cheek bones and beautiful, soulful eyes. Tom was waiting with his wife on the wharf. "Mr. Wade wanted me to accompany you and my wife," he explained.

"Yes, of course." Houston, for all its phenomenal growth—nearly 12,000 people strong now—was still basically a city of unsaved and unsavory souls.

"I brought your parasol, Miz Sarita." Esther passed it to her as the three boarded the mule-drawn trolley bound for Market Square.

The Freedmen's Bureau shared offices with City Hall, located on the second floor of the Municipal Building. The first floor was allocated to a fish market. The Freedmen's Bureau, established to help slaves make the transition to freedom after the War Between the States, was being phased out, but it still contained vital records.

Sarita took a seat before the subassistant's commissioner's desk. Completely bald, Harold Bittermeyer wore beer-bottom spectacles. He folded veined and liver-spotted hands on his desk. "How can I help you, Miss—Miss—?"

"Mrs. Wade Paladín." She planted her parasol tip between her high-laced shoes and folded her hands atop its tortoiseshell handle. "And we will need two more chairs. For Mr. and Mrs. Tom Wheelwright."

His bushy brows shot up above the rims of his glasses, but he stepped to the door and ordered two chairs brought in, then returned. Nodding at the Wheelwrights, he turned back to Sarita. "Now, clothing, food, health care, jobs—what is it they want from the Freedmen's Bureau?"

"Realizing the Freedman's Bureau also helps reunite families, we are here to find the daughter of Mr. and Mrs. Wheelwright. That would be a Miss Rebecca Wheelwright."

"The Oakland Sugar Plantation last had her papers," Esther put in anxiously. "That was eight years ago, when her father and me were sold to Master Allen. Becky would be fifteen by now."

Bittermeyer sighed. "What you are asking, these bills of sale can present rather a convoluted trail, when—"

He broke off, waiting as a young man in vest and sleeves chivied two straight-back chairs through the door and Tom and Esther seated themselves. "Clark, get me the Harris County File of Enslaved Africans."

"What I am asking," Sarita said after the young man left, "is for an egregious wrong to be righted per the orders of the President of the United States."

"Ma'am, President Johnson also ordered the Bureau to find steady employment and help the freedmen establish themselves on their own lands, as well as a small directive of restoring social order. And that's a mighty big order in itself."

Clark reappeared, file in hand.

The old man opened it, flipped through the pages, rubbed a hand over his balding pate. "Well, Mrs. Paladín, it appears that The Freedmen's Bureau has, indeed, done its job in documenting property ownership and transfers." He paused, his horny finger anchored on one line, and looked up at her. "The last owner of Rebecca Wheelwright was a Mr. Guillermo Obregon."

Wade sailed his Stetson onto one of the horns of the burly, wooly bison head mounted on the office back wall. He had located the Secretary of State's tiny office at one end of the capitol's multi-forked corridors. "Nice trophy."

"Property of the last occupant." Grinning widely, Kerry rounded the desk to deliver a wallop of a hug despite his missing left arm. "You should see Governor Davis's office, Wade. Or—hey, better yet—the Governor's Mansion. Davis is hosting a fundraiser tonight for the upcoming primaries. He's campaigning for re-election. Is Sarita with you? You two can come with Cat and me!"

Wade slouched into the spindle chair and stretched out his legs. "I left her off with your beloved. Catarina tells us it's going to be a wing-ding affair, but I let Sarita handle our social calendar."

Kerry returned to his chair, tilting it on its back legs. He looked happy. Wade didn't know if he would ever get used to that frockcoat's knotted sleeve. "I've missed you. Who's minding the shop?"

He laced his fingers behind his head. "Billy and Esther. Which is why I'm here in Austin. By the way, that railroad The Barony's invested in takes a sorry second place to traveling by horseback from Houston."

"But it got you here a damn sight quicker. So, what's so important you had to hightail it here?"

He leaned forward, forearms braced on his thighs, hands clasped between his knees. "It's about Tom Wheelwright, Kerry. He's in jail, awaiting trial next week. I've done everything I can to spring him, but I keep meeting dead ends."

Kerry hiked a brow. "What's he charged with?"

"A couple of months back, a professional gambler running the river on our steamer made a pass at Sarita—had hold of her dress and wouldn't let her go when she tried to leave. If I had known about it, I would have stomped a mud hole in him. As it was, Tom stepped in—simply tugged the dress from the gambler's fingers.

"No one thought any more about it, until two days later, when a sheriff boarded the *Bayou Queen*. Seems our riverboat gambler was the one who filed charges against Tom. Claims Tom stole his pocket watch."

"Any proof?"

He expelled a breath. "Yeah. Sheriff found the watch in Tom's coat pocket."

"Do you think Tom did steal it?

"Not a chance. You've met him, Kerry. I think to get

even, Winthrop pulled one of his sleights-of-hand tricks and fobbed it off on—"

"Did you say Winthrop? *Bram* Winthrop?"

"You know him?"

"No. Heard of him, though. He's a Republican appointee. Some insignificant office. Don't remember which one at the moment. What I do remember is hearing that he is a lackey of Guillermo Obregon's. Despite the size of our Texas, its political cronies are a petty tight bunch and word does get around."

"If Obregon has Winthrop in his pocket, Kerry, then Tom will swing. Damn, Obregon just will not let up."

Kerry tunneled fingers through his red locks. "Since I'm not a Republican, I don't have much pull, but I will investigate it and do what I can."

"Thanks, man." He did not want to ask the next question, but he could not help himself. "Have you heard anything from Dad?" The years without contact were a stone in his heart. He knew he could make the first move, but it would have to be on his father's terms—and groveling just plain stuck in his craw.

"Only through infrequent letters Cat and Thérèse exchange. Invitations to Thanksgiving dinners—which, of course, I have ordered Cat to decline. Ranch news—Dad's investing in the lumber industry. Sawmills, some box and cross tie factories. He's banking on the railroad boom."

"Yeah, and I'm banking on the steamboat bust."

"You're getting out of the rivercraft business?"

He crooked a lopsided grin. "Hell, no. It's in my blood

now. Just got a hunch. With the railroads stealing some of our passenger load, I believe that barges are the way to go for the future. At least in the Buffalo Bayou area. I've taken out a note to purchase a pair of small, powerful rigs to tow heavy lumber and cotton barges down to Galveston."

"Just make sure Obregon is not on the board of the bank that made your note."

"Yep, Sis wrote me about that fiasco with her note. Looks as though he's tightening the screws on us Paladíns. I'd written her back about Becky—Tom and Esther's daughter. As if The Barony didn't already have enough problems with Obregon. With it being so close to Brownsville, I'm hoping that Tara—"

"I never knew the Wheelwrights had a daughter."

"I'm told she's fifteen now. But about eight or so years ago, Obregon bought the child outright. I'm hoping Tara can keep an ear to the ground for any news of the Wheelwright girl."

His brother's green eyes grew solemn. "Did you know that sadness has winnowed Sis? She has always been slender, but Thérèse writes she is but a shadow of herself."

He glanced up from his clasped palms, confusion knitting his brows. "No. Why? What sadness?"

"Cat tells me that we males have a tendency to overlook the obvious when it comes to emotions. Seems our sister is pining away for Max. Only Max got engaged last year. Wedding is slated for this spring."

"Well, I'll be damned. That's a pretty long engagement. What does Uncle Karl say?"

"You know Uncle Karl. The original man of few words."

"Sure 'nough, but his actions always seem to speak up pretty loudly."

"Oh, he's well respected here in Austin circles . . . ."

"But? What did your pause mean?"

"I'm not sure, Wade. Ever since Jamie died You would think it was Karl's son who had passed away, not Niall's. I sometimes sense something rustling, like dead leaves, just behind Uncle Karl's eyes."

WITH MARIA ELENA ON HIS arm, Karl paused in the wide entry of the palatial Governor's Mansion and eyed the magnificent room. Directly in front, an impressive grand staircase curved to the left, climbing nineteen feet to the second floor—but it was the crystal chandelier overhead that nailed his attention.

*"Dios, mio, "*Maria Elena breathed, her cushiony hand going to her bosom and her round eyes following his upward.

"Yes, that is gas lighting, dear one."

And she was dear to him. All these years, she had been there to ease the pain of lost courtroom battles, friends' deaths, the mercurial temperament of a lawyer's finances— and to celebrate cases won, to provide savory dinners, and to devote comfort in bed. "It would seem the world is moving on without us."

Double parlors opened off the entry and he escorted her to the right, into a less crowded one. Light chatter, laughter, and tinkling wine glasses greeted their arrival. "Perhaps we'll find Max and Ingrid in here."

Lime-green draperies framed floor-length windows and color-matched seating was provided around the room's perimeter. A Negro in livery carrying a silver tray moved among the guests. Max and his fiancée were not among them, but he spotted Catarina with Kerry—and Sarita and Wade.

A surprise, as it had been some years since he had seen Wade. An unsettling surprise, because the young man looked so much like his father. Tall and dark, with that hard stamp of confidence in chiseled features. Except Wade's features were softened somewhat by his imperturbable attitude, where Alex's countenance was always pure intensity.

If he regretted anything—and Karl figured he owed a legion of regrets—he regretted most giving in to the temptation to kiss Rafaela on that fateful night. Yes, that precipitous act had strained the relationship between him and Rafaela for a while, but time had transformed their momentary passion into an easy friendship, enriched by mutual respect.

But Alex . . . . Though his friend had never mentioned the indiscretion after that night, the constraint between them festered in Karl's heart like a bullet wound—a wound he was certain would never heal. He knew there was no way he could possibly redeem himself with Alex.

"Uncle Karl!" Wade greeted him with a hearty handshake. "Do you know I still have tucked away somewhere that yo-yo you gave each of us kids?"

At that, Catarina grinned. "Kerry kept me from falling head first from the hitching post when I was trying to play with mine." She slid her husband a saucy glance. "But you didn't keep me from falling head over heels in love with you."

"You did not," he teased back. "You were only seven and you hated me because I took you to task for such a foolhardy risk."

She thumped her fan on his chest. "I was embarrassed, Kerry Paladín! You had me upside down."

"Children, children!" Max grinned as he and his fair-haired fiancée joined the small group. "Stop your arguing this instant!"

Max introduced his fiancée to Wade and Sarita. Wearing an expensive watered silk bustle dress with train, Ingrid Dreschner smiled politely. She was the refined and lovely daughter of one of San Antonio's affluent German families, but Karl sensed she felt uncomfortable among the boisterous Paladíns. "We are only lacking Tara now," Catarina complained.

At the mention of Tara, Karl flicked a glance at Max, but his handsome features mirrored nothing. Karl could only feel his own deep disappointment. Without knowing exactly how, he strongly sensed Max had cared deeply about Tara. But his self-serving adopted son had clay feet. Max would never appreciate the role that was his to play.

"I remember when Thérèse had the three of us cooking Thanksgiving dinner," Sarita said, "and Tara tossed down the shot glass of brandy Thérèse had reserved for the pecan pie."

Catarina snapped open her fan, her gaze sweeping over the circle of faces. "I imagine by this time, Tara is on her way to Brownsville. I must admit I am a little worried."

Max merely grabbed a flute from a passing servant's tray. "Brownsville?"

"Why?" Karl asked.

Sarita sent Wade an apologetic look. "Well, between our concern about the Wheelwright's daughter—and then Tara's bank note disaster—" She paused and glanced at Catarina. "Do I have it right, Catarina? You are the one Thérèse wrote."

Catarina's fan swished. "Yes, her letter arrived in today's mail. It seems our Tara has reached her limit with Obregon. She has it in her head that, as a female, she stands a better chance of ferreting out where Rebecca Wheelwright might be. Since Dad was fit to kill after Tara drove cattle to Saint Louis last year, she swore Thérèse to secrecy. But Thérèse is wor—"

At that moment, Governor Davis joined them, clapping a hand on Kerry's shoulder. "Well, Son, have you made up your mind about making a run with me for the gubernatorial bid?"

Kerry grinned. "Yes, sir, I have."

"What?" Karl and Wade spoke in unison.

"I have asked young Kerry to be my running mate." The gaunt, goateed Davis grinned.

"I'm going for it."

Max shot a questioning glance at Karl, but Karl strove to keep his countenance bland. Kerry had said nothing to him about any interest in the gubernatorial race.

Kerry's political views weighed more toward a moderate populist platform—and Davis was about as arch-conservative as any politician could ever be. Was the taste of politics eroding Kerry's focus on Texas itself?

"Good decision." Davis clapped him on the shoulder again. "The Republican Party will be most delighted."

"I sincerely doubt that," Kerry told the governor. "I am running on the Democratic ticket—only not for lieutenant governor. The office of Governor is my only objective."

Tension buzzed between them loud enough to be heard over the room's conversations. Recovering quickly, Davis glared at Kerry. "You are digging your own grave, son."

Karl could only agree.

WHEN KERRY FLICKED THE buggy reins, the bay broke into a trot beneath the newly erected gas streetlights. Catarina laid her head on Kerry's shoulder. He buried his nose in her hair and delighted in its lavender aroma. "Tired, honey?"

"Hmmm," she nodded, huddling deeper into her satin and velvet cloak. "And this is only the beginning of the campaign. I don't know how you do it, Kerry. How you keep up such a pace."

It had been a grueling five days since the clash with Davis at the Governor's Mansion. Three speaking engagements—one a lost cause at a state dentists meeting held at the Smith's Hotel, as only five dentists were present. Those meet and greet engagements were interspersed with his frustratingly tedious and fruitless duties as Secretary of State.

Most of the time, when he left his office for the day, he felt as if he had accomplished nothing worthwhile, nothing that made any headway in what he wanted for Texas—a vigorous action to balance the budget and an improved educational system, especially the establishment of an agricultural and mechanical college.

The only glowing aspect of his busy days was the release of Wade's Black friend, Tom Wheelwright, accomplished with significant haggling on Kerry's part—with both the Republican and Democratic partisans.

And haggling—compromising—had never been part of his personality. He was too much like his father in that regard.

He could only hope his grass-roots campaign would be as productive as Tom Wheelwright's release had been. For the first time, Kerry was selling himself—his word, his integrity. A yoke of responsibility had settled heavily onto his shoulders. He could always withdraw. But there was an obligation to the people of Texas that clung to him like a leech the moment someone trusted him with his vote. It was not easy.

Austin's gas lights faded behind them. Although the horse barn and feed bag were still some distance away, the bay broke into a canter toward the limestone home that was only slightly larger but more substantial than their first home, the little adobe in San Antonio.

When the buggy rounded the corner onto Shoal Creek, Kerry could see the glowing orange light flickering above the houses scattered among the oaks along the creek. The bay whinnied and began shying beneath the reins. A knot spasmed in Kerry's gut.

"Oh, God!" Catarina breathed. Her fingers gripped his thigh.

In front of their stone home, three tall wooden crosses burned like the fires of hell, lighting up the night. He shivered despite the heat toasting his skin.

So this was what it meant to buck the Ku Klux Klan.

BROWNSVILLE

A decade earlier, the *Brownsville Ranchero* had described its border town as one in which "fandangos are held every night and women as beautiful as houris exhibit their charms without the least reserve. Here congregate desperadoes, the vile of both sexes, adventurers, numberless groggeries, and houses of worse fame. Vice in its ghastliest form holds high carnival at all times. Ship masts stretch across the water as far as the eye can see."

However, by 1872, Brownsville was still struggling to recover from the war years—which had been buoyed up by the smuggling trade—and from the hurricane of 1867, which had wiped parts of Brownsville from the face of the Texas map. Union troops had reoccupied the town and were launching a massive construction effort to repair war damage to Fort Brown.

Tara swung down from the dusty stagecoach and headed for Miller's Hotel—a longtime popular establish-ment in Brownsville—but because of the housing shortage, even it was booked up.

"Try the *Whiteville*," a walleyed desk clerk suggested. "Down on the river."

The *Whiteville* turned out to be an old, out-of-service steamboat converted into a makeshift hotel. Once settled into one of its tiny, grimy cabins, she first made the rounds in the customary fountains of gossip—the billiard parlors and saloons.

The Rampant Colt Billiard Hall and Reading Room was a two-story brick affair between Elizabeth and Washington Street. There, a pimply-faced youth shook his head slowly at her inquiry about a young Negress, Rebecca Wheelwright. "Can't say I ever heard of the gal."

When two more billiard parlors rendered similar results, she began to make a round of Brownsville's thirty-three saloons.

Maybe it was her height—as tall as most men—or maybe it was the pocket Colt that settled disputes, which she carried in her leather fringed jacket pocket, but few saloon patrons hassled her.

Then, too, she was not the only woman to be found in the saloons. Texas had a huge German population, and their beer halls were kept by the owners' daughters or wives, occasionally serving as barmaids and waitresses.

She was just the only woman in men's clothing.

Neither the saloon patrons nor the soiled doves who plied their trade at the establishments had heard of Rebecca Wheelwright. Tara could only hope that Obregon had not sold the girl across the Rio Grande to work the Mexican brothels. If so, the Paladíns would have yet one more score to settle with Guillermo Obregon.

After fruitless inquiries at the first five saloons, she decided to try a different tact—this time, most reluctantly, asking for one of the two Brownsville contacts Thérèse had provided. The Frenchwoman's acquaintances were most unlikely to be working the seamier side of Brownsville society.

"An old friend, *ma cherie*. A former Texas Ranger who won't be stampeded. Buck McHenry served under Rip Ford in the '58 campaign in the Comancheria." Thérèse's beautifully painted lips formed a *moue* of regret. *"Helas,* Buck McHenry has no permanent address for me to give you!"

At the Occidental Saloon, the clatter of thrown dice and the click of the spun roulette wheel welcomed Tara. Above an oak-paneled bar, bordered by spittoons, its wall exhibited the prerequisite painting of a voluptuous naked lady and a pair of mossy steer horns mounted to either side of her.

The Occidental was jammed with miners, cowboys, soldiers, and railroad workers looking for a chance to tempt fate and fortune.

She scanned the room, trying to match Thérèse's description to one of the many faces in the saloon.

An old codger in spectacles and suspenders nodded at the back of a man in a faded red gabardine shirt slouched at the bar. "That'd be Buck McHenry."

Peering through the glaze of smoke, she did not hold out much hope. From behind, the bow-legged man, his rangy frame barely exceeding hers in height, looked hardscrabble. As he downed a mug of beer, his shaggy gray head was tilted back. Only his six-shooter and big rowel-spurred boots, one propped on the gleaming brass foot rail, lent him any semblance of authority.

She halted beside him. "I understand you're Buck McHenry. Thérèse told me—" Her eyes slammed to a dead stop as they moved from the tin mug in his hand to the man's suntanned profile—smooth as a baby's bottom. Though prematurely gray, he couldn't be much more than thirty or so.

"I've been called by that name . . . and a few others." Above his gray horseshoe mustache, contrasting black-as-coal, sloping brows framed old-soul blue eyes. They inventoried her from her scuffed boots up past her worn denims and leather-fringed jacket to her single thick braid slung over one shoulder.

Dazed, she nodded at his nearly empty mug. "Can I buy you another?"

"Harvey," he called to the aproned bartender, "I'll have another round of your tarantula juice."

He turned his flashing eyes back to her. "Can't say as how I have ever had a female—at least, you're purported to be, Miss Paladín—offer to buy me a drink."

He rattled her badly, knowing about her, as he did. She ignored the insult spoken by his deep Western drawl. At least, he was educated. "I'm looking for someone. A young Negress—Rebecca Wheelwright. I'll make it worth your while if you help me find her."

"And I'm looking for a nice spread to settle down on, ma'am." He paused as the bartender set before her a mug and then refilled his. "Get your pa to part with a section or so, and I might consider helping you."

"Paladín land ain't for sale."

"Neither am I." He turned his back on her to exchange words with a Chinaman—his black queue as long as her braid—who had sidled up to the bar on the other side of him.

"Jackass is another name you could be called by." She hefted her mug and sloshed its contents on the back of his red shirt. She stalked off, slamming the saloon's batwing doors wide, opening onto the boardwalk that flanked the dusty street.

Dejected, she sought out her remaining source supplied by Thérèse—Mrs. Moses Solomon. Tara could only hope this source proved more hospitable than Jackass McHenry.

She barely remembered Charlotte Solomon and her husband, the owner of Matamoros's Emporium, from a visit they had made to The Barony the summer Jamie died.

Blonde ringlets gone nearly gray but with a complexion still resembling peaches and cream, Charlotte Solomon sat in her rocker with a cup of tea and regaled her with stories of the old days.

"I came to Matamoros from Liverpool, 1833 I think it was, with my brother, a parson—Thérèse's second hus-band. Like all Matamoros females, I swooned over your father, Tara. So tall, so dark, so devilishly handsome. Yet it was the short but oh-so-impassioned Moses I gave my heart to."

The Solomon parlor was crowded with knick-knacks.

Tara folded her long legs under the settee in an effort to find a place to tuck her dirt-crusted boots. She took a sip from the porcelain cup. "I imagine Matamoros must have been much wilder than it is now."

"Oh, yes, my dear. Drunkards loitered everywhere and some men died of drink. Grog shops, taverns, and barrooms lined the few streets. Between the Mexican bandits and the Indians, we were constantly taking shelter. After the Mexican-American War, we moved across the river here to Brownsville. Nowadays, McNelly's Texas Rangers take care of the bandits and Indians outside Brownsville."

At the mention of the Texas Rangers, Tara's mind flitted to Buck McHenry.

Jackass.

Charlotte continued. "And Mr. Obregon keeps Brownsville itself orderly. Why, not long ago, when a dozen cowboys got out of hand and started shooting up the town, he had his men take them down and then stack their bodies like cordwood in the square."

Tara's teacup rattled in its saucer. "Obregon? *Guillermo* Obregon?"

"Why, yes, dear."

She felt a trill of anticipation, which she trusted would be satisfaction by the time she left Brownsville.

"You might say the Mayor, the sheriff, and the town councilmen all answer to Mr. Obregon. These days, ruffians steer clear of troublemaking. Else they face Mr. Obregon's form of justice."

"And that form of justice would be?"

Charlotte's seamed lips twisted in a wry smile. "Branding . . . bullets . . . hanging . . . family members going missing . . . ."

Tara set aside her cup and saucer and leaned forward. "That is precisely why I am here, Mrs. Solomon—a missing family member."

THE NEW ORLEANS FRENCH-STYLE convent served as a day and boarding school for girls. Occupying a full block in Brownsville, it was enclosed by a ten-foot, white-plastered adobe wall and housed the cloistered teaching order of the Sisters of the Incarnate Word and Blessed Sacrament. Here—so Charlotte had indicated—Tara might find Becky.

Tara pulled on the rope beside the heavy wooden double doors and a bell rang somewhere inside. Within the fortress-like stone walls, the smell of incense was pervasive and heavy, and so was the muted patter of shoes on polished wood.

On the convent's second floor, behind full-length shutters, Reverend Mother Maria St. Jerome met with Tara. At the sight of the Colt's grip protruding from Tara's coat pocket, the nun raised a grizzled, bushy brow.

"My apologies." She removed the pistol and eased it onto the modest desk besides the flickering taper. "For protection, Mother."

"The Blessed Virgin protects us here, my child."

A perfect opening. She slid into the hardback chair.

"I'm seeking to find out if, some years ago, the convent offered protection to an eight-year-old girl, Rebecca Wheelwright, Reverend Mother. She'd be about fifteen by now."

The nun pursed her wrinkled lips. "Within the Lord's House, there is such a thing as discretion."

"Discretion and donations are the very foundation of The Barony's success, Reverend Mother."

Within minutes, Rebecca Wheelwright appeared at the Reverend Mother's door. The flat-chested black girl, with her wiry ebony hair caught in a topknot and huarache-clad feet, was as regally composed in her threadbare gown as Nefertiti must have been in her royal robes.

"Enter, my child." Mother Maria beckoned with an imperious finger. "It would seem you have family wanting you. Now, if only you have the various objects you have pilfered that the Convent is wanting back."

Huge brown eyes with lashes as thick as a quadroon's fan blinked innocently. "Reverend Mother, I have only taken what I consider mine."

Tara had to grin. Here was embodied the Paladín creed.

A FLEECE SHAWL BUNDLED what goods the Reverend Mother had missed confiscating from Rebecca. Tara glimpsed remaining among the meager clothing a silver candlestick holder and a small bronze chalice.

Quickly, she collected her own gear at the *Whiteville*. She was anxious to leave Brownsville behind, as was Becky. Apparently, Obregon trafficked in slaves and had planned to sell off Becky before the girl had made her escape.

Tara felt a crushing disappointment that she had yet to accomplish the rest of her mission, to investigate Obregon thoroughly on his own turf—to find his Achilles Heel. And everyone—even Guillermo Obregon—had that weak spot, hers being that damnable Max. But getting Becky out of Brownsville, safely, was her priority.

Together, she and the girl, her bundle of goods balanced atop her head, set out for the stagecoach depot.

They got no further than the *Whiteville's* gangplank, anchored in the levee dirt.

A bulldog of a man in a bowler hat greeted them, sweeping it off and bowing. His face evidenced hard won skirmishes with the pox. "Mr. Obregon requests the honor of your presence."

She should have expected this. If Buck McHenry knew of her presence in Brownsville, then it stood to reason that Obregon most certainly would. "And if I have other plans?"

"You will be unable to keep them, regrettably."

Her hand dropped to her jacket's pocket, only to find it empty. Then she remembered—she had left her Colt on the Reverend Mother's desk. Son of a bitch!

The look in the cold eyes of Obregon's henchman convinced her now was not the time to quibble. She felt a shiver of apprehension but smiled agreeably. "I must say I have been looking forward to meeting with our family's foe."

Behind the Moorish-arched gates and corbelled brick walls of a Spanish Colonial hacienda, set a mile or so from town, presided Guillermo Obregon himself. He was nothing like the ogre Tara had conjured.

In a way, he possessed Max's Greek God-varnished looks, only not as tall. There was something cankerous in Obregon's features, though she could not quite say what. Where his henchman had that gimlet glaze, Guillermo Obregon's eyes were alive with unnerving pleasure.

He greeted them in his studio, sunlit by windows set high in one whitewashed wall. His paint-splattered smock was partially open, revealing a cream-colored silk vest. Setting aside his palette and brush on a brass-hinged *tabaret*, its three drawers pulled out to reveal hundreds more of his paintbrushes, he smiled. "What a rewarding encounter."

Rather than acknowledge him, she canted her head, eyeing the canvas behind him. She made out only what appeared to be a maelstrom of dust against a desert backdrop. "I'm no art critic, Mr. Obregon, but your latest work must, indeed, be a masterpiece—at least in your humble opinion."

Ahh, I see you possess your father's gift for sparring— and your mother's commonplace humor." He looked past her and Becky at his henchman. "Smythe, step outside and tell Beatriz to bring us tea."

"We won't be staying that long. I just wanted to see what a totally unprincipled human looks like."

"Oh, I do believe you two will be staying for some time. Stealing two females from Paladín should equal the theft of my daughter, Sarita, do you not agree? You see, it is now a matter of family honor. Of justice, if you will." He shrugged. "Or perhaps merely revenge—for I possess attributes besides painting—infinite patience, for one. This meeting has been a long time coming."

"You can't keep us here."

"Not only can I keep you—I can kill you. Quite easily. On the other hand, why should I not simply turn a nice profit—sell you into Mexico, where the two of you will surely become lost forever in the slave trade?"

At that moment, his henchman stepped back inside the studio. "Smythe, would you escort our two . . . *visitors* . . . to the carriage house for the time being. They can take their tea there."

Once they were in the tiled corridor, Tara thought of making a run for it, but she knew both she and Becky could never escape. Obregon's human mastiff of a guard could easily bring them down. Better to wait for a more promising opportunity.

The carriage house looked like a fortress. Its darkened interior smelled of human sweat, excrement, and abject fear.

"Enjoy yourselves, ladies." Smythe swept another bow with his bowler.

The pure panic Tara experienced surprised her and she clenched her teeth against the hammering impulse to scream. But before the last shaft of sunlight was extinguished by the closing door, an explosive noise reverberated in her ears—and Smythe the bulldog crumpled to the floor.

Still stunned, Tara gaped at the man whose bowler remained clutched in his hand. A hole was pumping blood from the crown of his head.

A glimmer of glee lighting her dark brown eyes, Becky handed Tara her Colt. "Figured the convent had no need of your pistol, Miz Tara."

THE BARONY
MARCH 1873

'*Bon Dieu!* Thérèse flung the invitation back onto Alex's desk. "Refusing to attend the celebration party—your grudge will gain you nothing but grief, Alex Paladín! You must keep open the lines of communication."

Alex picked up the invitation to the Democrats' celebration of Kerry's uncomfortably close gubernatorial nomination victory. Wadding it, he perfectly arced it into his office cuspidor. Amazingly, Kerry's more realistic platform had won his heated primary battle over a Democrat candidate "devoted to destruction of the foul Republican Reconstruction."

Alex's indifference to the discarded invitation brought on her fury. Magenta skirts in hand, she crossed the intervening space and slammed her palms onto his leather-topped desk. Her gaze scorched his. "Grief, *bon sang*, Alex! Do you hear me? Your season of mourning for Fiona has become a lifetime of mourning."

He raised a brow. "Just what has this invitation to do

with Fiona's death?"

Her eloquent eyes entreated him. "It has to do with your life. If someone or something has died in your life, do not die with it, Alex."

He scanned her flushed face, its exotic beauty more pronounced by her remarkable wrath. "What is this really about, Thérèse?"

Surprising him, she buried her face in her palms and mumbled something again about life.

"What?" This woman he had taken as a wife profoundly perplexed him. Fiona, he had been able to understand, at least sometimes, but Thérèse's Latin temperament left him bewildered more often than not.

She raised her head and looked at him through eyes glistening with tears. "I am carrying within me a life we have created, *mon amour*."

AUSTIN

Buck McHenry fingered the antique gold parchment of the invitation, replete with wax seal. Eyeing the flourish of the script, he wondered just what on God's green earth he was doing attending a function that promised nothing but ennui, superficiality, and arse-kissing.

Politics—the magician's grand illusion. Or was it delusion. He was well versed in the politician's power of persuasion.

As a naive West Point cadet, he had returned home that first year to celebrate the Christmas holidays among Dallas's elite echelon of society. His father was a distinguished

Dallas banker who made a fortune hauling freight by ox teams from Houston—and who later made an even greater fortune by embezzling his bank customers' funds. When that corruption was uncovered, Buck's father committed suicide.

As for Buck . . . he supposed he had committed his own version of suicide. His hair had then turned gray overnight. He had dropped out of West Point, where honor and honesty were everything, and disappeared into the wilds of West Texas to live with the nomadic Mescalero Apaches. He reappeared whenever he felt he could no longer resist his compulsion for experiencing some intellectual stimulus.

This time, however, he was reappearing at the behest of Thérèse del Valle Engler Paladín. Once she had learned her stepdaughter had, indeed, made contact with him in Brownsville—and no telling what the hellcat stepdaughter had shared—Thérèse had immediately written, requesting his assistance.

Years before, that freshly widowed Frenchwoman had taken him in, a war-weary renegade, and taught him a great deal about the rudiments of lovemaking. He supposed he owed her this—representing her and Paladín at his son Kerry's primary victory party.

As Buck mounted the Driskill Hotel's steps to the Grand Ballroom on the second floor, he swore this would be the last time he would ever wear a penguin suit. He presented his invitation to the doorman and entered the Grand Ballroom's glittering ambiance.

A military band, from the newly established Fort Sam

Houston out of San Antonio, occupied the left wall. "The Yellow Rose of Texas" reverberated through the ballroom. Adorned with red, white, and blue bunting, a refreshment table occupied the center wall. To Buck's right, a receiving line was stretched along the third wall.

From his cadet experiences at West Point, Buck knew something about receiving line protocol, but he watched the guest ahead of him anyway. Accordingly, he removed his right glove. Once past the receiving line, he intended to head straight for the refreshment table.

When his turn came, he spoke his name to Andrew Jackson Hamilton, the introducer. Though the former military governor of Texas had changed his political views as expediency demanded, his friendship with Kerry Paladín remained constant.

Hamilton introduced Buck to the guest of honor, Kerry Paladín, adding, "Mr. McHenry is attending as Mr. and Mrs. Alex Paladín's designated representative."

No way in hell could Buck miss the crush of disappointment that blighted the younger man's features. Well, that was something they both had in common—fathers who had not cared enough to stay around.

Kerry Paladín had more disappointment headed his way if he somehow managed to be elected governor. The years since the Civil War had been particularly difficult for Texas. The state had been bucking for its own reunification, insisting it had the right to be an independent republic again.

While the U.S. Army attempted to enforce martial law,

and the Supreme Court battered the would-be empire, outlaws, freedmen, and carpetbaggers flooded the wild and wooly state.

Buck bowed over the hand of Mrs. Paladín. Kerry's wife, though quite lovely in a majestic way, wore the same stricken expression as her husband, stunned apparently by the old baron's rebuff. But she managed a charming smile that agreed with the glow of her face, as she was heavily with child.

He moved to her right, repeating his name to Kerry's brother, Wade, and his wife, a dimple-faced beauty. They, too, wore that stark, startled look of . . . of what? Dashed hopes? Hearts squashed?

Quickly, he moved to the last person in line and bowed over her extended hand, a ringless feminine one. "Mr. Buck McHenry, mademoiselle," he murmured appropriately, expecting the requisite reply of fripperies.

"Buck McHenry? Well, well, well. We cross paths again."

Immediately, he recognized that dry, derisive drawl, as slow as molasses.

Had sparks flown from the female's fingertips? He looked directly into the eyes of Tara Paladín. Then he blinked . . . and blinked once more.

That thick braid that had resembled a frayed rope when he saw her last had been transformed into a cluster of curls embedded with seed pearls sitting atop the crown of her head. Some kind of satiny pink silk affair swathed low on her bosom and tight across her hips and was then bundled behind her in the latest fashion.

"Tell me . . . where does the name 'Buck' come from? Buckley? Buck skin? Buck shot? Buck *naked?*"

"Buckminster. And no proper lady I know would ever utter the term 'buck naked.'"

She canted her head and batted spectacularly long lashes at him. "Then you might as well know my most obvious secret, Jackass McHenry. I shore ain't no proper lady."

"No," he said slowly, feeling as if his ribs had been tap danced on by a wild bronc. "You certainly do not resemble any lady I have ever met."

"Tell me, does your mustache wax melt when you drink your tea?"

"I drink only rotgut."

"The rum punch might improve your disposition."

"A good spanking might improve yours."

Over lips moist and parted, she glared at him. Others were log-jamming behind him and he felt relieved when he could make good his escape toward the refreshment table.

Not even the rum punch had any effect on the unpleasant feeling that he had just become transformed from disenchanted cowboy to one thoroughly, if instantly, enchanted—and that he would have to deal with the inevitable pain that always followed any major disillusionment.

BUCK MCHENRY'S GRAY horseshoe mustache had tickled the back of Tara's bare hand, but his deep voice tremored her spine. However much as she may have pined for the gallant—and worthless—Max von Hesse-Lippe, that yearning was vanquished by this man who had just stopped before her.

She had never told her father about her run-in with Obregon. Knowing her father, he would have ridden hell for leather to Brownsville and called the man out—without heeding the dangerous fact that he would be trespassing on Obregon Territory.

Her eyes scanning the guests, she spotted Max and his fiancée. Nope, not so much as a tiny pang at the sight of that beautiful couple, clustered with Uncle Karl, Aunt Maria Elena, Uncle Niall, and Aunt Rafaela. The presence of the two older and distinguished couples lent stature to that evening's celebration of Kerry's primary election coup.

Tara's eyes swept the rest of the guests looking for that singular shaggy gray head. Representing Alex and Thérèse Paladín was he? Thérèse had adroitly sidestepped the fact that they would not be attending. But why had Thérèse not informed Tara, before she left The Barony for the celebration in Austin, she was designating Buck McHenry rather than her as their absentee representative?

Unless . . . . ? Could Thérèse be matchmaking on Tara's account?

Well, in that case . . . Tara decided to mix and mingle with the guests. If she had learned anything from that wily French siren, it was that presentation was everything, and not only within the cordon bleu culinary realm.

Unfurling her lace fan, she smiled and nodded graciously as she moved around the room. To her disappointment, Buck McHenry was not to be found among the guests. With a sickening wrench to her stomach, she recalled Thérèse's words—that the former Texas Ranger no longer kept a permanent address.

He came. He went. Obeying only his own internal time schedule. Tara realized she might never see him again.

Where could he have gone to so quickly? And she knew. Or had a good idea, anyway. A man who preferred rotgut over rum punch might well seek to appease his gullet at the first-floor bar. At least, she hoped a hardscrabble man like Buck McHenry would.

She snapped her fan shut and, whirling, edged through the crowd and out the Grand Ballroom's double doors. Voluminous skirts in hand, she dashed down the staircase, dodging guests coming up, and came to an abrupt halt at the dining salon doorway.

Inside, only a few guests patronized the bar, but she would recognize that bow-legged man with his rangy frame anywhere. One big rowel-spurred boot was prompted on the brass railing and his shaggy gray head was tilted back, downing doubtlessly a mug of rotgut.

As before, in Brownsville, she halted beside him. When he did not turn to acknowledge her, she rapped him on the shoulder with her fan. He turned his head to fasten those old-soul blue eyes on her. Showing no surprise to find her there, he merely raised one coal-black brow.

She wouldn't let him rattle her. "You once told me you were looking for a nice spread to settle down on. My pa wouldn't part with Paladín land, but I have a few sections of my own."

Beneath his handlebar mustache, a slow smile spread. "The question, Tara Paladín, is would you be willing to settle down with me?"

"With a solitary buckaroo like yourself?" She tilted her head, as if considering. "I don't know. I think I'd have to take you for a trial ride first." Eyes dancing, she tilted her head skywards. "Let's say, in my room above."

KERRY FLICKED THE BUGGY reins, nudging the bay through the frosty night. Behind, Wade, Sarita, and Tara followed in the buggy Wade had rented from Altman's Livery in Austin.

The small, time-worn stone house on Shoal Creek would barely sleep all four of them. Kerry often felt he should have done grander by Catarina. Yet she never complained. Never let him feel sorry for himself following the amputation. Would not accept any offered parental financial help from Niall and Rafaela.

Of course, Kerry's father had never offered any. Not that Kerry would have accepted. Still, he would have felt happy had he known that his father had Kerry's best interests at heart.

Close beside him, Catarina huddled against the chill of the night. The cold wrapped the city like a fist. He smiled down at her upturned face. "You have two of us to keep you warm, sweetheart."

She dimpled. "Maybe even three." She patted the enormous mound of her stomach. "Big as I am, it could well be twins. And soon, I hope."

He grinned. "Twins would mean more votes on my behalf."

He would certainly need them. He should have been happy that night. He was soon to be a father. Against all odds and predictions, he had won the Democratic primary. But running against the solid Republican party of carpetbaggers and scalawags would be almost a farce.

As the token candidate for the weakened Democratic Party, Kerry knew he would be kicked in the teeth, ridiculed, and ultimately defeated.

After all, everyone knew that incumbent Governor Edmund Davis had the Republican ticket and the office of governorship all sewed up. Kerry figured he might well be a Banty hen fighting a chicken hawk.

As usual, his bay abandoned its normal clip-clop pace, breaking into a canter as it rounded the corner onto Shoal Creek. The bay's barn and feed bag beckoned.

When the bay took the corner a little too fast, Kerry hauled on the reins. As soon as he did, one broke completely away from the harness. Trees flashed past. The bay was up to an all-out gallop. He leaned over the dash, grabbing with his one hand for the dragging rein—and when that proved impossible, he went for the brake.

But almost at once came the rolling, tumbling, tossing. Like the ball on a roulette wheel.

As Kerry began to lose consciousness, he heard Catarina's piercing scream.

THE BIG THICKET
APRIL 1873

A life for a life. Or something like that, according to the Good Book. His sister-in-law, Catarina, and her newborn son might still be clinging to theirs, but Wade reckoned that shouldn't hinder him any in taking the lives of the scum buckets who rigged Kerry's buggy incident.

One good thing about running the river, you met lots of people—so you could ask a few questions without seeming too nosey. Provided you were careful, of course.

Wade's destination that day was neither Galveston nor Houston, at opposite ends of Buffalo Bayou, but the Big Thicket north of Houston and southeast of Austin.

While that vast area had never been clearly mapped, Wade knew it was roughly forty miles long and twenty miles wide. It consisted of great stands of yellow pine five and six feet in diameter, dense vegetation, and cypresses bogged down in oozing swamps. The core of the habitat supported deer, bear, panthers, and wolves, as well as plenty of gators.

The Thicket was also renowned for harboring fugitives,

among them Confederate deserters. Soldiers on duty during the war, eager to avoid the gory risks of battle, took to its environs, living off the land, often trading goods with locals while evading lawmen and military guardsmen, none of whom had ever been popular in the lawless Thicket.

Fugitives were not the only specters haunting the place—tales of swamp ghosts and mystery lights enriched its folklore.

So did tales of the Hog Boys, offspring of families that had interbred, who often ran hogs and cattle inside those backwoods. The core of its population was mainly white, with a few Cajuns scraping by on its southeastern edges.

The Hog Boys had roots generations deep in the Thicket's loamy soil. They were Southerners by sympathy and migration—and most of them were devoted followers of the KKK.

Wade had little to go on. The nearly severed harness straps of Kerry's buggy indicated obvious tampering. Wade overheard along the Bayou that Hubert Grimes, grandpappy of the Hog Boys clan, was the power who controlled the Klan all over southeast Texas.

Wade decided now was the time for old man Grimes himself to encounter a higher power—the barrel of Wade's six gun.

Griffin, Catarina's son, born too soon following the buggy accident, was still struggling to survive. Catarina had hemorrhaged for seven long hours, and Kerry's good arm had been snapped at the wrist. With his election battle looming, Kerry had neither the time nor the energy to accomplish his own retribution.

Wade decided he would supply both the time and the energy. If their mother taught them nothing else, she had taught them family was everything.

Cypress Creek's elevation was high, but the stilted shack of Hubert Grimes's was even higher. Under the cover of a canopy of old trees, Wade pulled his canoe ashore, concealing it and his paddles with cypress fronds before wading among the cypress knees to sneak up on the Grimes's shack from behind.

Weak sunlight conspired with a thin morning mist to shroud bearded and buckskinned figures going to and from the hog pens, but Wade heard their voices plain enough.

"Rode her till she bled."

Snickering reverberated through the marsh.

Another voice chimed in. "I'm telling you, Bert, she was a-squealin' like a stuck pig."

That comment alone riled Wade further, but it was the sight of a dozen hooded white sheets pinned like diapers to the wire line, strung from a porch post to the beam of a nearby shed, that really steamed his blood.

Three of the Hog Boys? He could take them on. Where were the others? The womenfolk? The children?

A fourth voice bled through the mist. "Cut that nigger wench some slack, Jake. We got us bigger fish to fry. Kerry Paladín's harping on expanding rights for them monkeys. Time's now for his midnight rope party."

Wade inched toward the shack corner and peered carefully around it.

Bram Winthrop, dressed like a dandy in the midst of all the slop, was helping transfer rifles from the porch into a *bateau*. That bastard wasn't man enough to kiss the hem of Sarita's dress, much less to touch it. He had most certainly earned what was coming to him.

Pop. Pop. Pop.

The shots sounded, like slamming a book on a desktop. The Hog Boys each dropped into the mud, all three shot through a knee.

"Goldurn sumbitch!" Grandpappy was screeching through his grizzled beard, grabbing at the bloody white knob that used to be his right knee.

Jake, whichever of the other two he was, and the other had folded like puppets in the muck and were lying there screaming.

Bram splashed toward the *bateau* and jerked up a carbine. He spun around and pumped the lever. By the time he tried to cock the hammer, Wade had him in his own Colt's sights. "Put it down, Winthrop. No point at all wasting a bullet on you. You're going to swing if I have anything to do with it."

Bram's lips curled in a charming smile. "I think even you would call this a stand-off, Paladín." His carbine barrel still trained on Wade, Bram began to nudge the bateau off the bank into the river.

Shit! He couldn't let the bastard get away. "Bram! Look behind you!"

Bram chuckled, wading backward with each careful step. "You can't be serious, expecting me to—"

Suddenly, he went down, floundering in the murky stream. "Help! Omigod!" His arms thrashed, his gargled screeches ripped the air. "Help me!" Under the water he went. The water spewed and frothed. Foam and blood whirlpooled during the brief tussle between man and alligator. After a few more frenzied moments, Cypress Creek's misty surface was placid once again.

Wade's mood wasn't placid, however—wouldn't be until he reassured himself about Kerry, Catarina, and their infant son. He rode straight through a rainy night that lasted through the next morning to reach Austin.

At Kerry's house on Shoal Creek, a weary-looking Aunt Rafaela met him at the door and all he could do was stutter like a simpleton. "Catarina? She's . . . is she going to be?"

The patrician woman bit her lip and nodded. "She'll be all right. Doc Swanson just dropped by to check on her again."

He took off his rain-soaked hat, beating it against his thigh, then shrugged out of his poncho. "That old boozer?"

Her lips curved in a pitiful attempt at a grin, but her eyes teared up.

He wrapped his free arm around her. "The baby?"

"He and Catarina are both sleeping. Kerry's in the study."

Wade jammed the soggy hat and poncho on the hall tree and headed down the hallway to find Kerry muttering imprecations. Awkwardly, he was wielding his splinted wrist in an attempt to dip his nib pen into the inkwell. "Goddamnit to hell!"

He hurled the pen and Wade inclined his head an inch to avoid the missile. Picking it up where it rolled against the brass spittoon, he reached across the desk to pass back the pen. "Glad it wasn't a knife."

Kerry grunted, laid aside the pen, and slumped back into his chair. "Thanks, Wade."

"Got here as soon as I heard—well, after making a detour."

He grunted. "I can't tell you what a nightmare this is."

"This particular nightmare of yours is forever over." He tucked his thumbs into his belt loops and grinned. "That detour I mentioned took me through the Big Thicket, where I gunned down its Klan."

Slowly, Wade's full implication took hold and a wry smile tipped Kerry's lips. "Our momma always said clan is everything—pun intended. Thank you, brother."

AUSTIN
JULY 1873

At every turn, Kerry confronted roadblocks—if not from the Republicans, then from the Ku Klux Klan. And if it wasn't them, it was his own party acting against him. Elements of the Democratic Party were not happy with his platform of expanding rights for the Negro. All the while, Edmund Davis, his incumbent Republican opponent, was busy looking for mud to sling.

So Kerry supposed he should not have been at all surprised by his visitor that afternoon.

Retired army sergeant, Bob Woodhouse—the assistant

supplied to Kerry by his election team—had been hovering in front of a wall map, sticking tacks into various Texan counties. With the countdown to the election now a matter of weeks, he and Kerry were working Sunday morning at the office in their shirtsleeves, vests unbuttoned.

"There are three basic voting blocs." Bob jammed a scarred finger to the southwestern area of the state. "There, in El Paso County and in Cameron County, are the Rio Grande Democrats—with mostly Spanish surnames. Then there are some widely dispersed Republicans with no single concentration."

The erect sergeant pointed to Travis County. "Austin has a high-grade cross-section of our nation. Their vote could swing either way. These statistics bear out what we believe is possible, sir. With a couple months left to campaign, it seems possible that we just might unseat Davis."

"Possible but hardly probable," a voice proclaimed from the opened door. "In fact, to win this race, Paladín, will take you nothing short of a miracle."

Kerry turned to face a man standing negligently just inside the doorway. He possessed golden good looks, appeared to be in his late twenties, and was well dressed in frockcoat, vest, and straw boater hat. Kerry tried to recollect where he had seen that arresting face. "Your confidence could be daunting, but I am not one to give up easily, Mister . . ."

"Obregon." He dropped casually into the chair in front of Kerry's desk and draped an arm over the chair back.

"Rod Obregon."

"Bob," Kerry rebuttoned his vest, "give me a few moments alone with Mr. Obregon."

Bob nodded his grizzled head and stepped outside the room, closing the door softly behind him.

Well, well . . . . He hooked one hip onto the edge of his desk. After all these years, he was once again meeting the son of The Barony's nemesis.

"You're a man who could carry the burden of authority well—provided you're extra careful."

"Careful?" Eyes narrowed, he canted his head. "Meaning what, exactly?"

"Look, Paladín, it's plain to see your campaign is floundering. Your Democrat platform to end Reconstruction in Texas is, simply put, ludicrous. But I can guarantee you that Obregon Enterprises will be your miracle rescuer."

Kerry lifted one brow and smiled at Rod. "Now why does the phrase 'Fool me once, shame on you, fool me twice, shame on me,' come quickly to my mind?"

"I take it you're referring to our initial meeting so many years ago."

"I find it rather stretches my imagination to envision you and your father as miracle rescuers."

Rod Obregon brushed his knuckles alongside his jaw. "There would, of course, be a price for our financial support."

"Of course." Kerry planted his palm on the edge of the desk next to his hip and stretched out his legs, crossing them at the ankles. Only a yard separated his shabby brogans from Obregon's shiny patents. "And what might that price be?"

"The price for my father's support? Your signing over to him the twenty-one percent of The Barony left to you by your mother."

Kerry nodded slowly. He glanced once more at his well-worn brogans. Their soles were definitely the worse for wear. Some folded newspaper covered a hole in one sole. He looked back at Rod Obregon. "So, now your father is angling for total control?"

"Angling? That's far too weak a word. My father is a man of immeasurable persistence—and eventually, he will have his way. Then The Barony will belong to the Obregons—and rightly so. If not this week or this month, then later this year. I would predict certainly by November and election time."

Kerry's look settled on the wooly bison head mounted above where the man sat. He felt like that bison—an element from another era. He thought too of Cat, who was wearing dresses far long after their style had passed. Now there was their baby, Griffin, who quite possibly would go without a better education because of bickering politics—as well as Kerry's own ineptitude as a wage earner. "Suppose I refuse your generous offer?"

Elbows on the chair arms, Rod pyramided his finger-tips. "We know about an eight-year-old boy who's right now digging through garbage in Brownsville alleys—much as my father did in Five Points as a child. This eight-year-old—he resembles you more than a little, you know."

Kerry cocked his head, puzzled.

Then the implication punched through his work-weary mind. He fought back a gasp and cleared his throat before managing to hold onto his calm. "I don't believe you."

"Of course, there's no way to know for sure if you fathered that brat. Magdalena has already birthed a whole passel of them. She lost what few looks she ever had whoring for a living. But you had better know that my father has in his possession a powerful bargaining chip. He has indisputable evidence of your philandering—your Confederate campaign hat, its brim pinned with your late mama's four-leaf-clover brooch."

Kerry understood this quandary, almost too intensely. Obregon would see to it that his political career and his family life were ruined by the revelation of his philandering with the Mexican girl while he was wed to Cat.

An utter weariness settled on his shoulders. He thought about the heartbreak his foolish indiscretion would cause Cat. This decision should be a cakewalk. He felt no obligation to his estranged father, and besides, his aspirations as governor-elect would be assured with Obregon's backing. Why should he not fall into cahoots with that powerful entrepreneur? Common sense alone dictated that course.

Kerry's convictions, the ideals nurtured in him with his own mother's milk and refined in him by her powerful sense of righteousness, pushed him over the threshold.

Fiona's ideals were the ones the Texicans at the Alamo

and at Goliad had forfeited their lives for. Their ideals created a moral landscape for all Texicans by instilling a deep reverence for their lands. Those patriots' ideals about family and land and the life one leads—that power could never be confused with strength because the moral strength of one's truest nature trumped all.

Knowing he was about to act the fool, Kerry stood tall. "I will not toady to your father. Since you are his flunky, you can deliver this message to him. I decline his blackmail. Furthermore, if you are not out of here in ten seconds, I will throw you out. I have only one arm, but it has compensated for my lack of the other, and I guarantee would give you a run for your money. Now, get your reprehensible ass out of my office!"

Rod Obregon stood. Surprise—and something else— hovered behind his pale-green eyes. He tipped his hat. "You can find my father and me over at Smith's Hotel through noon tomorrow."

Later, the drive home to Shoal Creek seemed to Kerry to take seven years. He tried out a dozen things he could say to Cat. Yet, ultimately, he chose the simple truth—he had betrayed her and his marriage vows.

Losing the election would be terrible enough . . . but losing Cat? To Kerry, that was an inconceivable loss. She was his rock, the prime source of every bit of his strength.

She met him at the door, cradling a fussy Griffin in one arm. "He's got the colic." She shrugged, standing on tiptoe to kiss Kerry. "And were running late for Griffin's christening this afternoon."

All he could think was how utterly beautiful she was, despite her drab daydress. Unruly strands of taffy-colored hair escaped the knot at the back of her neck. He bent and kissed Griffin's talcum powder-fresh forehead. "How was your day, sweetheart?"

She looked at him through narrowed eyes. "Maybe I should ask you how your day was. What's wrong now, Kerry?"

Oh lordy, she knew him so well. "Sit down, Cat."

She appeared to freeze—all but her eyes. They roamed his face, looking for clues of what was coming. Then, slowly, she backed three steps and sank onto their well-worn sofa. When Griffin began crying, one by one she opened the buttons of her daydress to give the baby her breast—not so much as to soothe their infant son, Kerry suspected, as to stave off the bad news she must know was coming.

He looked down at his Madonna and child. Infinitely beautiful. What a god-damned mess he had made of his life! What folly! He hunkered before her, one knee resting on the rag carpet so they were eye to eye, and so she had nowhere to look but at him.

"Cat, all these years . . ." He was surprised at the tears that choked the back of his throat. "All these years, I have kept from you the sordid secret that I was unfaithful to you—nine years ago, during a trip I made to Brownsville with Brighton."

How had he ever managed to blurt the admission of his guilt to her so boldly, yet so crudely? To him, it seemed that an infinity spaced each of his scarcely breathed words.

He waited for her reaction. Fury, a flood of tears, shock and outrage at his weakness . . . . He was not at all sure what to expect from her, but surely not this—not her peal of merry laughter. As it gradually subsided, she wiped her eyes with the knuckles of her free hand.

"La, Kerry. I thought you were going to tell me the doctor said you had some grave disease and did not give you long to live."

"Did . . . did you understand what I just told you, Cat? That I—slept with another—"

"Woman? You mean Magdalena Herrera? What a dunce I have been, Kerry. All these years, I thought by saying nothing of my knowledge, it would keep you from suffering. Instead, you had to carry that guilt like an albatross around your neck."

Now it was he who was shocked. "How . . . how did you know?"

She flicked a hand, as if whisking away a pesky fly. "Geoffrey Brighton, of course. Whenever that idiot was in his cups, he liked to make himself feel important. You know how he was."

He captured her hand. "There's more that you may not know. I may have sired a child with the woman."

She sighed, compressed her lips, and shook her head. "Well, if that is indeed the case, then you will simply have to win the election if we have to support another mouth beside this darlin' child's."

At that, Kerry displayed a rueful smile. "I wish that were

the end to the bad tidings I bring you today. There is more. Rod Obregon came to my office this morning. He told me the election is in the bag—but only if I agree to surrender my twenty-one percent of The Barony Land and Cattle Company. If I don't agree, newspapers across Texas will learn of my disgrace. The shame and embarrassment I have brought upon you."

She was studying him closely. "What did you say to him?"

He drew a deep breath and peered at her reluctantly. "I sent him packing."

She dimpled. "Good for you, Kerry Paladín. Now get up off your knee. With the election all but lost, it would appear you will need to get busy learning a more lucrative trade than teaching. Would you ever consider horseshoeing?"

He gently squeezed her chin between his thumb and forefinger. "I will tell you what I consider, Kiddy Kat— simply put, I am the luckiest poor man in the entire world."

She smiled at him as she focused on Griffin's hungry mouth once again.

Yet a nagging thought poked his brain. Guillermo Obregon was a man who never gave up. That certainty created a skin-crawl that began at the base of Kerry's spine and coursed rapidly upward.

What would Obregon do next, if he couldn't get The Barony from Kerry?

AUSTIN

St. Mary's Cathedral was a beautiful basilica. Passing through its massive wooden doors, parishioners and visitors crossed the threshold from the distracting outside world into a muted space that whispered echoes of the Creator's eternal love for His creations.

Attending the private christening service that followed afternoon mass, Alex Paladín experienced none of that eternal love, but instead sensed his own burden of self-loathing.

Fiona would have told him that feeling could only have originated from his finding himself, a heretic, inside any church. Alex knew she would have been correct if she were present.

On this day, Thérèse must have reached a similar conclusion—that today, at least, that feeling of self-loathing also derived from the tornadic realization that his rancor, his pain, had laid waste to everyone and everything he encountered. He could hardly count the lost years he had inflicted on his own blood.

And yet his beloved Thérèse has given him another chance at connecting with his bloodline through the new life she was carrying within her. He was insanely, obnoxiously thrilled with the prospect of being a father again. And so he gave into her incessant, persistent badgering, agreeing to attend his grandson's christening.

"Bon Dieu, chere. Kerry and Catarina have named him after you—Griffin Alexander. If you do not have the decency to show up, then you are not the man I thought you to be."

As if in unison, one by one heads turned, jaws gaping, as Alex escorted Thérèse to a pew at the front of the nave. All his own family were equally aghast—Kerry and Catarina, Wade and Sarita, Niall and Rafaela, Karl and Maria Elena, Tara, too.

Hmmph, so that was Buck McHenry beside her—the name on the tongue of both Thérèse and Tara these past weeks—and clearly the reason for Tara's earlier departure for Austin ahead of him and Thérèse.

The Texas Ranger better be worth his salt, Alex grumbled under his breath. His predatory sixth sense laid twenty to one Buck and Thérèse had been more than mere friends. Which, if so, meant his dearly beloved Thérèse had a hell of a lot of explaining to do.

After Alex seated Thérèse, already starting to show with their forthcoming baby, the priest asked parents and godparents to come forward with the infant to be christened. Alex watched as Kerry and Catarina, their white shawl-swaddled baby in the crook of her arm, moved to stand before the wooden altar. To either side were Tara and Wade, the godparents.

When the priest asked them, "Do you believe and trust in the Holy Spirit, who gives life to the people of God?" Alex instantly recalled a scripture passage from some long ago moment of his own childhood.

" . . . For I will restore the years the locusts have eaten . . . ."

Even on this solemn occasion, Alex sincerely doubted that outcome. Despite his misgivings, here he sat, dining on crow. Maybe anything was possible. Perhaps even the restoration of relationships with his own that his pride and arrogance had so befouled—for all of them, Karl, Wade, Kerry, and too many others.

There was one more circumstance he intended to rectify. Leaning close to Thérèse, he told her in his raspy whisper, "If it takes getting votes from names on cemetery headstones this November to get Kerry elected, I vow that I will."

She smothered her gasp with a gloved hand. "You will do no such thing!" she snapped in a tense whisper.

"Well, maybe not that cemetery part."

Afterward, his family adjourned to Smith's Hotel to partake of its private room's sideboard buffet. All the out-of-towner Paladíns attending the ceremony were staying there.

With his and his sons' reunion still on tenterhooks, Alex's and their own stuttering attempts at conversation remained uncertain and stiff. As his sons and others well knew, their patriarch had never been known for flowery discourse.

In Alex's judgment, actions always counted more than words, even as he admitted to himself that his own actions had been an insult to his more traditional chivalrous nature.

The sideboard was laden with chafing dishes and mounded platters of food. Clam soup, baked fish drizzled with Hollandaise sauce, roast goose simmering in apple sauce, baked potatoes swimming in butter in their jackets, southern cabbage, and—for dessert—charlotte russes and a plum-pudding varnished with hard sauce.

He knew Thérèse would have appreciated the epicurean delights, had her appetite not been compromised by being with child.

Once everyone present was seated, Kerry rose, his champagne flute aloft. "A toast. To the two most important males in my life today—Griffin, who has just arrived in it, and my father, who has just returned to it."

Glancing up and down the length of the table, Alex thought he saw tears glistening in the eyes of his family. Then he realized he was blinking himself. He swallowed hard, knowing he should respond to Kerry's toast—not only to Kerry, but to everyone present—but, hell, was not his showing up in church penance enough?

Shaking his head and sighing, he rose, holding his own flute high. "To our Paladín family—soon to be increased by the arrival of yet another family member." He turned to Thérèse seated to his right. "Thank you, my dear, for your sacrifice."

In reality, her condition more than worried Alex—because it did represent a sacrifice. At her age, the risk of surviving childbearing did not bode well—and that thought alone terrified him.

He, who had never ever feared anything. Fiona's early departure from his life had almost destroyed him and his children. So, saints be praised for Thérèse's reappearance into his life—and for saving him before he lost all of his children, too.

After his toast, it seemed all prior restraint evaporated. Conversations blossomed. Anecdotes were exchanged. Laughter burst out everywhere. Sarita, Rafaela, and Tara were plying Thérèse about the newest family member she was carrying.

Alex listened, slightly bemused by realizing that this year would mark him both as a father again and a grandfather. How astounding was that!

To his left, Catarina turned to him in a whisper. "There is something you should know, Alex—about Kerry's own sacrifice."

His dark brows nearly met above his aristocratic nose. "You confound me, Catarina."

She shifted Griffin against her shoulder and patted the babe's back gently. "The Obregons—father and son—are here in Austin. At this very hotel."

Alex's eyes narrowed dangerously. That those two even dared to venture into his territory . . . . "May I?" Without waiting for her response, he lifted his grandson from her shoulder.

Christ's thorns, the smell of burped milk was clinging to his grandson—and his diaper was soggy. Even with that conflicting sensation, when Alex glimpsed the tuft of Fiona's red hair his grandson sported, he hugged the tiny bundle, damn the dampness.

"You were saying?"

"Sarita's brother, Rod, paid a visit to Kerry's office this morning." Biting her lower lip, she glanced anxiously toward Wade's wife.

"Please continue, Catarina." His attention divided between his grandson's less-than-fragrant diaper and his son's imbroglio with the Obregons.

"He said Rod offered Obregon public and financial support in the election in exchange for the twenty-one percent of The Barony Land and Cattle that Fiona left to Kerry."

Hearing Catarina's words, Alex almost dropped his grandson. "And what did Kerry tell him?"

"Pretty much what you would expect from a Paladín. Kerry turned him down. Flat. Then he threw Rod Obregon out of his office. Which seems to forfeit even the already slim chance Kerry had of winning the governorship."

Relief left Alex's lungs in an audible whoosh. Gingerly, he patted Griffin's increasingly soggy bottom. "Then the Obregons can head back to Brownsville with their tails between their legs?"

"Maybe not." Catarina's brows lowered over her lively amber eyes. "As leverage, if Kerry does not accept their offer before noon tomorrow, Guillermo Obregon is threatening to go to the newspapers with evidence of an indiscretion of Kerry's."

His hand ceased its rhythmic patting on his grandson. "Is there any truth to this, Catarina? To this . . . this charge of infidelity on Kerry's part?" His lips flattened into a severe line. "I find that beyond my comprehension. I know my sons. Kerry is one of the most honorable—"

"Guillermo Obregon is holding Kerry's campaign hat that he apparently left behind in that saloon—" Catarina blushed as she went on. "The one where he . . . where he had a drunken assignation with a woman, one Magdalena Herrera."

"The south is littered with old campaign hats."

"Not one pinned with a lucky four-leaf-clover pendant, the one you gave to me as a wedding present—Fiona's— that I later pinned on Kerry's campaign hat."

A blood vessel pulsed hard and furious in his temple. Only one other person, outside the family, would have recognized Fionas pendant after all the bygone years and known its significance to Alex. He passed Griffin to his mother and reached for his champagne flute, gulping its contents.

"But all that is in the past," she rushed on reassuringly. "I just thought you needed to be reminded that Kerry shares your own love for all that Texas is. And all it is becoming. Not even to ensure his election, would he ever—"

"Excuse me," he said, first to Catarina then to Thérèse. He rose, only pausing long enough behind Niall's chair to whisper in his friend's ear.

DUELS HAD LONG BEFORE BEEN outlawed in Texas—which made no difference at all to Alex. Honor was now satisfied by a mere drawing of some blood, but Alex was in a mood to demand the death of his longtime enemy.

Guillermo Obregon might mean for any death resulting from their combat to be Alex's, but even if the Irishman fired a bullet straight into Alex's brain, Alex knew he would still find a way to kill Liam O'Brien.

Alex could only wonder how he had not known—not *guessed*—the true identity of his foe. Just one more example of his own overbearing, obtuse arrogance—so sure of himself that he questioned not his arch rival.

Amidst the towering magnolias behind Smith's Hotel, where cloying tropical flowers ran riot, Alex met with Liam. His son served as his second—Niall as Alex's.

Per the unspoken rules of the Texican Code Duello, any firearms, except for the actual dueling pistols, were excluded from an appointed dueling arena—just in case agitated friends or family members of either of the duelists decided to take matters into their own hands. So, those attending the duel were required to leave their firearms in their hotel rooms.

"You're getting a might too old, Paladín. You can no longer depend on your quick reflexes."

Alex ignored Liam's taunt. He hardly recognized the boy he had once known and befriended. Oh, the handsome features were present—his blond ringlets, the bird-bright eyes—but they now seemed slightly out of focus to Alex, as if greed and mean-spiritedness had created a distorting optical illusion.

Surely, Liam, although a good fifteen years younger than he, could not possibly believe he was any match for Alex's skill with a pistol. Liam must surely realize he was a dead man even before they began to pace off.

From the hotel proprietor, Niall secured a brace of pistols. Alex waited while Niall and Rod verified that only a single ball was loaded in each. The two seconds then handed each duelist a weapon. Alex accepted his, hefting it in his palm and testing its balance.

Torches around the garden perimeter revealed a row of spectators—some known, some strangers. A few eager, others apprehensive.

But no family—and that was the way he wanted it. He and Niall had taken only Karl into their confidence—informing him of the impending duel and asking him to keep the family and guests occupied inside the hotel.

Retaining his Old World manners, Alex ignored the crowd, which was shifting about like milling cattle. His total focus was concentrated on the unfamiliar pistol. He went through the motions—raising his arm, then lowering the weapon in a strong, steady arc, sighting it in—all until he was satisfied.

The count was settled on by the seconds—twenty paces, then turn and fire. Niall returned to Alex and reported the arrangements. "You're sure you want to do this, my old friend?"

Alex nodded, well beyond being influenced by anyone else's reasoning. His mind was locked on this single act, one that had taken years before arriving at this inevitable climactic moment. Nothing outside the arena of those twenty paces could possibly distract him.

"I'm sure." Alex nodded curtly toward Liam, who stood across the garden with his son and an entourage of minions.

A slight mist rose out of the damp earth. Not a whisper of a breeze stirred live oak leaves or the ghostly white magnolia petals.

When the proprietor dropped his handkerchief, Alex stepped off his paces.

One . . . two . . . three . . . four. . . .

From the effects of this too-long-raging conflict, sweat sheened upon his brow. Alex knew that the man Fiona and Thérèse believed him to be did not belong on this false 'field of honor.' But to walk away would invite a bullet in the back. He knew well Liam's lack of any semblance of honor.

And Alex had never been a man who walked away or backed off from any threat.

At ten paces, he spun and fired—straight up into the air. The *delope,* as Thérèse's French would have it—throwing away the first shot to abort conflict.

He then dropped his pistol on the ground and began to stride away.

"Paladín!"

Alex kept walking, only to hear two shots ring out—one after the other. He felt the impact of the bullet fired at him from behind. He was thrown face forward onto the fecund earth. His last coherent thought was what better grave than Texas soil.

FACES WAVERED IN AND OUT of Alex's awareness. He was stretched out on a divan . . . but where?

"What in . . . consternation . . . is going on?" He was surprised by the lack of authority in his voice.

"You're inside Smith's Hotel, in its parlor, your silly goose."

His wife's voice sounded hoarse, fuzzy, too close to his ear. Dimly, Alex realized Thérèse was kneeling at his side. He saw tears had reddened her eyes.

"A doctor will be here soon, *mon amour.*"

Beyond her, he saw other faces—Niall, Kerry, Wade, Tara—others hovering. Among them, the former Texas Ranger—what was his name again? Yes, McHenry.

"Liam shot you, Dad." Kerry supplied, his freckles all but blanched white from concern. "A shoulder wound. Not any worse, it appears."

"I half expected that. Expected that bastard would never abide by the Code Duello."

"Liam's dead," Niall put in his usual no nonsense tone. "A fate that just about everyone there would agree the coward deserved."

"What?" Alex struggled to prop himself onto the elbow of his uninjured side and winced at the sharp pain he felt. "How?"

"Took a plug dead center through his heart."

Alex fired Wade an accusatory look.

Wade held up both palms. "Not me, Dad."

At Alex's inquiring brow, McHenry shook his head in the negative.

His glance swept past Karl, who never toted a gun, to meet that of Niall's, who also shook his head. "Remember, we all left our pistols in our hotel suites."

Then who in tarnation had fired that fatal shot?

DURING THE DISRUPTION caused by the astonishing events surrounding the duel, Karl von Hesse-Lippe had no difficulty slipping into the Obregon's hotel room. He removed the four-leaf clover brooch from a battered gray campaign hat and soon restored the pendant to Alex's room. Lastly, Karl sheathed Niall's pistol in its holster, draped from his hotel suite's bedpost.

Karl would carry to his own grave this deed and, with it, ownership of the bullet he had fired, killing Liam O'Brien Obregon.

A deplorable deed that went against his very fiber, but it was for his longtime friend, Alex.

It was for his beloved Rafaela. Although she would never love him as he wished, he would die a happy man knowing that he had made her life—and her children's—easier.

And it was for Texas.

His old friend, Robert E. Lee might say, "The Eyes of the South are upon you," but Karl knew differently. It was the Eyes of Texas!

AUTHOR'S NOTE

INTERESTINGLY, THE FIRST BATTLE OF the Mexican American War (1846) and the last of the Civil War (1865) were both fought within mere miles of Brownsville, Texas.

I gratefully wish to acknowledge the use of *Kings of Texas: The 150- year Saga of an American Ranching Empire* by Don Graham and *The Master Showmen of King Ranch* by Betty Bailey Coley and Stephen J. (Tio) Kleberg in my research. In addition, I am grateful for the use of Skip Hollandsworth's "When We Were Kings" in *Texas Monthly*.

ABOUT THE AUTHOR

PARRIS AFTON BONDS is the mother of five sons and the author of more than fifty published novels. She is the co-founder and first vice president of Romance Writers of America, as well as, co-founder of Southwest Writers Workshop.

Declared by ABC's *Nightline* as one of three best-selling authors of romantic fiction, the award-winning Parris Afton Bonds has been featured in major newspapers and magazines, in addition to being published in more than half a dozen languages.

The Parris Award was established in her name by the

Southwest Writers Workshop to honor a published writer who has given outstandingly of time and talent to other writers. Prestigious recipients of the Parris Award include Tony Hillerman and the Pulitzer nominee Norman Zollinger.

She donates spare time to teaching creative writing to both grade school children and female inmates, whom she considers her captive audiences

Parris would love to send you a free e-book. Visit her website at www.ParrisAftonBonds.com today and claim your free book!